TATTOOED TO DEATH

Heather Redmond

This first world edition published 2020
in Great Britain and 2021 in the USA by
SEVERN HOUSE PUBLISHERS LTD of
Eardley House, 4 Uxbridge Street, London W8 7SY.
Trade paperback edition first published
in Great Britain and the USA 2021 by
SEVERN HOUSE PUBLISHERS LTD.

British Library Cataloguing in Publication Data
A CIP catalogue record for this title is available from the British Library.

ISBN-13: 978-0-7278-8951-5 (cased)
ISBN-13: 978-1-78029-738-5 (trade paper)
ISBN-13: 978-1-4483-0460-8 (e-book)

All Severn House titles are printed on acid-free paper.

Severn House Publishers support the Forest Stewardship Council™ [FSC™],
the leading international forest certification organisation.
All our titles that are printed on FSC certified paper carry the FSC logo.

Typeset by Palimpsest Book Production Ltd.,
Falkirk, Stirlingshire, Scotland.
Printed and bound in Great Britain by
TJ Books Limited, Padstow, Cornwall.

ONE

'I could just kill her,' a woman griped. 'Worst massage ever.'

Mandy Meadows scowled as she recognized the voice coming from the front counter of the University of Seattle Hospital coffee bar. Hidden in the bar's prep room while her boss, Fannah, manned the counter, she ignored the tantrum, tucked her tongue into the side of her mouth, and carefully drew the red lacing on a baseball cookie with a piping bag. When she had finished, she adjusted her Seattle Mariners blue headband, encouraging her curls away from her lip gloss.

Fannah had decided they should enhance their house-made offerings with frosted sugar cookies since Mandy's creations were already their bestsellers. She did what she could to keep their profit margin way above the cafeteria's.

Mandy's new co-worker, Houston Harris, shot Mandy a look of horror through the door as he tied a clean USea Hospital apron over his Mariners T-shirt. 'I guess the new chair massage service isn't a hit with someone. Why are they complaining about it at the coffee bar?'

'That's my friend, Reese,' Mandy explained. 'She's a nurse in the podiatry office next door. Total pussycat with their child patients.'

'Umm, that's great, but shouldn't you intervene before she attacks Fannah with a plastic knife?' The Alaska native had only worked at the coffee bar a few weeks.

'Don't be silly. It's not Fannah she's mad at and I need to get these done.' Mandy angled the frosting tip over another cookie.

'Aren't you curious about what happened?' Houston asked.

'Nah.' Mandy winked at the kid and pressed frosting through the bag. 'Reese lives across the street from me. I can hear about it after work.'

Houston hunched his narrow shoulders and walked out of Mandy's view. Just twenty, he still had the look of a newborn colt despite having a face that checked all the cuteness boxes.

She appreciated her new steady seven-to-three-thirty work schedule, but Wednesdays were always extra hectic, because Fannah worked her oddball shift for inventory purposes and the lead weekend barista, Beverly, swapped in for the first part of the day. The hospital's board of directors met on Wednesdays too, and since the coffee they served in the boardroom wasn't very good, the directors usually came in a clump during the half hour from nine thirty to ten when all four of the employees were jockeying for space in the tight area.

'Mandy!'

She shot to attention when she heard her boss's voice. After setting down her frosting bag, she removed her gloves, washed her hands, and went through the back room into the coffee bar.

Fannah extended a model-slim arm at her and gestured gracefully. 'Please fill out a catering order for Miss O'Leary-Sett. I need to make a phone call.'

She glided past Mandy as if on the catwalk she used to call her professional home. Mandy was left facing Reese – nurse, neighbor, and fellow journaling video blogger.

Stunning half-Bengali, half-Irish Reese, however, wasn't at the top of her form. One shoulder was hunched up to her neck, which was tilted at a strange, canted angle.

'What's wrong?' Mandy asked. 'I could hear you all the way in the prep room. My daughter didn't yell that loudly when you buddy-taped her broken toe.'

Reese fluttered her eyelashes. Mandy suspected they were real, despite their lush length, even though Reese had been a movie makeup recreator in a past phase.

'I just had the chair massage from hell in the hospital lobby. How am I going to survive the afternoon like this? I'm due back at work in five minutes.'

Keeping her gaze locked on her friend's face, Mandy gently placed her hands on Reese's shoulders, then pressed down on the one that had crept up. She heard a pop somewhere around Reese's shoulder.

'Wow, you aren't kidding,' Mandy said.

Reese sniffed and rubbed her shoulder. 'My friendship with Coral is over.'

'Who is Coral?'

'Coral Le Charme? The massage therapist? I never should have recommended her for the job.'

'I didn't know you had anything to do with the new chair massage people.' Mandy pulled out a catering form.

Reese's lips tightened. She bent her head forward, her neck crackling as she lifted it again. 'I could kill Coral for hurting me so much.'

'I'll fix you right up,' Houston said, as two elderly customers shuffled away, their smoothies tucked into the holding pouches on their walkers. He grinned at Reese and lifted his hands into the air.

She ignored him and kept her eyes on Mandy.

'Let's not talk about killing people,' Mandy begged. 'It's been less than a month since the attack on me, and I'm just starting to feel comfortable here again. Now, you wanted to make a catering order?'

'Fine,' Reese groused. 'I'm throwing a little party in the office at the end of the day.'

Houston leaned in. 'I hope you invite me.'

Reese spoke as if Houston wasn't there. 'Baby shower for the office manager.'

'You didn't plan ahead?'

Reese's shoulder made crackling noises as she tried to shrug. 'I have all the shower stuff and the cake. I just need the drinks. You're open until six, right?'

'Can you send someone to pick up the drinks?' Mandy asked.

'I'm off at five,' Houston broke in. 'I can deliver them.'

'We close at four,' Reese explained, turning her big, beautiful eyes to Houston for the first time. 'I need the drinks then. Mandy, can't you?'

'I can bring them after three thirty,' Mandy offered. 'Vellum has a yearbook meeting so I can hang out.' Divorced, she lived with her daughter in the upstairs of her house, and rented out the daylight basement.

'Stay for the party,' Reese invited. 'I'll buy you a drink, too. Just add yours and I'll pay for it all now.' She handed Mandy a list of eight drink orders.

A line had formed behind Reese at the cash register, so Mandy pulled her friend to the side to finish while Houston took care of the next customers. Mandy added a tall mocha to the order for herself and took the credit card Reese offered. 'Thanks for the invite.' Maybe cake and the excitement of a little one coming would be just what she needed.

'Should we invite Fannah, too?' Reese asked. 'Does she have friends in the complex?'

'She works until six,' Mandy explained. 'I'm the only one free.'

Reese slowly bent her head from side to side. 'I just think we should all stick together, after what happened to you.'

Mandy nodded and handed Reese her credit card back. 'Then maybe you should be nicer to Houston. I know he doesn't fit your Hindu dating profile, but he's a decent kid.'

Reese rolled her eyes. 'Come on, Mandili. We have to have some standards.'

Mandy laughed despite herself. 'OK, you don't have to be friendly with him, but I do.'

'You'll be fine.' Reese shuddered. 'He's not much older than your daughter.'

Mandy chuckled. Houston and Reese were closer in age than she and Reese were.

Fannah sent Mandy on her lunch break just before noon. An elevator door opened to the lobby before she pushed the button to go to the cafeteria floor, disgorging a couple of nurses from the coronary care unit.

'What's the special today?' one of them asked as Mandy held the door.

'Matcha latte, in honor of cherry blossom season,' she told them.

'That's green tea, right?' asked the other nurse.

Mandy nodded. 'It's earthy and addictive. It has about the same amount of caffeine as coffee but you get a more sustained energy boost due to the amino acid content.'

The first nurse laughed. 'You should write ad copy.'

Mandy beamed at the praise and stepped into the elevator. The door closed and she was blissfully alone for a few seconds. The placard on the left held the cafeteria specials for the week, which she'd already memorized since it was Wednesday, but a new announcement had gone up on the left. The hospital was being graced by a lecture on Mindful Meditation by a Bodhi Lee next Wednesday.

'Never heard of him,' Mandy muttered. Meditation wasn't for her. Art was her therapy and she was happy to know that what kept her sane also paid quite a few bills.

Her fateful art journaling class with Reese the previous year had led to a side hustle that was on track to pay her more than her barista job by summer. If only microbusinesses came with health insurance.

The best part about it, though, was that her social media presence, her classes and product sales could all be shared with fifteen-year-old Vellum. Even when things were a bit rocky in the parent–child relationship, they worked together well. Vellum didn't have to babysit the bratty Roswell twins next door for cash anymore, and Mandy had a professional partner-in-crime who added tangible and intangible benefits to her business.

Mandy bypassed the barbecue burger lunch special in favor of the salad-in-a-jar she'd packed, though she grabbed a paper plate. The nook along the windows overlooking the I-5 freeway was only lightly populated, so she settled into a chair and dusted crumbs off the two-top table. Just enough room for her planner and lunch.

She opened the notebook to this week's journal spread, then unscrewed the metal lid of her mason jar. Homemade lemon Dijon dressing filled an old spice jar she'd tucked inside. After dumping out her salad of mixed power greens, the kind you could eat raw or sauté or turn into smoothies, she stirred black beans, corn, chicken and cheese into the mix, then topped it all with dressing and a hospital pepper pack.

Her phone rang as she was pulling a metal fork from her purse. Her daughter's frowning face had appeared on the screen. 'Hi, honey.'

'Bad news, Mom.'

'Did your yearbook meeting get cancelled? I'm going to run late tonight, so you'll probably want to take the bus home.'

'No, all of the members on our new creative site have filled out the poll for May's theme.'

In order to secure a steadier stream of income from their business, Mandy had launched a membership on an internet platform, where her customers could pay a monthly fee to receive her stickers and classes. She had followed the model of other creators and set up polls to give her customers some say over the content they received. But that meant giving up control.

Mandy pushed her fork tines into her lettuce. 'What's the verdict?'

'It was a tie. May's theme is a merge of bunnies and tea.'

Mandy rubbed her nose. 'Uh-oh.'

'How did that happen? I know we have new customers signing up every day who could change the poll results. But you like to do our work six weeks ahead, so we're already running late for May.'

'Yeah, we need to get started. Do you really think our school-age customers will like that theme? It sounds like an old lady Easter mash-up.'

'The journaling community loves animal themes,' Vellum soothed.

'And beverage themes,' Mandy added. 'I guess the bunnies will have to drink tea.'

Vellum laughed. 'If this new platform causes more problems, we can always shut it down.'

'We already have enough new customers from it to add five figures a year to our bottom line,' Mandy said. 'Let's make it work. We don't have to give them options in the poll that we don't want to do.'

'We can change the rules to say no ties,' Vellum added. 'I mean, we can pick one if there's a tie.'

'Exactly. I'll rewrite the poll rules tonight.'

'OK, Mom. I'll see you after my meeting.'

'Sure thing. I should be home before you.' Mandy disconnected, then sent a kiss emoji over text. When she set her phone down, a man approached her.

'Is this seat taken?'

Mandy glanced up the lab coat to see Dr Tristan Burrell, a neonatologist who frequented both the coffee bar and, so he claimed, her social media videos.

His craggy features were punctuated by thick dark brows and piercing blue eyes reminiscent of actor Chris Pine, who Mandy had crushed on since his first *Star Trek* movie. The unattractive glasses the doctor wore hid his deserved hospital hottie status, and his nature was too unassuming to come on strong, but Mandy had learned what a great guy hid underneath the quiet pleasantry of their interactions.

'Hi, Stan, of course.' Mandy waved her hand at the other side of the table.

He placed his tray, with an iced tea and the barbecue burger, then took the seat. 'Your lunch looks much better than mine.'

'Brought it from home. I never like the Wednesday specials.'

'Burgers aren't their strong suit. But they do a good job with Meatless Mondays.'

Mandy nodded. 'That three-bean chili is better than what I can make at home.'

'Hmm.' The doctor grimaced at his lunch, then opened the mustard and ketchup packets he'd added to his tray and squeezed them on to his burger. 'I thought this might help.'

'I'd have added mayonnaise,' Mandy told him.

'I didn't think of that. It might have cut the vinegar.'

'Do you want me to grab you some?'

'No, no. I only have ten minutes to eat.'

'What's going on in the Neonatal Intensive Care Unit today?' she asked.

'We're watching a couple of preemies for pneumonia.'

'More than one? Are you afraid that infection is going through the unit?'

'I hope not. That's when we lose the really fragile babies.' He sighed. 'It's a rollercoaster ride for the families and I hate losing our patients.'

'It's one thing to know the odds aren't great, and another thing entirely to have the worst happen,' Mandy agreed. 'I get choked up just thinking about it. I guess that's why I'm the barista and you're the doctor.'

Dr Burrell lifted his burger. 'You brighten a lot of days with that smile of yours, not to mention the excellent coffee and cookies.'

'Thanks.' She watched him take a bite. It seemed like their customer–barista relationship had taken a turn toward something friendlier over the past six weeks, but she still didn't know if he was interested in her or Fannah. He flirted with both of them. His low-key nature made it hard to tell. Because Mandy had yet to start dating since her recent divorce, she left the field to Fannah.

But Dr Burrell undeniably appealed. A man who spent his career saving babies – who could compare with that?

Her alarm went off after several minutes of companionable eating in silence. She dropped her fork and dressing container inside and screwed the lid back on her jar.

'That's a great idea,' the doctor said, gesturing at her jar.

'No plastic,' Mandy agreed. 'My daughter found the salad recipes online.'

'Smart kid,' Dr Burrell said.

'Do you have any?' Mandy asked as she stood.

'I do actually.'

Mandy paused, surprised. 'Are you divorced, too?'

'No, never married.'

She pointed to the corner of his mouth.

He wiped off a small glob of turmeric-yellow mustard. 'My daughter is seventeen. She's out there somewhere. An open adoption.'

'Oh.'

'She was premature, born almost three months too early. It was more than we could handle, so we let her go to a family that knew what they were doing. My ex gets photos once a year.' Dr Burrell nodded. 'Painful stuff, but a long time ago.'

'Do you see photos, too?'

He pointed to her phone. 'You'd better get going. I don't want Fannah mad at you on my account.'

How could she not want to learn more? But shift workers couldn't be late from breaks. Taking a deep breath, she strode away, shocked by this new dimension to the handsome doctor.

At least she now had her curiosity satisfied about his career choice.

At three thirty, Mandy grabbed her purse, slung it over her shoulder, then picked up two drink holders. Fannah made a throaty noise when Mandy glanced at the third drink holder doubtfully.

'Don't go anywhere until I return,' Fannah told Houston, then picked up the other carrier.

Mandy followed her boss up the escalator to the next floor, where a glassed-in sky bridge led over the front driveway to the office building. The complex was built as three sides of a square, with busy Madison Avenue making up the fourth side.

Reese's podiatry office was on the same floor as the bridge. Fannah walked confidently across the tiled floor to the right side. Her catwalk stomp remained from her model days, as had her spectacular glowing skin, though she was a couple of years older than Mandy. The soothing tones of her voice came from her native tongue – Amharic.

'You know where you're going.' Mandy trotted behind the floor-eating stride of her taller boss.

'I've been to the podiatrist a couple of times to have my foot wrapped.'

'Plantar fasciitis?'

Fannah nodded. 'Too many of my careers have involved standing. Reese can be abrasive as a customer, but she's a great nurse.'

'I haven't needed her services so far, though she helped Vellum,' Mandy said, smiling at a little boy coming out of a children's therapy office.

'You will if you stay a barista.' Fannah shrugged, making the ice in one of the drinks she held rattle. 'When I had the chance to get off my feet, I took it, but they were already damaged.'

'Food for thought,' Mandy said. 'Though, other than people trying to kill me, I've enjoyed working here.'

Fannah said nothing, just ran a manicured nail along her forehead, under her headwrap. They had never talked about what had happened. Mandy had buried her feelings during the days she'd been given off, then returned to work. Her attacker, and others involved, were awaiting trial somewhere in the region, and she simply chose not to think about it. Fannah must have decided the same, although Mandy had noticed they had three security cameras installed above the coffee bar now.

Mandy had fun at the little party and ended up in an extended discussion about an exhibit at the Seattle Asian Art Museum with the office manager. Long after dark, Mandy yawned as she walked across the sky bridge from the office building to the parking garage. She noted the sign which proudly declared that the entire sky bridge circuit was a half-mile long, and made her usual unfulfilled pledge to walk the circuit a couple of times during the day, to get her steps in.

She chuckled at the thought. A teenage boy gave her a quizzical look as he saw her laughing face, so she touched her ear, pretending she was laughing at something on earbuds hidden behind her curly brown hair. People talked to themselves all the time these days. It was rare anyone even bothered to notice.

She turned off the bridge at the elevators and rose up to the top floor, partially uncovered to the rainy March sky. A gust of not-quite-freezing wind blasted her as she walked out of the overhang to her car, half an aisle down. Happy first day of spring to her. The streetlamps were coming on as twilight deepened.

She had parked in her favorite spot, next to the dumpster in a triangular space created by one corner of the garage. She never lost her car when she parked there.

Her neck spasmed as she reached her car. She winced as she unlocked her trunk and dumped in her bag of party favors and the slice of cake Reese had insisted she take for Vellum before she had rushed off somewhere.

Mandy rubbed her neck, wondering how she'd managed to be roped into a conversation that kept her at the party longer than the planner herself had stayed. *Ugh.* She never should have agreed to carry heavy trays all the way to the podiatrist's office. Walking while holding them had been too much after a day at the espresso machine.

She tucked her chin into her chest, stretching the back of her neck as she stepped around her car to unlock the driver-side door.

With her neck in that position, it was no surprise she saw the foot.

TWO

Mandy did a double take as wind whipped her hair in and out of her eyes. The foot was clad in vertical black-and-white striped fabric. Mandy's mocha threatened to reappear as her disbelieving eyes followed the foot to the attached leg, then past the thigh to a short black skirt. She swallowed hard as her gaze passed a brief expanse of belly with marks on it, to a black shirt. A black jacket, office-style, opened over the torso.

Mandy's hand went to her mouth. It shook when she saw the face leaning away from the dumpster, unfamiliar to her with a slack mouth painted vermilion, half-closed eyes.

She knelt down, scarcely noting the freezing concrete under her knees, and wrapped her fingers around the woman's wrist. Unable to find a pulse, she noted that the woman's skin still felt warm.

After discovering her cousin's body last month, she had learned how to feel for a pulse. She didn't know if this woman was dead exactly, but she was close to death at the very least. Horror hit abruptly.

'Call nine-one-one!' she screamed into the parking garage, hoping someone unseen would hear her. 'Hello! Hello!'

She tilted the woman's head back and blew two breaths into her unresponsive mouth, following ancient CPR training that she probably remembered wrong.

Nothing happened. Mandy felt for the woman's sternum and began to compress her chest, trying to remember the rhythm of the Bee Gees' 'Stayin' Alive.' Wasn't that what she was supposed to do? Suddenly, she realized her hands were wet.

From her first compression, they seemed to stick to the fabric. She stared down at her hands in confusion and, in the fading light, saw blood coating them.

The dark garage spun with stars for a moment. *Oh no.* The woman's black clothing had hidden serious wounds. This wasn't an overdose or heart attack. Mandy shook her head a little, trying to stay focused. She pulled up the untucked shirt. A nightmare of thin cuts was sliced across the woman's chest. Tattoos, too – black bullseye tattoos on her belly.

Mandy reached for her phone, buried in her coat pocket, and dialed 911. She'd lost track of time, but no one seemed to be coming to help her.

While she talked to the operator through the speaker, she turned on the flashlight app on her phone. She hadn't been imagining it. The woman really didn't have any shoes on. Mandy still didn't recognize her, but she was young. Fashionable too, with dip-dyed hair, cotton candy blue over blond. Her even features and smooth skin had probably been lovely, though Mandy had smeared her lipstick.

Realizing what that meant, she dropped her phone and scrubbed at her mouth with her wrist. Her lips felt greasy against the soft skin of her inner arm. Nausea rising, she skittered back and wound up leaning against her tire, hands covered in blood, her wrist and mouth dabbed with a dead woman's lipstick.

'Hello? Hello?'

No one answered. She'd managed to disconnect the emergency operator. When she glanced down, her phone screen had left the call function and now displayed her daughter's smiling face, along with various apps. Vellum's face was full of life, compared with the slack face of the victim.

Mandy had to do something to help. She ripped off her coat and pushed it against the woman's chest, then hit the call app again. This time she dialed the hospital operator and explained her situation, hoping they could come to her aid. Would the hospital insurance policy allow it?

Tears pricked her eyes and the piece of cake she'd eaten at the party seemed to churn in her stomach. How could this be happening again? Tentatively, she touched the woman's hand. Still warm. Should she do more compressions? Was this crumpled figure's life completely extinguished?

'Mandy Meadows?'

She heard her name called, almost before she heard the sound of the elevator door opening. 'Over here, by the dumpster!' she called.

She struggled to her feet and held her phone in the direction of the elevator, creating a beacon. Two people carried a stretcher, and an emergency room medical resident ran alongside them. She thanked the operator and hung up, not paying attention to what the woman said.

Mandy recognized all three of the respondents since they were customers of the coffee bar.

'Are you hurt?' the resident, Dr Anderson, asked.

Mandy pointed. 'No, her. Thank you for coming so quickly.'

The young doctor's eyes went wide when he looked past Mandy, then he barked out orders. They treated the victim as if she was still alive, though Mandy pointed out the stab wounds. She wondered if they had any hope of saving the woman's life.

Dr Anderson told her to wait for the police, then followed his team as they headed back to the elevator with the woman on their stretcher. The trio had worked with lightning speed. Maybe there hadn't been enough blood to be certain she was irrevocably dead? Except a pool of it remained on the concrete, now that the body had gone.

Mandy wished she'd stayed in school, maybe majoring in nursing instead of art as she had before she dropped out, so she would have known the basics of medicine and the human body. Then she could have offered more help.

A minute later, the high pitch of a police siren wailed. A patrol car roared up the parking ramp. Just underneath the wail, Mandy heard the elevator open. Her name was called again. Running footsteps revealed Keawe Kim, the security guard from the ER.

'Are you OK?' The heavy-set man wheezed, putting his hands on his back as he came to a stumbling stop ahead of the police car braking.

Uniformed police officers climbed out of their car. Strobe lights flashed garishly, illuminating the dumpster. Behind them, an ambulance appeared.

'Just light-headed.' Mandy put her hand to her forehead. 'I tried to do CPR.'

'All you can do is try,' Keawe said. He looked exhausted by his race through the hospital.

'You found the victim?' asked the officer, an older, long-faced man who'd been on the passenger side. She'd seen him before in the hospital. This must be his usual beat.

Mandy nodded, starting to shiver in her long-sleeved tee. 'I think she's dead, but they took her away.'

The officer frowned. 'Who?'

'Doctor Anderson was in charge.' She registered the police officer's confusion. 'I lost my connection to nine-one-one, so I called the hospital. I guess they are allowed to send employees into the parking garage. I wasn't sure.'

The officer ignored all that with a little flip of his head. 'Why did you think the person was dead?'

Mandy gestured to her chest. 'Mostly the stab wounds. She didn't have a pulse when I tried to find it, either.'

'She did CPR,' Keawe interjected.

Mandy wiped at her mouth with her sleeve, remembering the lipstick again. 'I didn't see the stab wounds at first.'

'Where were they?' asked the second officer. Mandy didn't recognize her. Younger than the first by twenty years and biracial, she wore her straight black hair in an unflattering collar-length pageboy.

'Her chest. She has a black shirt on.' Mandy shuddered and pointed to the pavement. 'I felt the blood sticking to my fingers when I did chest compressions.'

The two officers shared a glance. The woman took out a notebook as the other spoke into his body cam.

'There's a chaplain on duty,' Keawe said. 'Do you want me to get him for you, Mandy?'

'I—'

'Take her to your office if you have one,' the second police officer said. 'We'll secure the scene and send someone to interview the witness.'

Keawe didn't allow Mandy to wash, saying she'd have to ask the police for permission in case they needed to collect evidence. She sat on the guest chair in his windowless office, dried blood on her hands and lipstick on her face and arm, for the better part of an hour, with nothing to do but watch the output of the surveillance cameras Keawe had up on his computer screen. He had one camera loaded from the employee part of the parking garage, so she watched the police and their technicians scurry around her car until the security-office door opened.

She recognized her tenant, homicide detective Justin Ahola, and his partner, Detective Craig Rideout, with a sinking feeling. Was she being treated as a witness or a Good Samaritan, or, as she increasingly felt, a suspect? 'Did you come to rescue me or is the woman I found dead?'

Justin, just a year younger than Mandy and possessing the looks of a Viking warrior, gave her an exasperated nod. 'I'm afraid she didn't make it, Mandy. How did you, out of everyone who works here, manage to be the one who found her?'

'Was she still alive when I got there?' Mandy said querulously.

'Does it matter?' Justin asked.

'Of course it does. I want to know if I could have saved her.' She swallowed hard. 'You know, if I'd done something differently.'

His eyebrows knitted together. 'How long was it before you called for help?'

'I yelled for help but no one responded. Then I tried to do CPR until I realized how wounded she was. A minute or two, I guess.'

'I doubt it would have mattered,' he said.

She didn't like the word 'doubt.' 'Are you sure? Because—'

Justin grimaced.

Detective Rideout, heavy-set with graying black hair and terra-cotta skin, held up his hand as if to forestall Justin's irritation. 'Let's take Mandy to the station and get her statement out of the way.'

'Can I clean up first?' she asked.

'At the station, please,' Justin said. 'You knelt in the crime scene, handled the crime scene. If you don't mind, I'd like to collect any trace evidence we can.'

Mandy was relieved by his tone of request, rather than demand. She hoped the security cameras would show the murder and she'd be completely exonerated. 'I thought she might be alive. She was warm despite the wind.'

Detective Rideout's wife was fighting late-stage cancer. Mandy never saw her housemate's partner without a rush of sympathy and the desire to bake something Mrs Rideout might be willing to nibble on. 'They pronounced her dead soon after arriving in the ER, but at least you tried. She had a lot of deep wounds, Mandy.'

The sight of that cluster of stab wounds danced across Mandy's vision. And the bizarre tattoos. But it could all wait for the inter-view room at the police station. She didn't have it in her to talk about it just then. Maybe they'd offer her a hot drink. She needed one. A change of clothes too, since they might want hers.

'Did you find the murder weapon?' she asked, touching her hip pocket to make sure she still had her phone.

Justin narrowed his eyes at her. 'They're searching the dumpster now. But you need to forget about this. It isn't your problem.'

Not a chance. 'It's my hospital,' Mandy said. 'Does this have something to do with the drug operation we learned about last month?'

'Nah,' Detective Rideout said. 'Criminal Investigations cleared out those bastards last week. Kept it quiet.'

Mandy rose from the office chair, feeling as if she'd aged a decade since she carried those drinks to the baby shower. 'Very. I'm amazed. They must not have had to close any departments.'

'I guess they can keep going with limited staff in the affected area,' Justin explained.

'I forget how big this campus is sometimes.' Mandy felt for her car keys. They were still in her possession.

'What were you doing here so late?' Justin asked. 'I thought your schedule was the same every day now.'

Mandy walked between the men out of the security-room door. The office was tucked in behind the cafeteria on the second floor. 'I was at a baby shower,' she called behind her.

Justin took Mandy's arm as they went to the elevator. The other detective frowned at his partner.

'I hope this doesn't look like I'm under arrest,' Mandy said.

She heard Justin snort but he released her arm. 'Where's Vellum?'

'I texted her. She's going to my mother's.' Unlike the last time she'd found a body, the police had no need to confiscate her phone. Since her mother lived across the street from her Maple Leaf neighborhood home, Vellum could easily change course.

'I made pizza for dinner,' Justin said. 'I should have known better, since we were on call.'

Mandy rolled her eyes. 'So exciting. I'm sorry I ruined your pizza.'

'It wasn't from a box,' Justin said. 'I bought a cauliflower crust and topped it myself. Better than the endless tofu stir-fry you live on.'

'It's far more flexible than pizza,' Mandy rebutted.

'Children,' said the other detective when the elevator opened. 'Can it. This is a murder investigation, not a night at *casa* Meadows-Ahola.'

At least he had put her name first, Mandy grumped to herself.

'*Casa*,' Justin muttered.

'What's wrong with "*casa*"?' Mandy asked. 'We can use a Spanish word.'

'His ex was Latinx,' Detective Rideout said. 'He takes all Spanish like an insult now. It used to be cute.' He nudged Justin. 'Remember when you thought it was cute?'

Justin growled, his thick brows furrowing together over his pronounced eye ridges. 'I'm way past the cute phase.'

His partner quirked his lips. 'He didn't want to sell his house. I don't know why he didn't simply get a housemate like you did.'

They walked into the sky bridge. 'Good question,' Mandy said. 'I never asked why you didn't do that.'

Justin grimaced. 'I didn't have the time to keep up the yard and the house.'

'Big yard,' Detective Rideout agreed. 'With a hill. Hard to mow. But you could have afforded a cleaner if you'd had a housemate.'

'I would have had to do a lot of work on the basement before I could have rented it out,' Justin said. 'And I didn't want someone on the same floor as me. It's irritating.'

'Does sharing my kitchen irritate you?' Mandy waited for Justin to unlock the police car's door. She had to sit in back with the doors that didn't open.

'I'm coping.' He smiled at her and shut the door.

Mandy had appreciated the tension release that came from teasing her housemate, but as soon as they reached the station, the detectives were all business again. They walked her through her statement and collected all the evidence they could, apologizing for her discomfort, then a young patrol cop drove her home, since her car was still part of the crime scene.

While she rode through Seattle in the back of another police car, she texted Reese and asked if she could drive into work a little early the next morning, so Mandy would have a ride to her shift.

After a few noncommittal exchanges, Reese said she'd let her know later. Mandy downloaded a ride app just in case. Vellum's surviving grandfather, Mandy's ex-father-in-law, had just said he might buy Vellum a car for Christmas, but that was nine months away. This was the first time Mandy had considered that a two-car household might be a good idea. Then again, insurance cost the earth, and how often was her car going to be trapped in a crime scene?

Never again, she hoped. When she asked, the police officer kindly pulled around to the driveway behind her house to let her out. No need to have her neighbors think she'd been arrested. The

Roswells next door were particularly irksome: a depressed and druggie single mom and her two shiftless middle-schoolers.

Mandy had no sooner exited the car than she heard the clip-clop of shoes crossing the side street. Her neighbor and close friend, Linda Bhatt, had reconciled with the local dentist lothario, George Lowry, two weeks before, and he'd been showering her with gifts, including the loud, furry slipper-shoes.

Linda's mouth dropped open as she watched the police car reverse out of the driveway. She trotted forward, holding a plastic container of her signature treats. 'What happened this time? Did your car break down?'

'What do you mean "this time"? I've never come home in a police car.'

'Not true. Justin picked you up when your car was in the shop last week.'

'That's different. That was just housemate kindness.'

'And this wasn't?' Linda frowned. 'That wasn't Justin at the wheel?'

'No. He asked someone to drive me home from the station. I had to give a statement.'

Linda sighed and handed her the container, then crossed her arms over her ample chest. 'Any minute now it's going to be fine to leave the house without a coat, right?' She shivered.

Mandy peered through the clear plastic. 'Why is the frosting green?'

'It's the last of the St Patrick's Day brownies.'

'Ooh, are these the boozy ones?'

'Yes. I didn't want them around Vellum, but I saw her go over to your mother's.' Linda's house looked out at Mandy's on one side and Barbara's, which was on the other side of the arterial, Roosevelt Way, on the other. Mandy's mother had been widowed shortly before Mandy's marriage had fallen apart, and with Linda being long divorced, all three of them kept an eye on each other.

Reese appeared at the foot of the driveway, then walked briskly to Linda's side, her fabulous mane of black hair bouncing with each step. 'What's going on? After all those text messages I thought I'd better walk down and check on you.' Reese, who lived next door to Mandy's mother to the south, had only become Mandy's rival in online video blogging for art-focused journaling because she'd failed to find an audience with her first vlog, which was recreating famous makeup looks from the movies. They had taken the same journaling class a couple of years earlier. 'What happened to your car? Were you in an accident?'

'No, it's stuck in a crime scene in the hospital parking garage.' Mandy shivered in her borrowed clothes. 'Why did you leave your party before I did?'

'I had a message to return and you looked like you were having fun talking to Kenya.' Reese frowned. 'A crime scene?'

'Let's go into the house. Reese is the only one of us with a heavy coat.' Mandy led the way across the flagstone path in her backyard and up the steps to her back door.

'What happened to yours?' Linda asked.

'I used it to try to help,' Mandy said, the image of the dead woman flashing through her mind. She blinked to suppress tears. What a waste of a life.

Inside the back door was her built-in bill-paying desk, and across from that, a wall with a pegboard for everyone to hang up the various coats, hats, and scarves a household needed to survive the Seattle seasons.

She set down the brownies, her purse, and her tote bag. Reese hung her light burgundy puffer coat on an empty peg. Linda just shivered.

'I'll make some tea,' Mandy said, as Linda grabbed her brownies and followed her into the kitchen.

'Just a tisane, please, if I have to be up early to take you to work,' Reese announced.

Mandy loaded her electric kettle with Seattle's clean-tasting water directly from the tap. 'Linda? Is herbal tea OK?'

'I'd rather have English Breakfast. If you have it in decaf, that's fine.'

'I have some Canadian Breakfast tea from Murchie's that's decaf.'

'Perfect, but hurry up. I want to know who died this time.'

'Died?' Reese gasped.

As Mandy prepared the tea, Linda waved her arms. 'You know that's what happened. Justin is involved, and he's a homicide guy. So spill, Mandy, and not the tea.'

'I went to Reese's event after work.' At Linda's look of hurt, she added, 'A co-worker's baby shower. I had to deliver drinks. Anyway, after I left, I found a dying woman by the dumpster next to my car.'

Linda gasped. 'Oh, had she been released from the hospital too soon?'

'Or never made it in,' Reese guessed.

'No, she'd been stabbed. But I didn't see the wounds in the dark, and her shirt was black.' Mandy shuddered. 'I tried CPR.'

'Someone dumped her there,' Reese suggested. 'It happens.'

'Disgusting.' Linda grabbed a knife and cut savagely into her treats, dividing the rectangle into three large pieces.

Mandy waved her hands. 'Four pieces, please. You don't want to hurt Vellum's feelings.'

'Or Barbara's,' Reese added quickly. Mandy knew she wanted a much smaller piece. Reese was proud of her curvy but sleek figure.

Linda sighed and recut the brownies. She slid three on to plates and left the last one in the container. 'Not for Vellum this time. Too boozy. I should have made a double batch.'

'This is perfect,' Mandy assured her, guessing that the alcohol had burned off, but not wanting to override her friend. 'Anyway, I don't know how the woman in the garage got there.'

'Did you know her?' Reese inquired.

'No. She was young, Goth kind of outfit.' Mandy described the black ensemble. 'Orange-red lipstick.' Her stomach flipped at the memory.

Reese frowned, a tiny movement that expressed displeasure without causing unattractive wrinkles. 'How young? What about her hair?'

'Not a teenager,' Mandy said. 'But young enough to spend a small fortune on pop star hair.'

'Blue dip dye?' Reese repeated after Mandy gave a full description.

Mandy nodded and pulled teacups from her grandmother's wedding china from a cupboard. Reese would expect no less. Mandy added the saucers, before reaching for the matching tray with a prefilled sugar pot, then added milk to the small jug. She carried the tea tray into the dining room, which was mostly used as her 'Mandy's Plan' business's print-and-mail station.

Linda set out brownies and forks. Reese, who had only recently become a regular guest, acted like one and simply took a seat, her gaze wafting over the printers and sticker cutter machines, the postage meter, paper, and ink supplies, not to mention the envelopes of various types and the rubber stamps they used to make their packages look inviting.

'What's that?' Linda asked, pointing to the box at one end of the table.

Mandy set down her tray. 'Notebook samples. I decided to follow Reese's lead and invest in products with my logo on them. I thought I might put together an art journal starter kit since we have so many student journalers. They can ask for the kit as gifts.'

Reese harrumphed. 'But back to the dead woman.'

'Yes, of course.' Mandy poured tea and passed it around.

'It sounds like Coral Le Charme. She was wearing Goth-style clothes when she gave me that massage, and she had blue dip-dyed hair,' Reese said, grimacing slightly at the memory.

Mandy's hand froze over her teacup. Steam coated her hand with moisture. 'Isn't that the massage therapist who hurt you?'

'Yes, but—' Reese wrapped her hands around her cup. 'I liked her. I got her that job.'

That was news to Mandy. Had she found the corpse of Reese's friend? 'How did you know her?' Linda grabbed Mandy's cup and added milk and sugar.

'Coral used to work at a massage place by the mall, but it closed down because of the National Hockey League construction. She was a great therapist there. I don't know why her skills seemed to have vanished.'

'That mall's really changing this area.' Linda pushed Mandy's teacup into her hand and forked up a big bite of brownie. 'As if traffic isn't bad enough.'

'Since we'd become friendly, I suggested that Coral apply at the chair massage alcove in the hospital.' Reese lifted her cup to her lips. 'I can't imagine what happened.'

'You threatened to kill her today,' Mandy pointed out. Her voice sounded shaky. 'You couldn't even stand straight. Maybe she hurt someone else – someone with a murderous temper.'

'That seems extreme.' Reese wiped under her eyes with her

napkin. Mandy noticed her hand tremor slightly. 'But something was definitely wrong with her technique today.'

'Eat, Mandy,' Linda ordered. 'You're pale.'

'They have security cameras in that part of the garage. I watched them work the crime scene after Keawe stuck me in his office.' Mandy slowly picked up her fork. 'I'm sure they'll be able to identify the killer.'

'Are you sure it was her?' Linda asked. 'I mean, I've seen that hairstyle around.'

'It's not just the hair. I'm sure Coral was wearing the outfit Mandili described today,' Reese said emphatically, then looked sadly at Mandy. 'I can't believe she's died.'

'It's horrible.' Mandy pulled out her phone and pulled up Justin's number. It went straight to voicemail. She passed her phone to Reese. 'Leave a message for Justin.'

Reese explained her identification concisely, reminding Mandy that she was a registered nurse, used to transferring information in a calm manner. She must have been in a lot of pain to be so dramatic at the hospital.

'There's nothing more we can do until he calls back.' Linda's brownie was already gone. She pressed the back of her fork to a stray crumb.

'Let's please change the subject. I can't bear the thought of poor Coral.' Reese lifted her gaze to Mandy's face. 'How is it going with the new tenant in the basement?'

'I don't think he likes being here,' Mandy stated, confused by Reese's half-concerned, half-indifferent behavior. 'But he's stayed out of my way. I doubt he'll live here for long – just until he can finance another house.'

'Why do you think that?' Linda asked.

'From what his partner said today.'

Reese pushed her brownie toward Linda. 'I'm not hungry, what with finding out my friend died and all. Do you think it's worth the money to have a stranger in your house?'

'I don't have a choice if I want to keep investing in my business,' Mandy explained. 'Fannah gave me a raise after all the drama. I'm the lead barista now. Mandy's Plan is doing great, but if I'm going to hold inventory, I can't take all the profit out for my living expenses.'

'Do you need to hold much?' Linda asked.

'If I stock up in downtimes, it saves me a lot of time. It's crazy how long it takes to print and cut stickers. And then I want to add other products like the starter kit, build my brand. Maybe even license my art. I have to update my classes and keep my membership systems fresh.'

'I was thinking about renting out my basement,' Reese interjected.

Normally, Reese would have jumped on any discussion of Mandy's business plans, ready to mimic her, so Mandy knew something was wrong.

Linda asked the question first. 'Why would you want to rent out your basement? You said your parents paid for your house and you have a good salary.'

Reese exhaled through her nose. 'I'm having cash flow problems.'

Mandy winced. 'Been there. One thing you have to cut out is restaurant meals.'

'Did you buy that Tesla yourself?' Linda asked.

'I'm having a little conflict with my parents,' Reese explained. 'Besides, they are out of the country right now. I have to make a few decisions on my own.'

Mandy knew how close Reese was to her parents. Some conflict was inevitable in family relationships. Was her parental dispute the reason why Reese suddenly seemed so emotionally deadened, or was she more affected by Coral's death than she was letting on?

THREE

'One more day to go, huh,' Houston said, leaning through the doorway to the back room as Mandy took off her apron at three thirty the next day. 'Do we ever get offered overtime, like on the weekends?'

'Hasn't happened yet. Overtime's only offered when there's some kind of emergency. We don't have a big staff.'

Houston pushed floppy black hair out of his eyes. 'If you get the flu, I get more hours?'

'You might be asked to come in at seven thirty instead of nine,' she agreed. 'But mostly it's Beverly who comes in, so we have another warm body in the coffee bar.'

'Got it.'

'Cash flow problems?' Mandy asked, pulling her purse from her cubby.

He shrugged. 'Moving expenses.'

Mandy grabbed her time sheet. 'You could try to pick up a weekend gig somewhere. Not here.'

'You have another business. Need some help?'

'I have my daughter for that. Sorry.'

'Mandy?'

She recognized Reese's voice coming from the coffee bar. Mandy clocked out and went through the side door into the lobby and came up behind Reese. 'What's up?'

Reese shrieked and jumped back. 'Where did you come from?'

Mandy pointed. 'I was in the back room.'

Reese put her hand to her chest. 'Mean. I need you to go to Lynnwood with me.'

'Lynnwood?' Mandy echoed. 'Why? The traffic is horrible at this time of day.'

'That's where Coral lives – I mean, *lived*. I want to pay my respects to her husband and sister, but I don't want to go alone.'

Houston leaned over the counter. 'I'll go with you after my shift. I don't think Mandy is interested.'

Reese ignored him.

Mandy sighed. 'Don't you need to focus on prepping your basement for a tenant?'

'Pay respects,' Reese repeated. 'I need to do this.'

Mandy knew she'd end up being roped into this since she'd found Coral. 'What are you bringing?'

'Bringing?' Reese asked.

'You know, food for the bereaved.'

Reese shrugged. 'I hadn't thought of it. People my age rarely die.'

Houston put his hand to his cheek. 'You need to bring something.'

'Flowers?' Reese asked Mandy.

Houston interjected again. 'No, that's for the funeral. You need to bring food.'

Reese glanced at the pastry display case. 'You don't have much here.'

Mandy turned her back to the counter, attempting to shut Houston out of the conversation. 'The cafeteria could sell you an entire pizza, or a few pints of soup. Today is jambalaya day. A big salad? Or you could go to the grocery store on the way. A cheese plate, muffins?'

Reese rolled her eyes. 'You must be hungry. I can't show up with a Styrofoam box of salad.'

'Is that what Coral liked?'

'I don't know. She was my massage therapist. We didn't eat meals together.'

Mandy felt confused. 'Do you really know these people well enough to visit them today? How do you know where she lived?'

Reese put her fingers to her temples. 'Mandili, I feel responsible. I helped her get this job, and she died here. Her résumé had her address on it. I have to do something.'

Sadness rushed over Mandy at the thought of Coral's body. For the sake of their mental health, she changed the subject. 'She was fit. Probably a healthy eater.'

Reese brightened. 'A fruit basket. They have Easter baskets in the gift shop and fruit in the cafeteria.'

'Sure,' Mandy agreed. 'You do that.'

Reese's perfectly made-up eyes narrowed. 'You have to come with me. I can't do this alone.'

'It will take you at least fifteen minutes to do the shopping,' Mandy said. 'I'll go upstairs with you and sit on the bench outside the bathroom. I can at least get through my email while you shop.'

Reese's tiny frown appeared. Mandy wrapped her hand around Reese's elbow. 'It's a win-win. I get a little work done and you get a bereavement companion.'

'Fine.'

'Bye,' Houston called loudly as they went toward the elevator.

'Boring afternoon at the coffee bar,' Mandy said. 'Usually, the regulars abound at this time of day, but everyone who came through at three wanted something easy. Meetings keeping everyone away?'

'Must be,' Reese agreed.

Reese rejoined Mandy with a pink basket and an assortment of apples and oranges a little before four. They went across the sky bridge. At the elevator in the parking garage, Reese hit the button to the second floor and Mandy punched the top.

'Aren't we going in one car?' Reese asked in an exasperated voice.

'Justin called at two and said my car had been released,' Mandy explained.

'We don't both want to drive. What's the point?'

'Do you want to get up early again tomorrow to drive me here?'

'If I have to,' Reese said with a sigh. 'It's a lot of work being friends with you.'

Mandy tactfully changed the subject to monthly theme ideas for their journals.

Reese laughed heartily at the upcoming bunnies-drinking-tea theme. 'I would never let some common online viewer dictate my theme to me.'

'That's what you do when you gain an audience. You give them a voice. Your own journal is one thing, but you have to give your customers what they want.' They reached Reese's new car. Mandy admired the deep-blue exterior.

'My journal comes first,' Reese said stubbornly as she unlocked the car doors. 'It's for my personal use.'

'You like to do giveaways. Do two spreads in two different journals each month. One for your audience and one for yourself in your personal journal. That way it's no one's business what yours looks like.' Mandy set her stuff in the massive trunk and slid into the electric car's black interior.

'You have to do the flip-through of your pages from last month,' Reese said. 'People want to see your spreads filled out. That's why it's a bad idea to do everything in advance like you do.'

'I've been successful without including it.' Mandy considered. 'Probably because I always include recreations in my videos. Customers would rather see their work displayed on my videos than my scribbled-over pages. Or Vellum's.'

'I guess we all have to be a little different.' Reese switched topics as she reversed out of her parking space. 'I'm excited to load our tulip videos this weekend.'

'Me, too. I loaded my first April "Plan with Me" with the cherry blossoms last week and it's selling really well. With our next set of sticker releases, it's going to be a bonanza month.'

They had taken the unusual step of recording Mandy, Vellum, and Reese doing journal spreads together with Mandy's stickers, then a second video of Mandy and Reese doing more spreads with Reese's stickers. Usually with channel trades, one artist recorded a standalone video for their trade's channel and vice versa. In this instance, their geographic proximity had allowed them to team up. Despite Reese's youth, she'd become part of regular tea and brownie hang-outs with Mandy and Linda over the past month, and she'd been on hand to gently tend to Vellum when she'd tripped on the back steps and broken her toe a few weeks before.

For the rest of the drive, Reese chattered about the animals and flowers she liked to draw and which ones she was actually good at drawing, which apparently weren't the same. Then she talked about color stories. Breaking into the monologue, Mandy explained that her color choices were part of her style, and therefore if she did a penguin theme, for instance, the penguins would probably be blue or red or yellow.

'Wouldn't that turn off customers?'

'Not when I've set the expectations of my work being bright and colorful. No one comes to me for color realism.'

'You did snowflakes and snowdrops,' Reese pointed out.

'The snowflakes were silver and gold to the extent that my printer could handle the colors. And with the snowdrops, only the flowers were white. Everything else was bright. You won't see me doing a basic brown bear or a basic white bunny.'

'What are you going to do for bunnies drinking tea? I wanted to do a teddy bears' picnic, remember? How is this idea any better?'

'Customer choice,' Mandy said. 'I'm going to do navy-blue bunnies. Blue bunnies are a real thing. It's the entire theme that's bugging me. Real bunnies don't have any body part that can hold a teacup.'

'Maybe baby bunnies in a teacup?' Reese suggested.

'Hmm.' Mandy considered. 'That's good, Reese. I was thinking perhaps bunnies frolicking around a set-up tea service. Maybe with that colorful Mexican pottery.'

'Is that going to appeal to your school-aged audience?'

'That's what the fans voted for. At least if it's a big fail, I went into the May selling period with great sales for April to balance it out. Trust me, I'm doubting the theme, too.'

The car wound through two-lane roads in an off-the-beaten-track part of Lynnwood. Eventually, Reese turned across the lanes of traffic and pulled into a driveway on a rectangular piece of land that lay next to the side of the road.

Mandy saw two buildings on the lot, both of the prefab variety. One was a temporary home of the kind for sale along the I-5 freeway where she used to have to drive to Portland for archery camp. The other appeared to be a duo of businesses. One burned-wood sign said *Viking Forge* and on the opposite side of the long building the sign announced *Portilla Tattoo*.

'Do you have any tattoos?' Mandy asked.

'No.'

Reese looked up at the buildings. 'Coral told me about the setup here. Her husband owns the forge. Their friend owns the tattoo shop, but Phuc Trong Pham runs it. He specializes in traditional Vietnamese and Cambodian tattoos. And war stuff. She showed me a photo of a tattoo with helicopters landing over rice paddies. Really realistic.'

'What does Portilla mean?'

'That's the owner's name. Rod Portilla. He's Coral's husband's business partner.'

'Who owns the land?' It was an odd oblong-shaped lot, but nothing came cheap in the Seattle area.

'I think Tom inherited it from his great-aunt.' Reese frowned. 'Well, someone inherited it from someone.'

'Tom's the husband?'

'Yes, Tom DeRoy. Coral kept her name – Le Charme. She said it was too cool to give up.'

'So Coral was married to a blacksmith? Or is he a farrier?'

'Bladesmith. He makes custom kitchen knives.'

The word sent chills through Mandy. 'Last I heard, they hadn't found the knife that was used on Coral.'

They shared a glance, then Reese shook her head sharply. 'Not Tom. He adored her.'

'What about this Rod guy? Did he adore her, too?'

'He's around a lot, but it's not like he lives with them. He has an apartment somewhere. Coral and Tom do live with their siblings, though. Darci and Peony. Peony is Coral's sister and she's disabled. Cerebral palsy. Darci is a hair stylist, and she's Tom's sister.'

Mandy glanced around the property. The grass was mowed and the driveway showed only the usual amount of wear. The buildings were utilitarian, and the street noise was irritating, but the setting didn't have a negative quality. 'Did Coral have a lot of friends and acquaintances outside of her family?'

'I doubt it,' Reese said. 'She grew up in Alaska and I think she's spent a lot of time caring for her sister.'

'There are so many Alaskans around here. Houston, my new coworker, just moved down from Anchorage.' Mandy stared into Reese's eyes. 'Who do you think killed Coral? Could it be someone who lives or works right here?'

She glanced away. 'That's for your housemate to figure out, not me.'

Mandy touched her arm. 'You're obviously more friendly with Coral than a mere acquaintance. You know these people, Reese.'

'I bet a stranger killed her,' Reese said, pulling her key from the ignition. 'Not one of the family. Someone might have killed her for her wallet.'

Mandy clutched her purse and followed Reese out of the car, trying not to think about the events that had led up to Coral's death. If she'd gone to her car a few minutes earlier, she might have saved Coral's life – or been the murder victim herself. She shivered.

Reese pulled open the door to the forge building, holding the fruit basket with her other hand. They entered a small anteroom with an appointment table that held brochures and an appointment book. A cell phone had been left there. Cubbies along the wall were empty.

'Maybe we should have gone to the house?' Mandy asked.

Before Reese could respond, the shop door opened and a man came into the room.

'I thought I heard voices,' he said.

Mandy guessed this was Tom. Slim, he wore a leather apron

over a utility kilt and a T-shirt. His long black hair was braided back and he had an anvil medallion strung on a leather thong around his neck. She checked his arms for tattoos but his skin was dark enough that she couldn't make out more than black lines on the inside of one forearm.

Reese held up the fruit basket. Her lips trembled. 'I'm so sorry for your loss.'

Tom closed his eyes for a second, then he nodded. 'Thanks, girl.'

She shoved the basket in his direction, then put a handkerchief to her eyes.

Mandy suddenly wondered if she should even be there. Why had she let Reese talk her into this? Tom had to be the chief suspect in his wife's death, unless the police could tell it was a robbery as Reese had theorized. From what little she knew about crime, the husband was the first one to be checked out. Besides, this guy knew knives.

He looked at her expectantly. The pink basket looked utterly idiotic in his hand.

'I'm Mandy Meadows. I gave your wife CPR. I tried to save her.' Mandy's voice cut out on a squeak. She swallowed. 'I didn't know her, but I'm so sorry. I did everything I could.'

He frowned. 'Do you work in the ER or something? You a doctor?'

'No, I'm a barista. I found your wife in the parking garage.' She glanced from Reese to Tom, feeling her body shake with remembered adrenaline from the night before.

Tom worked his jaw. 'Umm, I've been wondering, did she suffer? I mean . . .'

Tears flowed down Reese's cheeks. Mandy's voice shook as she answered. 'It was pretty dark, but I think . . . well, she seemed peaceful. I'm just sorry, is all.' Everything that wanted to come out of her mouth seemed inappropriate to say in front of the widower, whether he was a murderer or not.

He set the basket on the appointment table, then ran his fingers over the top of his head, dislodging coarse strands of hair. 'I guess we all need therapy after something like this. I keep thinking she'll walk in. Her shift ended at three. She ought to be home any second now.'

Mandy wished she understood psychology. Why was he in his forge instead of his house? Was he behaving like an appropriately grieving husband? But even if he was, that could mask some kind of psychopathy. Like Ted Bundy, the scourge of Seattle for a time in the 1970s, or someone like that. The Green River killer. But those were serial killers, not some random wife killer. A person could probably kill their wife and not anyone else. 'We shouldn't have come here today. It was insensitive.'

'No, no. I've met Reese a couple of times.' He nodded at Reese. 'It was kind of you to bring, er, food. Coral had a massage table here at the house and she took private patients on Sundays when her old clinic was closed. I got used to seeing you around.'

That explained why Reese was familiar with the situation here without considering Coral a friend. Mandy nodded encouragingly at Tom, hoping to learn more information that Reese seemed to be reluctant to share.

'I found her the new job. It was a rotten commute, but what isn't around here?' Reese said.

Tom's voice lowered, as if realizing this conversation was far too normal for the circumstances. 'I'd have thought, if you had to get hurt, being at the hospital was the best place for it, but I guess she was hurt too bad, huh.'

Mandy fought to keep her voice steady. 'I called nine-one-one and then the hospital switchboard. Help came fast, and I'd already tried CPR. It was just a couple of minutes before they had her inside. But I don't know how long she was there before I found her.'

Tom took a shuddering breath. 'Did you see who hurt her?'

Mandy shook her head. 'No. She was alone. I was hoping the security cameras picked up what happened.'

He shook his head. 'Blind spot. The police came by last night. You really didn't see anyone in the garage?'

Oh no. 'No. That means the police have nothing to go on?' Mandy asked.

A bang startled Tom before he could answer. Two young women came in from the forge, a heavy door swinging shut behind them. One, lovely despite teenage acne, wore a tank top and cut-offs that displayed muscular limbs. She had braces on her ankles and knees, and walked with a stiff, uneven gait. The other woman had long black hair, braided like Tom's, and looked a bit older than the teenager. She wore a thin summer sundress but was sweating.

Mandy guessed they were Peony and Darci, from the descriptions she'd heard earlier.

Reese made a visible effort to pull herself together. 'You're working today?'

'Got an order for a new restaurant in Fremont,' Tom said. 'Chef knives. There's a waiting list for autopsies. It's not like we can plan a funeral just yet.'

'She wouldn't want one anyway,' Peony said in a clotted, dull tone. 'Coral was an atheist. Dead is dead.'

'How sad,' Reese, a devout Hindu, murmured. 'I hope you'll have some kind of celebration of her life.'

Tom fluffed up his hair again. 'Yeah, maybe here at the forge.'

The door to the outside opened again and another man popped in. His skin had a yellowish cast under the tan and his hair was dark, with thick eyebrows and a day-old beard. Handsome, to be sure, but Mandy never liked the covered-in-tattoos look, or men wearing white tank tops.

Tom glanced at him, then at Reese, then at the man again. 'Rod, I don't think you've met Coral's friend, Reese. And this is the woman who found Coral yesterday. Sorry, I don't remember your name.'

'Mandy.' She shook the man's hand.

'I could use some help with the power hammer. It's on the fritz,' Tom said.

'Anything you need,' Rod said. 'But first I need to help Pham. There's something wrong with the power supply.'

'I'll take a look,' Tom said. 'Girls? Why don't you grind edges on to the last batch of knives?'

They nodded dutifully and went back through the forge door.

'We should go,' Mandy murmured. 'We just wanted to pay our respects.'

'Oh, stay,' Rod invited. 'I'll show you around. It will take my mind off the tragedy.' He grabbed an apple from Reese's fruit basket and strode out of the front door.

Mandy expected Reese to make her excuses, but she followed Rod out. Mandy shrugged and tagged along.

'Have you ever been in the tattoo shop, Reese?' Tom asked as they walked alongside the building.

'Not this one, but I did go into one once.' Reese touched the tiny diamond in her nose piercing. 'I had this done and my friend had a butterfly tattooed on her ankle.'

Rod held the door open for them, then checked out Reese's piercing as she walked by. 'Looks like they did a good job. It's exactly in the right place. Who did the work?'

'It was years ago.' Reese tucked her handkerchief away. 'The shop is long gone.'

Mandy, her nose wrinkling from the heavy antiseptic smell of the shop, noted that Reese showed no interest in Rod, despite his interest in her. Or maybe it was merely the sad circumstances that had tamped down her usual flirtatious way with attractive men.

'Hey, Pham,' Tom said, with an exhausted-looking wave. 'What's wrong with the power supply?'

The tattoo artist patted the shoulder of his client, a slim young woman getting a tramp stamp. Mandy didn't have a chance to see the design before it was covered up with cream and a bandage. 'I finished manually.'

'I'm all done?' The woman displayed discolored teeth.

Pham nodded. 'Follow the tattoo care instruction sheet I gave you.'

The client weaved unsteadily out of the front door.

'I hope she isn't driving,' Reese said.

'A friend's waiting.' Pham gave Reese the once-over. 'You want a tattoo? You'll have to wait. Come back in an hour.'

Tom crouched on his haunches while Pham spoke, pulling cables from a cabinet against the wall. 'She brought food because of Coral.'

'Oh,' Pham said. 'Well, I'll show you anyway, OK?'

'You think it's a bad cord?' Rod asked.

Tom shrugged. 'First thing to check. Not that my luck can get any worse.'

Mandy glanced between the two men. Reese was distracted, attempting to fend off Pham. He had out his design book and was assuring her that they were all his original art.

Rod glanced at Mandy. 'Is Pham going after the wrong customer? Do you want some ink?'

'No, thanks.'

'It will help out the business. Tom can use the trade.'

'What about you?' She took a step in Rod's direction. 'Your name is on the shop.'

'We own the businesses together.' He winked at her. 'C'mon sweetheart, just a little something?'

'I don't think so.'

'I'll take you out for dinner after,' Rod urged. 'Make a night of it.'

'My daughter is waiting for me,' Mandy said. 'I just came along to support Reese.'

'I can't believe she did that,' Tom muttered, ripping a cord free of the power unit and throwing it against the cabinet.

'What's wrong?' Rod asked.

'Darci. She took the good cord for her salon station and left us with the frayed one. I don't have a replacement.'

'Why are you still letting her live here?' Rod puffed out his chest.

'She isn't making enough for her own place.' Tom swore.

Mandy wondered if he was taking his grief over Coral out on this seemingly minor problem.

'Then it's time to get rid of Peony,' Rod said. 'She's eighteen next month and her sister is dead. Two weeks' notice, that's all.'

'You know that'll never happen. Darci is much harder to live with,' Tom said, staring at the group of cables. 'She's so messy. At least Peony makes sandwiches.'

'I don't know how you can live like this, man. Two chicks under your roof, eating your food, and no one to—' He made a rude gesture.

Mandy was repulsed by the casual misogyny, and in front of a stranger, no less. Poor Peony. She hoped the disabled teen had a case manager to help her.

Tom stood up and picked up the frayed cord, then hunted around in a drawer until he found some duct tape. He wrapped it securely, then plugged it back into the power source. When he flipped a switch, a light turned on.

'There you go!' Rod said, delighted. 'I knew you could make it work.'

'I have another client in twenty minutes,' Pham said. Reese

took advantage of the break in his attention and dashed to Mandy's side.

Rod nodded and went to the iPad docked on the cabinet. 'I have a free night. C'mon, ladies, what do you say? Beers and wings?'

Mandy shook her head slowly. 'No, I have to get home to cook for my daughter.'

'I'm her ride.' Reese forced the words through tense lips. 'You can use the time to buy a new cord somewhere.'

'Or wring it out of Darci's hide,' Rod growled.

'Go easy on her,' Mandy interjected. 'She's bereaved.'

With that, Mandy followed Reese out of the door. They didn't speak until they reached the car.

'Good grief,' Mandy said.

'Rod is a creep,' Reese added.

'And Tom's a mess. Poor Peony. Do you think he'll really kick her out?'

'I think they live pretty much hand to mouth. Now they've lost whatever income Coral made, and her burial arrangements will cost something.'

Mandy huffed out a breath, thinking about what the family faced. 'Tom will probably have to take time off from work to deal with all of it. I just hope he doesn't take it out on Coral's sister.'

'Me, too,' Reese agreed.

'What do you think?' Mandy asked, when Reese had driven back on to the street. 'Did any of them murder Coral?'

FOUR

'Yum, Chinese is good,' Vellum cooed as she forked up a chunk of Szechuan tofu, her thick blond hair tucked into the back of her school logo sweatshirt to keep it away from her dinner.

Mandy chuckled from her spot on the opposite end of the living-room coffee table. Mother and daughter were perched on beachy striped cushions on the floor as they ate the takeout she and Reese had picked up on the way back from Lynnwood.

'It's nice to be able to comfortably afford it again, that's for sure.' Mandy pressed her lips shut. She'd learned the hard way not to bring up the subject of money around her daughter. A month ago, Vellum had briefly moved in with her father's family and had just about broken Mandy's heart. Vellum had quickly discerned that her father wasn't very parental and her grandmother, with whom he lived, was deeply rigid. But the whole unfortunate situation had occurred because Vellum had worried about her mother's finances.

'I'm glad Justin is here,' Vellum said. 'I like having a cop around the house. It's as though we have our own personal watchdog.'

'That's not a very polite way to put it,' Mandy said. 'No one likes being called a dog.'

'That's not what I meant, Mom.' Vellum rolled her eyes.

'Words have power,' Mandy cautioned. 'Just saying.' She forked up an extra-large broccoli tree from its pool of garlic sauce and was about to bite down when the doorbell rang.

No packages were due to be delivered. With the knowledge that nothing good came to her front door, Mandy set down her broccoli and went to answer.

She glanced through the security peephole and saw a familiar face, albeit belonging to one who was out of place and shouldn't know her address: Houston Harris.

'Who is it, Mom?'

'A co-worker.' Mandy opened the door, unsure how to greet him.

A wide smile that looked twenty percent too big for his jaw beamed goodwill at her. 'Hi, Mandy. Sorry to drop in on you like this.'

She frowned. 'I don't remember telling you where I live.'

'You said you were across the street from Shangri-La Bakery,' he told her.

'I'm not, exactly.' She folded her arms over her chest.

'And that your house is on the corner, and it's painted green,' he added.

She needed to be more careful about what she said at work. 'Right. What can I do for you?' A gust of wind hit Mandy in the face. It went right through to her sinuses. Pain flared. Against her better judgment, she stepped back to let him in.

Houston planted his feet right on the small rug on the floor and made a show of wiping his feet.

Mandy's stomach gave a little growl of irritation. At Houston's amused grin, she explained, 'We were just eating dinner.'

'You should eat.' Houston shooed her as he pulled off his coat.

'Yes, I should,' Mandy agreed, then stalked back to her cushion. 'What are you doing here?'

'This must be the famous Vellum,' Houston exclaimed, bestowing that overlarge smile on her daughter.

Vellum waved and returned to eating, obviously categorizing him as her mother's friend and therefore not worth being interested in.

Without invitation, Houston plopped himself down on Mandy's cranberry recliner, putting himself beside Vellum and above both of them. Mandy decided to ignore him for a minute in the interest of her stomach and forked up her broccoli.

Vellum gave her a disapproving glance. 'Do you want some?' she asked, tilting her head back. 'We have eggrolls.'

'Yum.' Houston dropped his coat to the floor and tore open the waxed paper bag in his eagerness to grab an eggroll. He dipped it into the open container of sweet-and-sour sauce, catching drips with his palm as he shoved it into his mouth.

Vellum's lips twitched. Mandy's stomach clenched with anger but she was starving. She'd moved on to fried rice when he spoke again.

'I stopped by because you mentioned your friend's possible rental.'

Mandy glanced up and saw that Houston was staring at Vellum's profile instead of looking at her.

'Reese is going to rent out her house? Where is she moving to?' Vellum set down her fork. 'I thought she was rich.'

Mandy shot Vellum a warning glance. 'She's just talking about renting out her basement like we do.'

'Is it nice?' Houston asked Vellum.

Vellum shrugged. 'Never been in her basement.' She snagged the last eggroll before he could.

His mouth turned down.

Buy your own food, buddy. 'I'll text Reese. I know she's home.' Mandy wiped her greasy fingers on a napkin and sent the message

before returning to her food. She hoped Reese would agree to
show him around right away since she didn't like Houston's fascin-
ation with Vellum, who was five years his junior.

He stared mournfully at the empty eggroll bag, then seemed to
shake it off and asked Vellum about her movie and book tastes.
She'd tentatively engaged in a discussion of a teen-focused Jack
the Ripper retelling when Mandy's phone beeped with a response
from Reese.

'You're in luck,' Mandy said. 'Let's walk over there.'

'No rush,' Houston said, glancing at Vellum. 'You can finish
eating.'

'I've had enough.' Mandy grabbed the table edge and pulled
herself up. Her elbow spasmed.

'You coming?' he asked Vellum.

'I've seen enough basements,' she said, and took another bite
of cooling fried rice.

Mandy, grateful that she showed no sign of interest in the older
boy, directed him toward the entryway. She shoved her feet into
an old pair of rainboots, then opened the front door.

'Reese is across the street and down a bit. Similar layout.'

'You didn't give me a tour.'

Mandy would have fixed him with a glare, but there wasn't
enough light on her front walkway for him to see it. 'I don't have
time to entertain unexpected visitors.'

His head hung down, but she didn't really buy his remorse.
After all, he'd eaten her eggroll.

Mandy led him across the street, then past her mother's house
to Reese's door. 'Sorry to interrupt your dinner,' Mandy told Reese
when she opened the door.

'I was about to run a bath and go to bed early, since I have to
get up to take you to work.' Reese fluttered her eyelashes.

Houston glanced from Reese to Mandy, visibly amused at the
grousing.

'You're looking to rent here?' Reese continued. 'Why not somewhere around the hospital? It makes much more sense for you.'

'Mandy seems to like the neighborhood.' He coughed. 'I'd like
to explore Seattle more.'

Reese frowned but invited them in. Her living room had an
uncluttered vibe, with a hardwood floor and no adornments other

than a long cream sofa and an incense and flower-decorated altar along the wall, featuring the Hindu goddess Parvati. Mandy admired the beautiful brass statue of the goddess, which stood out among other smaller god and goddess figurines, while Reese led them into the hallway.

Reese's deliciously scented leftovers were still on the counter. Her cat prowled by, then disappeared in the direction of the dining room. She opened the basement door and turned on the light. Her stairs looked steeper than Mandy's, with no turn, just a straight jaunt to the bottom.

'I didn't realize your layout was so different,' Mandy commented. Her elbow spasmed again.

Houston followed Reese down, with Mandy walking more slowly, massaging her joint.

'You'll see the full bath, along with a bedroom. Upstairs offers kitchen privileges, plus a separate entrance and laundry down here,' Reese said briskly, heading to the bedroom.

Houston paused at an open door. Mandy glanced in and saw a massive flat-screen television, in a room decked out like a movie theater. Reese even had a popcorn machine in the corner.

'Is this part of the rental?' Houston asked.

Reese glared at Houston. 'No.' Her hair bounced on her shoulders as she kept moving. 'What's nice about my downstairs bedroom, unlike Mandy's, is that the bathroom is en suite. It's very private.'

Houston glanced into the empty room. 'It's a good size.'

'About three hundred and fifty square feet including the bathroom,' Reese said. 'I could offer it furnished as well, if necessary.'

'I would want to use the TV room,' Houston said. 'We could work out a schedule. Like in the morning I could use it. I work nine thirty to six.'

'Hmm,' Reese murmured.

'What is your asking price?' Mandy asked, knowing what Reese's tone of voice meant.

Reese named a rental price, plus generous deposit, that sounded sky-high.

Mandy's eyebrows shot up. The price was ridiculous. Maybe it would be only a little overpriced if the TV room was included. Hadn't Reese done her research?

'No, thanks,' Houston said with a chuckle. 'I'm sure you know what Mandy and I make.'

'She's vague,' Reese drawled. 'I'm sorry the property is out of your price range.'

'Are you sure you don't want to lower it? For a co-worker.' He cocked his head and smiled that overly large smile of his again.

'I don't think we'd be able to work it out,' Reese said smoothly. 'I don't want to waste anyone's time, so I'll show you out, hmm?'

The nurse moved them out of her house with dexterity. While it wasn't like Reese to not even offer her guests tea, Mandy guessed she didn't want a young male stranger as her tenant. Did she disagree? Not really. She barely knew Houston herself.

Friday brought several waves of business through the coffee bar. Fannah kept Mandy busy making cookies whenever she could be spared from the counter. They were too busy for the new frosted cookies so she baked her classics – ginger thins and chocolate chip.

'I could smell the ginger from the elevators,' Dr Burrell said, stepping up to the counter.

Mandy grinned at him. 'I made them myself.'

'A fantastic job you do, too.'

Mandy colored and changed the subject. 'They must have changed the air flow in here again. No one has ever come sniffing from the elevators before.'

He tapped his finger on his upper lip. 'I bet they did. That gust right in between the elevator banks seems to be gone.'

Her fingers waited at the cash register. 'How about in Neonatal Intensive Care? I hear the waiting room is freezing.'

'No, that hasn't changed. Maybe I'll have a chat with Maintenance.'

Fannah floated in from the back and gently nudged Mandy out of the way. 'The timer just went off, Mandy. What can I get you, Stan?'

Mandy went back to her toaster oven. She was hardly going to face off with her boss over a very nice doctor.

Shortly after, Fannah's shift ended. Houston appeared at Mandy's elbow and complained about Reese's overpriced basement.

'She didn't even want me to use the TV? That's crazy.'

'It wasn't personal,' Mandy assured him. 'You saw how clean her house was. She isn't used to having a tenant.'

'Tell her she's overpricing that rental. Maybe we can still work something out.'

'I suspect she's just testing the waters and isn't serious,' she explained.

A trio of ER nurses approached as soon as their shift ended. They commuted together to somewhere in the south end.

'Have you heard anything more about the murder, Mandy?'

Mandy didn't know the name of the nurse who asked, because she flipped over her badge when she was in the lobby, but she knew Everly. The flaming red-haired nurse, a decade younger than her commuter friends, leaned against the counter.

'Coral was a terrible massage therapist,' Everly confided.

'I wonder how she was even hired,' said the first nurse.

'I know how she got the interview,' Mandy said. 'Maybe there weren't any other candidates. Are you having your regular orders today?'

They all nodded. 'I'll have to tell Amrik to be pickier next time,' Everly said. 'Otherwise I'm going back to my chiropractor's massage therapist.'

'Is Amrik the massage manager?' Mandy asked.

'I think he owns the business,' Everly said. 'He's the only guy.'

The third nurse rolled her eyes. 'Why can't we bring in a woman-owned business?'

'Maybe they should get a new company in here,' the third nurse shrilled. 'What if he's the one who killed that massage tech?'

'Why would he do that?' Mandy asked.

The nurse shrugged. 'I don't know. An affair gone wrong or something?'

'Have you ever had a massage in the lobby?' Houston asked while Mandy washed pitchers just before her shift ended.

The tables to the right of the coffee bar were filled with their customers, but no one was at the counter.

'I never had that kind of disposable cash,' Mandy said. 'Things were tight after my marriage broke up. I took this job, rented out my basement and started a business.'

'Didn't someone die in your house recently? I heard someone talking about it.'

Mandy had become used to casual comments about her cousin's death. He'd been an employee here as well as her tenant. But it still hurt. She missed her oldest friend. 'My cousin; he'd been renting from me. But I have my new tenant now and my business is growing, so I guess I could afford a massage.'

'I noticed you were rubbing your elbow last night. Barista elbow?'

'Is that a thing?' Just the thought made pain pulse in the joint.

'Yes. I knew someone about your age who had it at my last job. She was responsible for moving heavy milk jugs from the deliveries into all the refrigerators. Lots of lifting and bending.'

'I hope it doesn't become chronic,' Mandy fretted, ignoring his dig about her age.

'Get a massage,' Houston advised. 'See where the pain is starting.'

'You mean like in my shoulder?'

'Or your neck. Maybe you need physical therapy.'

'I'll do a web search for stretches to combat it,' Mandy said. 'But, yeah, I guess I could try that fifteen-minute employee special. They probably aren't that busy right now.'

She clocked out, grabbed her things, and walked across the lobby to the alcove that had been taken over by the massage people in January. Management had removed the grand piano that volunteers used to play, theoretically to soothe stressed-out passers-by. It seemed to have the opposite effect. One guy used to come in and do forty-five minutes of ragtime, which set her teeth on edge. Five weeks of constant Christmas carols had felt like a relief after that.

White fabric-covered temporary walls squared off the corner of the lobby these days, with a desk on wheels in front. She recognized the attractive, angular-faced Indian man who sat on a cheap folding chair because she'd seen him around, but he'd never visited the coffee bar.

'Do you have a fifteen-minute employee slot open?' she asked.

'I haven't seen you before,' he said, his elongated black eyebrows bunching up on his narrow, unlined forehead.

She pulled her badge out of her pocket. 'First-time customer. I work at the coffee bar. I'm Mandy. What's your name?'

'Amrik Kurmi.' His cheekbones popped dazzlingly as he smiled. 'I don't drink coffee.'

'We serve tea, and milk and alternative milk drinks, too.'

Without responding, he scribbled something down in his paperwork, then handed her a form to fill out. He waited patiently while she did so and then dug in her purse for cash. None appeared. She'd already given Vellum her allowance, so this indulgence had to go on her credit card. Now she really hoped that the extra themed set of April planner stickers would sell.

Amrik used a tablet to process her card and handed it to her to sign. Then he took her behind the wall, where a female therapist massaged a clothed nurse on a table. There were also two chairs with headrests. She expected that one of these had been Coral's station.

'Do you normally have four massage stations going at once?' she asked, placing her bags where he directed, then settling herself on the chair. Having second thoughts, she pulled off her sweater to give him more access. She really did hurt.

'You knew Coral,' he said evenly. 'I know you found her. I recognize your name.'

The other therapist glanced up at the sound of Coral's name, then went back to work.

'I didn't know Coral,' Mandy said. 'But you're right, I did find her. She'd been attacked next to my car.'

'I see.' He moved behind her and put his hands on her shoulders, gently squeezing.

Her right arm gave a twinge. She hoped she hadn't just given a murderer access to her neck. 'I have pain radiating down.'

'You have very tight muscles on the right.'

'That's why I'm here,' she said lightly.

'Did Reese O'Leary-Sett send you?'

'No, my co-worker Houston Harris suggested it. But Reese is a friend. She told me she recommended Coral for the job after her old business closed.'

'That's true.' Amrik massaged her arm, working out the kinks with firm strokes. 'Make sure you drink a bottle of water after this. I would also ice your shoulder and arm.'

'I never think to at this time of year,' she admitted guiltily.

'After you apply ice, you can apply heat if you are too cold,' he suggested, his talented hands moving down her side.

She sighed, relaxing. 'I should have done this a long time ago. How did you talk the hospital into putting your business here?'

'I have a cousin who works in Administration. I worked for a company that supplied massage therapists to corporations in the area, so when I had the opportunity, I knew how to start my own business.'

'Did you know Coral before?'

'No, but I was glad to hire her.'

'It sounds like she had trouble adjusting to clothed chair massages instead of table massages,' Mandy suggested.

'It's not for everyone.'

'Was she just having a bad day, that last day? Was she normally a good therapist?'

His hands left her back and he picked up a water container and took a drink. Then he moved in front of her and did more work on her shoulders. 'Her work was deteriorating. I suppose it doesn't matter now,' he said softly. 'Tom, her husband, abused her.'

'What?' Mandy lifted her head.

'On the towel, please,' he said.

'Right, sorry.' All her tension had reappeared. 'That makes no sense to me. Reese took me up to Tom's property to pay our condolences. We brought a fruit basket.'

'I'm sure she wanted to comfort Peony, not Tom.' His hands relaxed her again. 'After what Coral told me at our interview, I hired her out of pity so she could build up some cash to escape her marriage. Did you meet Peony?'

'Yes, she's a lovely, quiet girl. We met Darci, too. And the business partners.'

His voice softened. 'I'm really going to miss seeing Coral and Peony.'

'Did they have a good relationship?'

'Yes. Coral worked Saturday to Wednesday and Peony would bring her lunch on the weekends. They were two peas in a pod.'

'That's sweet. I met so many people so fast last night that I had trouble forming any impression, except of that Rod Portilla.'

'That's the husband's business partner?'

'Yes. He seemed pretty pushy.'

'Coral didn't say much about anyone other than her husband and sister. She was so proud of everything Peony accomplished despite her disability. I guess she wasn't expected to survive childhood and here she is about to graduate high school.'

'Oh my goodness. I saw her legs were in braces and her speech was impaired but I didn't know how bad the situation had been. Cerebral palsy varies so much.'

'She had trouble with swallowing when she was a toddler. Coral said she had pneumonia multiple times because she would get material in her lungs.'

Mandy shuddered. 'That's terrible. I hope she's doing better now. Is that why she moved here from Alaska? For treatment? It's such a big decision to leave your parents and move in with your sister.'

'Yes, but Coral was better equipped to deal with it, I think. She was a born caregiver. You are familiar with cerebral palsy?'

'My daughter had a classmate with it in grade school.'

'Well, Coral was under a great deal of strain. She didn't do her best work here.' Amrik's voice went hard. 'That husband of hers has it coming.'

Abuse would cause a lot of strain, and maybe pain too, and that would make it hard to give a massage. She wondered what could have set Tom off recently. Fears of a workplace affair, maybe?

'I admit I'm confused how the notoriously picky Reese could have liked Coral's services so much in her previous massage place, when everyone is saying Coral was so terrible at the hospital,' Mandy admitted.

'She didn't like massaging over clothing,' Amrik explained. 'She said it hurt her hands and she couldn't read the patient's body.'

Mandy considered. 'I guess that makes sense. How long did she work here?'

'Six weeks. She started just after I opened.' Amrik's strokes changed, and he went over her back one last time with soothing movements.

Mandy wished she'd paid for more than fifteen minutes. When his hands left her shirt, she said, 'That was lovely. I'm going to go over my finances and see if I can make this a weekly indulgence.' She sat up, feeling relaxed and mildly dizzy.

'Remember, water and ice,' he continued.

'I'll fill my water bottle on the way out, and ice at home,' she said. 'I promise.'

He nodded, unsmiling. While pleasant, he was a complete professional and Mandy didn't feel any sense of warmth from him. Despite the troubling conversation, he'd done an excellent job. She'd be back if she could afford it. Unless he was arrested. But he sounded more likely to have killed Tom than Coral.

'You look flushed,' Vellum observed as Mandy entered her kitchen through the mudroom door an hour later.

'Bathroom,' Mandy gasped, and zipped through the kitchen. Drinking twenty-four ounces during her commute wasn't her smartest move.

When she came out again, Vellum frowned. 'You OK?'

'I invested in a little chair massage because my arm was bugging me.' She opened the freezer and pulled out a soft rectangular ice pack. 'I drank a ton of water and now I'm supposed to ice.'

'Oh, OK.' A horn honking outside captured Vellum's attention. 'There's my ride.'

'Have fun at the movies,' Mandy said, kissing her daughter's forehead.

'Are you doing anything fun tonight?' Vellum asked.

'I'll give Linda or Reese a call. Or check in with Mom.'

'OK. If your arm is hurting, I can deal with our social media when I have time.'

Mandy appreciated that, but she'd have to pay Vellum for the hours. 'I'll try to keep it to a minimum, but you know we're going to get a ton of comments when I load the new video.'

'Load it now,' Vellum suggested. 'So we can spread out our responses. We can wait to fulfill orders on Sunday when I get home.'

'Yes, ma'am.' Mandy waved with her left hand as Vellum went out the front door with her backpack, then stood on the landing and waved again at Vellum's best friend Kate's mother, Olivia, who was on driving duty that night.

Mandy collapsed on to the sofa and tucked her ice pack inside her shirt, then molded it around her shoulder. After that, she loaded the new April 'Plan with Me' tulip video, and texted Reese to warn her it was going up, before turning on the TV to relax. Reese texted back, saying she would start her video load too, and the third vlogger, Tamika, who was doing tulips along with them was doing the same.

Mandy yawned and settled in. Her phone buzzed again. Reese, asking her to attend an impromptu memorial gathering for Coral at the family property. Mandy winced at the thought of being around Rod Portilla again, but she suspected Reese needed the support. She texted back to Reese to say yes, then texted Justin to see if her housemate knew about the event. His footsteps in the kitchen had woken her early that morning, but she hadn't actually seen him since giving her statement on Wednesday night.

A buzzing woke her sometime later. She blinked, disturbing images of targets flashing through her vision. Noise blared and she discovered the television was on. She turned it off. So much for catching up on *Top Chef*. Her phone buzzed again, a text notification. She picked up her phone, expecting to see a row of excited emojis from Reese, but instead it was her ex-husband.

Sorry babe, I can't take Vellum this weekend, Cory's text said.

Mandy growled. How could he do this so late? With a year having passed since their separation, she wished he had figured out the new routine by now. She quickly texted him back. *You're supposed to pick up the girls at the Varsity at nine tonight.*

Can't do it, he texted back.

Mandy gritted her teeth. She checked her phone and saw she'd have to leave right away. *Unacceptable*, she texted back, then shoved her phone into her pocket and went to get her coat. She knew perfectly well that no amount of dad-shaming would make him go to the movie theater. For all she knew, he wasn't even in town. What would it take to instill a sense of responsibility in her ex?

FIVE

Mandy stood alone at Coral's memorial service on Saturday. Even though four people lived there, the living room of the DeRoy/Le Charme house didn't contain much – just a television and one sofa. A couple of grocery store trays of finger food had been set on a card table, and a cooler of cheap beer hugged the carpet next to it. Maybe they had moved out furniture in anticipation of a crowd.

She counted twenty people milling around the house. A small group had been talking massages in front of the TV, so they were probably Coral's former co-workers. Then there were half a dozen men in kilts. She guessed they were students at the forge, or maybe tattoo clients. They all had at least one full sleeve of tattoos.

The front door opened. Amrik, Coral's employer, appeared, followed by a pretty woman around his age in a sari. Mandy moved in his direction. At least she'd met him, and she'd already fended off Rod once since she'd arrived. Reese had vanished into the kitchen, supposedly to help make tea.

'Hello, Amrik,' Mandy called, walking toward him.

He frowned, obviously unable to place her.

'Mandy from the hospital. We met when I had a massage,' she explained.

His expression cleared. 'Yes, of course. You have a sad connection with Coral.' He took the arm of his companion. 'May I introduce my sister? Nandini Kurmi, this is Mandy, one of my clients.'

Mandy shook the young woman's hand. 'I love your sari. That shade of lilac is a favorite of mine.'

'Thank you. You knew the deceased?' Nandini leaned her head closer, wafting sandalwood through the air. 'I never met her.'

'Ah.' Mandy glanced at Amrik.

Amrik whispered something in another language in Nandini's ear. Her mouth went slack. She squeezed Mandy's hand. 'Oh, I am so sorry. How tragic.'

Mandy couldn't bring herself to smile. 'Yes, it was.' Feeling uncomfortable, she glanced around the room and noticed Darci and Peony had come into the living room.

Peony wore a long black sundress with a light rose-colored sweater over it. It almost hid her leg braces. Her light makeup enhanced model-worthy cheekbones and full lips. Darci had donned a form-fitting black cocktail dress with cutouts and put her dark hair into a twist. She looked like Audrey Hepburn, only missing the pearls and cigarette holder.

Mandy sighed inwardly, but both of them were young and unlikely to have anything more appropriate to wear. Most everyone else wore jeans, and she realized she might be the oldest person in the room – even Amrik looked a couple of years younger than her.

'We should pay our respects,' Amrik suggested.

Mandy nodded and followed him to the girls, with Nandini at her side.

Amrik took the hand of each girl in turn, and offered his soft-voiced condolences, then introduced his sister. Darci gave Mandy a hug. Peony pressed her hand, her expression unfocused and stoic. Mandy wondered if she'd been given a tranquilizer.

'Are your parents here?' she asked gently.

Peony shook her head, then bit her lip. 'My throat is really dry.'

'Do you drink tea? Something warm might be good,' Mandy suggested.

'We like hot chocolate,' Darci said.

'I'll be happy to make some for you.' Mandy felt odd about making the offer but it wasn't as if she had anyone to talk to here.

'I'll come with you.' Darci wrapped her hand around Mandy's arm and directed her into the kitchen, leaving Peony behind.

Reese and Tom stood by a coffee maker. It glugged and spit out a thin stream of dark fluid. Mandy smelled cheap tea bags. Tom started when he saw Darci and Mandy, then he forced a tired smile. 'Thank you for coming.'

'Of course,' Mandy said, keeping her face blank. For all she knew, this guy had killed his wife. If the murder weapon appeared and was one of Tom's knives, she bet he'd be arrested.

He reached into the cupboard and started pulling out pottery mugs.

Reese filled the mugs. Her ease in the strange kitchen struck Mandy as unexpected and didn't match what she'd said about her limited history with the family. Darci took out a bag of sugar and a carton of milk and they poured the sugar into a cereal bowl and the milk into a juice cup since that was all they could find.

After Tom and Reese went into the living room, Darci found a box of Swiss Miss while Mandy microwaved milk and water together in the last of the mugs.

'How is Peony doing?' she asked, while the microwave hummed. 'It's so hard to lose a sister. Was Coral her guardian?'

'Until she turned eighteen, yes.'

'Is everything going to change now?'

Darci shrugged. 'Losing Coral's income isn't going to help.'

Reese had said the same thing. 'You work in a salon?'

'Yes, I rent a chair at a place near here. But I help out at the forge, too. I keep real busy.'

Mandy pulled out the hot mug, debating how to ask her question in the kindest way possible. 'Is there anything I can do to help Peony?'

'You must be a mom,' Darci said with a wry smile.

Mandy ripped open the hot chocolate packet. 'I have a teenage daughter. Can you find a spoon?'

Darci fiddled in a drawer and then handed Mandy a plastic stirrer.

'Here's the thing,' Mandy said, as she mixed the brown powder into her milk and water combination. 'People are going to gossip about Coral and her life under the circumstances.'

'I know.' Darci rubbed under her eye. A little of her heavy concealer came off on her finger, exposing the edge of a dark circle.

Mandy glanced around to make sure the kitchen doors were closed. 'Does Peony need help? Do you? I'm here for you.'

'What do you mean?'

'There's a rumor going around that Coral was an abused wife.'

'Oh.' Darci straightened. 'No, that isn't true. I'm sure people will ask questions. I mean, someone stabbed her, but I'm sure it was a stranger. My brother is a great guy.'

She wasn't surprised by the denial. 'I worry about how she died.'

'Because she was stabbed and we make knives,' Darci said flatly. 'I wonder if someone who came to a class here did it. Because she was beautiful, right? Someone could have stalked her.'

Mandy wondered who was lying about the abuse. Amrik? Coral herself? Darci, being defensive about her brother? She'd have to find out what Reese knew. Those strange tattoos on Coral's body haunted her. Surely no one would get them voluntarily. They had seemed to be spaced haphazardly, and the circles weren't even round or the exact same shade of black.

'Where do you work at the hospital?' Darci asked abruptly.

'I'm a barista at the coffee shop. I also have a home business. My daughter and I make stickers and teach online classes on journaling.'

'Oh, like to help with productivity? I'm so busy, I could really use that.' Darci smiled wryly.

'Search online for *Mandy's Plan*. We have more than a year of free videos along with paid classes. Peony might find our content useful too, since we vlog from both a high school student's and a working mom's perspective.'

'It sounds like something that might really distract us right now, which would be great. Does it cost much to start journaling?'

'Most people use A5 dot grid journals, and they will cost about twenty dollars. Other than that, you just need a black marker that dries quickly – in other words, not a ball point pen – and some cheap markers if you want to be colorful like I do. There are a million choices. You don't have to be artistic, but that's what I like. I like to be happy when I open my journal.'

'I love being arty. Maybe I could stop by the coffee bar on Monday to pick your brain?' When Mandy hesitated, Darci added, 'I have to collect Coral's things.'

Mandy nodded. 'My shift ends at three thirty. I can't talk while I'm working. My boss wouldn't be happy.' Maybe she could learn more about Peony's situation if she did a favor for Darci. She couldn't help but worry about the girl.

'Thanks.' Darci squeezed her hand. 'I'd better take Peony her drink.' She grabbed it and rushed out of the kitchen.

Mandy dropped the packet into the garbage can. At least the bereaved teenager had a slightly older young woman to lean on. She didn't see anything to verify Tom and Rod's low opinion of Darci.

An hour later, Mandy had had enough. Rod had asked her out again and she'd refused. She'd talked to Pham about art as long as she could, but he didn't have much to say, despite his obvious talent. When she caught Reese's eye and tilted her head toward the door, Reese said goodbye to Nandini, who she'd been chatting with for quite a while, and followed Mandy out.

They drove south with the radio off. They'd been quiet on the drive here, just listening to a classical radio station.

'Everyone seemed nice,' Reese commented. 'But no one talked about Coral much.'

'That was fine for me, since I didn't have anything to say,'

Mandy said. 'I'm sorry for you, though, since you actually knew her.'

Reese sighed. 'It has been a tough week.'

'Is something more going on? I know death is hard, but you weren't close.' Mandy paused, trying to get to the bottom of her slight unease with Reese's behavior. 'Are you feeling somewhat responsible, since you found her the job?'

Reese straightened her skirt. 'No. I'm sure whoever killed her had nothing to do with the hospital.'

Their eyes met, remembering the events of the previous month. 'Probably not,' Reese amended.

Mandy maneuvered around a curve. 'Regardless, you've been stressed. Why did you attempt to charge Houston such a ridiculous rent?'

'I don't want Houston as a tenant. That's why,' she snapped.

Reese's sudden ire sent Mandy's pulse racing. 'Do you have someone specific in mind? At least he's employed and he's cheerful enough.'

'It would be awkward. I'd have to be nicely dressed and in full makeup every second with a man in the house. Plus, I have no doubt he'd use the TV room when I wasn't looking.'

'I don't think you'd have to do that under any circumstance. But you might be right about the TV room.' Mandy turned on to a side road. 'Want to pick up some pho? There's a good place near here.'

'No, thank you,' Reese said, 'I have an appointment.'

Mandy waited for her to explain, but Reese remained silent. Mandy told herself she didn't care. She needed to work on her business anyway. And she could make her own soup.

'Hi, Mom,' Vellum called from the kitchen as Mandy walked in.

Mandy kissed her daughter's forehead. 'Quiet day?'

Vellum slid the top rack into the dishwasher. Mugs rattled against each other. 'We should try to figure out this "Plan with Me" design.' She giggled. 'Bunnies and tea.'

'And check sticker orders from the tulip "Plan with Me."'

'I did the orders this morning.' Vellum closed the dishwasher. 'When I needed breaks from reading *Animal Farm*.'

'Lots of orders?' Mandy asked hopefully.

'Not really. All the superfans ordered, and a couple who said they saw the video on Reese's channel.'

She frowned. 'Anyone from "Planning by Tamika"?'

'Not that I saw.'

'Odd. She has a bigger following than Reese.' Mandy took off her coat.

'I don't think her video is up yet. Maybe she had technical problems.' Vellum glanced at the refrigerator.

'OK. Did you check comments on our video?'

'No.'

'I'll look in a bit. I'm going to make a quick ramen soup. Want some?'

'Sure.'

Mandy set four cups of veggie stock to boil, then checked her social media. The video had great stats, even if it wasn't translating directly to sales. It had been a long shot, after all, to expect all her customers to buy twice as much product that month.

She cut up veggies and a couple of hard-boiled eggs, then cooked the ramen and assembled the bowls. While they were eating, she had a text from Tamika saying her video had been corrupted but everything was fixed now.

'You seem distracted, Mom,' Vellum said as she cleared their bowls away.

'Just wondering who the killer is,' Mandy said absently, her chin on her propped-up arm.

Vellum gasped. 'I'd expect that sort of thing out of Justin's mouth, not yours.'

'I haven't seen much of him this week.'

'I've heard the door downstairs at odd times. I don't think he's been home much.'

'I hope they know who killed Coral, even if they can't make an arrest yet.' Mandy straightened. She couldn't make finding the murderer her third job. Coral wasn't her cousin. She hadn't died in Mandy's house.

'Should we go into the studio?' Vellum asked.

'Yep. But I don't think there's any point in filming our work today. This won't be a theme that shapes up quickly.'

'That's OK. We've got weeks before it needs to be ready.'

Mandy felt a weight lift off her when she flipped on all the

lights in her art studio after she washed her hands. While her lamps
weren't expensive, they kept the shadows at bay where they filmed.
She even had an area where she could film herself doing intros
and outros for her videos.

For now, though, they had plenty of light at their worktable in
front of the window overlooking the gloomy backyard. Mandy set
out a sketch pad for both of them. She'd done watercolors for the
tulips, which made sense. This time, she expected she'd do digital
art, once they figured out their plan.

Vellum plopped down in her chair. 'Thanks for letting me help.
Usually you do the designing.'

'You're getting older.' They smiled at each other. 'Plus, you're
unexpectedly home.'

'Any ideas?'

'The teacups will be the most vibrant part of the design. I know
I want to do blue bunnies.'

'We love our reds, blues, and yellows,' Vellum pointed out.
'What if our teacups are red and yellow?'

'Perfect,' Mandy exclaimed. 'What kind of designs? Classic
British china? Mexican exuberance? American pottery?'

'What goes with a bunny?' Vellum mused.

'I'm going to start drawing bunnies in different poses,' Mandy
said. 'Why don't you choose our palette?'

Vellum selected markers from their extensive selection of expensive and low-cost items. Later on, if they found the perfect color,
Mandy could photograph their art and use software to capture the
actual colors and finalize the design digitally.

She drew two pages of bunnies frolicking, experimenting how
to give them fur with Vellum's two blue choices, a baby-blue and
a navy. They decided on china teacups with primary red poppies
and yellow gold rims. Vellum worked on the teacup designs, using
her markers.

'Why are rabbits so lucky?' Mandy asked.

'Huh?' Vellum set down a coral-colored pen.

'Because they have four rabbit's feet!' Mandy said. 'Remember
that old joke?'

'Gross,' Vellum said.

After a couple of hours, Mandy leaned back in her chair. 'I
don't think we've quite got it yet but we've come a long way.'

'Do you think you're ready to pull out the iPad and get started?'

'Tomorrow,' Mandy decided. 'I don't know what we're having for dinner yet. I'll have to check the freezer.'

'There's two packages of tofu in the fridge.' Vellum gave Mandy a playful poke in the arm.

'Yeah, but we're out of onions. Maybe I'll bake them in sauce.'

'Thai peanut?' Vellum suggested. 'Yum!'

'Yeah, I can do that.'

'I'll make cookies for dessert,' Vellum said. 'Could I text Houston? Maybe he'd like to eat with us, watch a movie?'

Mandy went cold. Had she been set up? 'You have his number?'

Vellum blushed. 'He slipped it to me when he was over here to look at Reese's basement, but he doesn't have mine yet. What do you think?'

Mandy forced her tone to stay level, despite her instant rage that Houston had tried to get her daughter to contact him. 'Sorry, hun. I have to say no because he's over eighteen. Five years is a huge gap at your age.'

'Just as friends?' Vellum tried.

'No.' She and Houston would be having a very tense talk at work.

Vellum's lips set. She pulled out her phone and typed away.

Mandy's body tensed. 'Who are you texting?'

'Dad. He knows boys are way more immature than girls. I'm sure my fifteen is close to Houston's twenty.'

Mandy stiffened even more. Immaturity was one thing, but a lot changed between high school and being out in the world. 'He's not a college boy. You should date more intellectual kids.' And her father had cancelled their plans as if they weren't important.

Vellum considered her. 'If a college man asked me out, you'd say yes?'

'Of course not. What college man would ask out a sophomore in high school?' Her tone went scathing on 'man.'

'I'm almost a junior,' Vellum whined.

Mandy cleaned up their pens and paper mess. Vellum's phone didn't beep with an incoming text. Eventually, she stomped out of the art studio, making sure her favorite clunky boots made the maximum noise possible.

'I'm sorry your father isn't getting back to you,' Mandy called. 'He didn't explain what emergency came up this weekend.'

Vellum just growled and stomped on through the kitchen. Her bedroom door slammed.

Mandy pushed aside her frustration with her unreliable ex. They'd divorced for a reason. When her father had died suddenly and she spent a lot of time comforting her mother, he'd decided to start an affair. He'd never really matured from the boy she'd met in college, in her opinion. She went into the kitchen and started assembling baked tofu ingredients. Downstairs, Mandy heard the basement door open and close. Justin must have arrived.

Usually, he stayed in his part of the house, but as she pulled a square baking dish from a lower cupboard, she heard his footsteps on the stairs. When the basement door opened, she smelled teriyaki sauce.

'Bringing your dinner up here to torture us?' Mandy asked as he came around the corner into the kitchen.

He chuckled and set two plastic bags on the counter. 'I thought you might have had a rough afternoon. You went to the wake or whatever it was at the forge, right?'

'It was at the house actually, but yes, I went with Reese. She's taking it hard. Didn't even want to get food after.'

He waved a hand over the food. 'Three orders of chicken breast.'

'That's very kind of you.' Where was he going with this kindness? 'I hadn't quite finished making dinner so, yeah, I'll just clean this up.' She grabbed her handful of prepped vegetables and tossed them back into the crisper.

He went into the hall and knocked on Vellum's door. 'Dinner is served.'

When he returned, Mandy said, 'I didn't see any police at the gathering.'

'A good chunk of the force was pulled into a multiple homicide at an apartment on MLK Way.' He yawned, and Mandy, with her fixings put away, finally took a good look at him.

'You're exhausted.'

He nodded. 'Up all night. An estranged husband decided to kill his family. Took out the wife, two kids, his mother-in-law, and a cousin.'

She shook her head and pulled plates from the cupboard. 'Get some food into you and go to sleep before you get called out for something else.'

'Thanks, Mandy.' He poured water into tall glasses while she opened the teriyaki clamshells and dished out food.

The next morning, Mandy woke to banging on her door and Vellum calling for her.

'What?' she asked groggily, pushing her blankets back.

Vellum opened her door and rushed in. 'Mom, something is going on down the street. I just saw it on social media.'

Mandy rubbed sleep from her eyes. 'Did you look out the window?'

Just then, the mudroom doorbell rang. She grabbed her robe from the foot of the bed and shoved her feet into hard-soled slippers.

'Oh gosh, is that the police?' Vellum fretted. 'Is Justin here?'

Mandy rushed through the kitchen, which still smelled faintly of teriyaki. At the back door, Linda was waiting, a plaid blanket thrown over her shoulders.

'The police are at Reese's house.' Linda's face was red from exertion.

The walls swayed. Mandy grabbed her bill-paying table for support. 'Not dead? Oh no.'

'Mom?' Vellum wrapped her arms around her mother from the back.

Linda shook her head. 'I don't think so. It's police, not ambulances or fire trucks.'

Mandy put her hand to her forehead. 'I need coffee. And answers.'

'I had mine already,' Linda said. 'You slept in, kiddo. My awake brain is telling me that Reese's house is probably being searched.'

'For what?' Mandy asked.

'Do you think she's being arrested for Coral's murder?' Vellum asked.

Mandy turned around in the cramped space. 'Back into the kitchen,' she told her wide-eyed daughter. Without speaking, she went to her coffee maker and turned it on.

'What should we do?' Linda fretted.

'While my water heats up, I'm going downstairs to look for the resident cop.' Mandy went into the hall, opened the basement door and walked down the stairs. She checked Justin's bedroom and sitting room. Both doors were open and he wasn't there. His digital clock read eight thirty.

She *had* slept in. At first, she remembered the family massacre and thought he'd had to go back to it early on a Sunday, but her sluggish brain connected the information Linda had shared. As far as she knew, Justin and Craig were still primaries on Coral's murder. And Reese had been acting strangely. Mandy had no idea where she had been right when Coral had been stabbed. She had left the party before Mandy did. Was she a suspect? Did the police have a search warrant?

'I have to find Justin,' she muttered.

'Your coffee is ready,' Vellum called down the stairs.

On autopilot, Mandy switched the laundry from washer to dryer and started a load of Justin's clothes that were in a basket, ready to go in. He'd been working too hard to even take care of the basics.

Once the washer had started to hiss with flowing water, she woke up enough to realize how ridiculous it was that she'd just handled her tenant's dirty clothes. He wasn't her cousin, not like Ryan. She stared into the mirrored surface of the washer, remembering that Vellum had insisted she'd seen Ryan's ghost here shortly after he'd died.

She shook her head. 'Wherever you are now, Ryan, watch over Reese. I know I suspected her of killing you, at least a little bit, but I can't imagine she murdered her massage therapist.'

She went back upstairs. 'Maybe she was robbed? I mean, why are we assuming Reese is in trouble over Coral?'

Vellum handed her a cup of the special edition coffee, her hoarded Starbucks Pumpkin Spice Latte with the dairy packet included.

'Too much of a coincidence otherwise,' Linda said. 'That smells good. What is it?'

Vellum explained. Linda looked thoughtful. 'Maybe I should try pumpkin spice brownies.'

'In March?' Vellum asked with disdain.

'Pumpkin spice is good in all seasons,' Mandy insisted.

'I dare you to make a pumpkin spice sticker series in the middle of summer,' Vellum teased.

Mandy regarded her over her coffee cup. 'I will and I'll use it for myself, but not release it until fall.'

Vellum rolled her eyes. 'Mothers.'

Linda chuckled. The mudroom doorbell rang again.

'I hope that's Reese,' Mandy muttered.

Instead, she found her mother at the door, her short cap of blond hair disordered from the wind. She was zipped into a windbreaker and a multicolored scarf was tied jauntily around her neck.

'Hi, Mom,' Mandy said warily.

'I remembered you being upset when the emergency vehicles were in front of your house last month and I didn't come over,' Barbara Meadows explained. 'So this time I came over.'

Mandy stepped back and took another gulp of coffee. 'Cool.'

'What is that?' Her mother sniffed. 'Smells good.'

Mandy handed over her cup. She'd downed half of it already. 'Can you grab our coats?' she asked Vellum, then went to dress.

The quartet walked across the street to Reese's, but none of the curious neighbors huddled outside knew anything. Mandy's texts to Reese and Justin went unanswered. She wondered if Reese was still in the neighborhood. Had she been arrested?

Finally, they gave up due to the lack of information and walked a few blocks south to a café. Over egg and cheese biscuits, they discussed Reese's prospects.

'I can't believe you never mentioned that Reese doesn't have an alibi when the massage therapist was murdered,' Linda fretted.

'I don't know that,' Mandy argued. 'I don't know where she was, that's all.'

'I don't like those tattoos you described on Coral,' Vellum said. 'They don't sound cute. Tattoos should be cute.'

'Not everyone agrees with you,' Barbara said. 'I've seen ladies with big dragon tattoos a couple of times.'

'What would a target tattoo be symbolic of?' Linda asked.

'A future murder victim,' Mandy said sourly. 'I wonder if the tats were related to a nickname?'

'Maybe she loved shopping at the Target chain,' Vellum suggested.

'They were black, not red,' Mandy said. 'Murders are usually committed by spouses or people the victim knew. Maybe it was someone at the forge like her sister-in-law thinks. But I'm still worried about her husband because of the knife, and then there's her boss – he might have lied to me about Tom abusing her.'

Linda nodded. 'Or the tattoo artist next door. Too much coincidence.'

After they ate, Linda had to run to her responsibilities at the animal shelter she baked for, and Barbara had a pottery class to attend. Mandy and Vellum did their livestream to set up their weekly spread for the next week with their fans. They used the tulip kit to increase enthusiasm for it, filled orders, and responded to comments online for a couple of hours, then Vellum did homework while Mandy made the tofu dish she'd started the day before.

Early that evening, Mandy was perched at her table in the art studio, recording herself sketching fifty floral doodles for a social media video, when Justin walked up the backyard path. She turned off her camera and raced through the house, managing to catch him before he went into the basement.

A little out of breath, she pointed at him to gain his attention.

'It's raining,' he said mildly. 'If you wanted to talk to me, why didn't you just go downstairs?'

'Trying to respect your privacy,' Mandy panted. 'I stay out of the basement unless I'm doing laundry.'

'It's OK, Mandy.' He unlocked the basement door and she followed him into his sitting room.

His movements weary, he opened a small refrigerator in the corner and pulled out a beer. 'Want one?'

'No, thanks.' She sat down on his tan leather loveseat and waited for him to uncap the bottle and take his first sip.

'So,' Justin said.

'So,' Mandy echoed.

'I don't know how much gossip you've heard at the hospital,' he said, 'but in the course of the investigation, your co-workers Houston, Fannah, and Beverly all reported that Reese had made threatening comments about Coral Le Charme.'

'I heard her,' Mandy agreed, 'but you know Reese. Being in pain made her not act like her best self. I don't know what Coral did to her that day, but it wasn't worth Reese or anyone killing her for.'

'We have to take a threat against someone who later died seriously.'

'That's not evidence,' she retorted. 'They were friendly. She knew Coral's family and we went to the memorial service. You know that.'

He sat on the lounge chair next to the loveseat. 'We have material evidence linking her to the murder, found in her house. The other case delayed this one, which is why the search wasn't executed until today.'

Mandy winced, but she wanted to cast doubt. 'I'm not sure that means anything, whatever you found. She has her basement up for rent so people have been in her house. At least, Houston from the coffee bar. And me.'

He glanced at her over his bottle. 'Where do you think we'll find his fingerprints?'

She thought. 'Probably on the door to the TV room in Reese's basement. He was really attracted to it.'

'Good to know.' He set his bottle against his lips. 'We already have yours.'

She warmed to her theme. 'Also, I saw the body, and I'm guessing you found the knife that killed her. But it's far more likely that those blacksmith guys would have knives than Reese. Coral's husband makes knives. And I'm not sure I trust her boss.'

'I am not at liberty to discuss any specifics with you.'

'Did they find the murder weapon?' she asked tentatively.

He shrugged.

'Do you even know what they found at Reese's or are you still too busy with the other case?'

'There's always other cases, Mandy. It's already been four days since Coral Le Charme died.'

'I know that's a bad sign,' Mandy said. 'Does her husband have an alibi? Did he explain her weird tattoos to the police?'

He leaned back. 'All you need to know is that he hasn't been arrested.'

'Has Reese?' Mandy asked. 'Did you actually arrest her for murder?'

'Yes,' Justin said somberly.

SIX

J ustin switched his beer to his other hand and leaned forward in his chair. 'Reese O'Leary-Sett has been arrested based on what was found in her house.'

'Oh no,' Mandy whispered, horrified. She covered her eyes with her hands for a moment. 'What was found? What can I do to help her?'

'Pray there's some other explanation for the evidence,' Justin said, tilting his bottle again. 'Because it isn't looking good for her. I can't tell you more than that.'

'I can't believe it. Reese has been acting a bit distracted lately, but she's not someone who would fly off in a rage and stab someone multiple times.' She shuddered. Admittedly, she had suspected Reese of killing her cousin, but that was only because she seemed to want to profit from his death at the time by buying Mandy's business at a discount. 'Next to a dumpster of all places.'

'Did Reese tell you that she'd known Rod Portilla for most of her life?' Justin said conversationally.

Mandy frowned. 'No. Tom introduced them as though they'd never met and neither of them said anything. I had the impression she and Coral were friends, then she said she just knew her from a massage place she used to work at by the mall, and then I discovered she'd actually had private massages at Coral's house.'

'Confusing, huh?' Justin emptied the last of his beer into his mouth. 'If you'd kept asking questions, you might have discovered that Reese and Rod grew up on the same block in Kirkland. They went to the same grade school.'

'Surely Rod is quite a bit older than Reese.'

'Thirty-two.'

She looked around Justin's sitting room. While he'd furnished it with bachelor basics, nothing hung on the walls. 'That's seven years.'

'Closer to six,' Justin said.

Justin had owned a home before, with his ex. Had she taken

everything after the breakup? 'That's a big gap in kid terms. They'd be unlikely to have interacted with that much of an age difference. And what does it matter? Coral was married to Tom, not Rod.'

'We'll figure it out,' Justin said. 'I just want you to understand there's more going on beneath the surface. How long have you known Reese?'

'She moved into her house two years ago, so I saw her around, but we only got to know each other last January when we were both in the same journaling class.'

'How well do you know your neighbors?'

'Some I know super well, like, my mom, Linda, the Roswells next door to some extent. George Lowry, the lothario dentist who lives behind Reese. Eugenia Knight, the nice old lady across the street by the bakery.'

'That's better than most, these days.' He yawned. 'I guess I can't prove my point about neighbors being strangers.'

'Yeah.' She pictured a map of the street. 'I don't know anyone in the apartment building directly across from us. And the bakery staff at Shangri-La across from Linda change jobs too often for much familiarity.'

'Well, there you go. I've got a really early morning, Mandy. I'm beat.'

'Fine.' She stood. 'I made extra tofu if you want some.'

He grinned sleepily at her. 'Thanks. I know you're upset about Reese, but please remember none of this is your fault. You can't fix what happened.'

'I know. Do you think I could go see her?' She wanted to make sure her friend was being treated well.

'I don't know where she is in the process. You would have to make contact with her lawyer to find out, then get on the jail's visitation schedule.' He lost his smile. 'Her family has money. I'm sure she'll have solid representation. You don't need to worry.' He scratched his stubbled chin.

She found herself unable to slip away. But he had nothing more to tell her. 'Thanks again for the teriyaki yesterday.'

He yawned again.

She had a thought. 'What about Reese's cat? It will need to be taken care of.'

'Does she have an exterior cat door?'

Mandy thought. 'Yes, into the gated backyard.'

'You can take food and water over and put it by the door.' He yawned again.

She nodded and went upstairs, puzzling over law enforcement's conclusions about the murder. Reese murdering Coral made no sense to her. When Ryan died, she'd discovered that someone she'd known her entire life had kept many secrets from her. What secrets were they missing about Coral? Or Reese for that matter.

She grabbed her keys and drove down Roosevelt to the grocery store a few blocks away. After purchasing some high-end cat food and plastic bowls, she drove to Reese's house and fiddled with the back gate until she made it into the tidy green yard. Reese tended neat hedges around the perimeter of the rectangular lawn and had a dormant water fountain near the back door.

Mandy set her bowls by the back door and poured a bottle of water into one, then scooped moist cat food from a pop-top container into the other with a fast-food spork. She figured the cat would come out of the house eventually and hoped strays wouldn't find the food first.

She stared at the cat flap. Maybe she could put the dishes just inside the door. Just then, the cat pushed out from the flap. Ignoring her, it dipped his head into the water bowl and lapped up some liquid. When he lifted his head, she held out her hand for a sniff.

She gave the cat a scratch behind the ears, then struggled into a standing position. 'I'll bring you some more tomorrow.' With a sigh, she went home.

After she took off her coat, she went into her art studio and sat down. When she'd been confused about her cousin Ryan's murder, using her journal had helped. She pulled it from the ledge and flipped back to Valentine's Day, then found her murder spread.

She winced at the splotches of ink that resembled blood on the page. Maybe she'd avoid doing that again. Instead, she poked through her rack of imperfect sticker sheets and found a page of Halloween stickers. A perfectly cut gravestone emblazoned with 'RIP' waited in the middle of the page.

'There we go.' She pulled it off the sheet and placed it carefully in the middle of the page, lining it up on the dot grid markings. Then she took a red pen and wrote 'Murder' on one side and 'Spread' on the other in her standard modern calligraphy font.

She'd used circles for people's names last time, but as she flipped through her stencils, the teardrop shape caught her eye. That seemed appropriate. Coral had only been twenty-six, from what had been said at Tom's gathering. She hadn't quite lived to see her sister grow up and ran out of time to have her own children. Terribly sad and worthy of tears.

Mandy stenciled the largest teardrop into the center of the page and wrote 'Coral Le Charme' inside with her Micron pen. Underneath she wrote what she knew – age twenty-six, married, massage therapist, tattooed.

After that, Mandy used the same stencils she'd used in February to make categories of 'family,' 'lovers,' and 'co-workers,' though she added 'clients' in this case, and 'neighbors.' Lastly, she added a banner for 'weapons' on the right-hand side. For family she put Peony and Darci into teardrops. The 'lovers' category only held Tom. She decided to put Rod and Pham into 'neighbors.' At least their business was next to Coral's house. Lastly, 'co-workers/clients' held Amrik, her boss, and Reese, her friend and client.

Why didn't she have a friend category? She flipped back to her first murder spread and shook her head when she realized it was because her deceased cousin only had friends who were also family or lovers. Loss punched her in the heart yet again, but she had to stay focused on helping Reese.

Coral's murder spread seemed pretty empty, especially with only one weapon, the knife. Had the police found it in Reese's home? She sat back in her chair, her eyes blurring over the page. Unless Coral had been sleeping with Rod or Pham, or even Amrik, there was no crossover between the categories. No one person appeared any more involved in Coral's life than anyone else.

Mandy closed her book, feeling grumpy. At least she had a place to stash more names as she came across them. She knew she didn't have the entire story on Coral. Not yet.

The front doorbell rang just as the sky was turning dark outside the art studio.

Mandy went through the house. Vellum peeked out of her bedroom door. She'd been working on her homework.

'Don't you just love Sundays?' Vellum groused. 'Who would come to the front door?'

'No one we want to talk to,' Mandy said. She peeked through

the security hole and recognized Houston. What was he here for
this time? Obviously, with Reese arrested, there was no hope of
renting her basement. Probably, he had heard the news somewhere
and had an interest in the story since he had been in her house.

She opened the door. 'What brings you by, Houston?'

He held up a plastic bag. Mandy couldn't see what was inside
and realized the outside light had not been flipped on. She illumin-
ated the space and saw the plastic bag was filled with water. A
goldfish swam in the water.

'Do you have a kid friend in the neighborhood?' Mandy asked.

He laughed. 'No, but I have a large fish tank. I'm not allowed
to have it in my apartment. That's one reason I want to move.'

Mandy wondered when he would've sprung that on Reese. He
hadn't brought up pet rules when he viewed the basement. Of
course, she did already have a cat. Maybe that would have been
enough for him. 'You're wandering the neighborhood with the fish
in a bag?'

'No.' Houston looked adorably confused. 'I brought this gift
for Vellum.'

Mandy frowned. 'You just randomly decided to bring my
daughter a pet without asking first? Not to mention giving her
your phone number the last time you showed up uninvited, which
was completely unacceptable. She's five years younger than you
are.'

He shifted from side to side as she pressed on.

'Do you have fish food? A bowl? I can't just leave a goldfish
in a bag and not feed it.'

Houston's expression remained adorably confused. 'I hadn't
thought about that. I have all the stuff at home. Don't you have
something you could use for tonight?'

Mandy put her hands on her hips. 'Seriously? You think I have
fish food just waiting around the house for a fish to appear? Who
would have that if they didn't have fish?'

'Sorry,' Houston mumbled.

Vellum came up behind Mandy and leaned her head on her
mother's shoulder. 'I heard something about a goldfish?'

Houston thrust the bag toward her as if he had never heard
Mandy express her displeasure. 'Hi, Vellum. I brought you a little
present. I hope you like it!'

Vellum glanced at the bag. 'That's really sweet of you, but it sounds like you already have a tank and you can take care of it better than I can. I have at least three hours of homework left to do tonight and I don't have time to get fish food.'

'I'm sure your mom—'

Mandy interrupted. 'Sorry, Houston. I don't have time. I work two jobs.'

'Well, all right then,' he said.

Mandy watched as testosterone flipped a switch on in his brain and he brazened out the next phase of his plan, in front of her no less.

He said, 'I haven't heard from you, Vellum. Maybe we can see a movie sometime?'

Mandy glared at him before Vellum could even open her mouth. 'Do not ask my daughter on a date. She's fifteen, Houston. I'm telling you this loud and clear. It's not acceptable.'

Houston raised his eyebrows and shoved his free hand into his pocket. After a long pause, he said, 'No problem.'

Mandy could scarcely believe her eyes, but he had the audacity to wink at her daughter before trotting down the steps to the pathway to her lawn. He disappeared through the arch down to the street. She waited. But she didn't hear a car start. Had he taken the bus? Or had the household gained a stalker?

She shut the door and locked it. At least Justin would make quick work of Houston if that became the case.

Where did he live? She doubted he was nearby. Something was off. With little interest in him as a person, she didn't even know why he'd moved here from Alaska.

In fact, maybe she should add him to her murder spread. There was something very odd about Houston Harris. A thought struck her. Alaska was a massive state, but could he have known Coral?

'He has surface charm,' Mandy said, 'but I'm trusting that kid less and less.'

Vellum curled her lip. 'Mom.'

Mandy put her hands on her daughter's shoulders. 'You're an attractive girl, and a great person. But any intelligent twenty-year-old knows there is a vast experience, knowledge, and maturity gap between twenty and fifteen and wouldn't go there.'

'It was sweet to bring me a gift.'

'No, it wasn't.' Mandy's gaze followed Vellum's until her daughter was looking at her. 'It was thoughtless. Did you hear him? Suggesting I could go out and get what was needed to keep an unwelcome pet alive?'

'It was thoughtless to you,' Vellum amended.

Mandy wasn't convinced she was getting through to her daughter. A cute boy was chasing her; that seemed to be her primary focus. 'Let me be clear. I don't want Houston in our house.'

'Right.'

Mandy kept her gaze on Vellum. 'I don't want you in touch with him, not only because of his age and behavior, but because of what's going on with Reese. We don't know who killed that massage therapist, and all of a sudden we have someone we don't know very well hanging around. Someone who came up with an excuse to get into Reese's home. We don't know what the police found there. And he's from Alaska, just like the murder victim.' She grabbed her daughter's hand. 'Come with me.'

She towed Vellum into the art studio and flipped on the light. Her planner was still on her desk. She grabbed her stencil and, as Vellum watched, drew another tear shape in the row for co-workers and clients. Her pen etched Houston's name in the new tear. 'There, he's officially on my suspect list.'

Vellum pointed her finger at Reese's name. Her cute bright green clover-leaf manicure contrasted unpleasantly with the red ink and gravestone sticker.

'You suspected Reese of being capable of killing our cousin not too long ago. Maybe she really is a murderess. Maybe you were right about her, just wrong about the victim.'

'Reese was one of a pool of possibilities then, but she isn't going to kill a bad massage therapist,' Mandy snapped. She tapped the big tear with Coral's name. 'That's not why people kill.'

Vellum's chin thrust out. 'Then why do they?'

Mandy took up the challenge, remembering a podcast she'd listened to in her car. 'Some reasons are sex, revenge, jealousy, money, abuse, lust for fame. Just the seven deadly sins, basically. Or, lust, love, loathing, loot.'

'Reese might have done it for revenge, since Coral hurt her. See, there's a motive. What might be the reason for Houston?'

Mandy nodded thoughtfully and wrote 'revenge' under Reese's name. She didn't buy it, but the exercise might be useful. 'I like where we're going. Keep this coming.'

Vellum glanced down. 'Is Amrik Coral's boss?'

'Yes.'

'Revenge or money? Because Coral might have hurt his business?'

'OK, good.' She made a note. 'Or maybe lust, for all we know.'

'Did Coral give Houston a massage?'

'Not that he's ever mentioned.'

'Who is next?'

'I have family. Her sister, Peony, and her sister-in-law, Darci. I know the tattoo guys complain about Darci being a scrounger.'

'Money and abuse?' Vellum suggested. 'What do you know about Peony?'

'She's soon to be eighteen. Hoping her sister's death doesn't lead to her being homeless, since Coral was her guardian. She's still in high school and somewhat impaired by cerebral palsy. Coral's death is devastating to her prospects. She's needed a lot of therapy for mobility and even swallowing.'

'Then she was better off with her sister being alive.'

'Exactly. So on to lovers. Just her husband so far for sure.'

'Any trouble with him?'

'No proof that we know of,' Mandy said. 'Amrik claimed there was abuse, but Darci denied it. The knife angle is suspicious. She was killed with a knife, and he makes them. Also, there are several men in the suspect pool.'

'Who's left?'

'Rod and Pham. Rod keeps hitting on me. Maybe he hit on Coral?'

'So something to do with lust?'

'Or revenge if she said no.' Mandy tapped her pen on the desk. 'The only problem is Coral and I weren't remotely the same type. She was a decade younger than me and very Goth.'

'I think you need to learn more about this Rod guy.'

'I don't know how, not with Reese being arrested.'

'If you think she's innocent, we have to help her. Though she does have a motive.'

'Not a good one.' Mandy closed her planner. 'Darci wanted to talk to me about journaling. She said she was going to stop by the coffee bar tomorrow. I'll ask her more about Rod then.'

Vellum licked her lips. 'Be careful, Mom. Darci is a suspect, too. If nothing else, if she's a people user, she might get her hooks into you. Besides, she has access to the same knives, right?'

'Or I might make a friend. I don't necessarily believe the grousing of some manly men to be an accurate representation of a woman's personality.'

'I guess.' She worried at her lip again.

Mandy saw her daughter's unease. 'OK, honey, you have all that homework to do. I'll make you some of that tea you like, so you can focus.'

'I don't have as much as I said. I was just trying to help you get rid of Houston.'

Mandy stared at Vellum who grinned, making her mother feel much lighter. 'OK, then go finish up while I make the tea and we can watch some old Bob Ross episodes for inspiration.'

Vellum nodded. 'I love him! We need some happy little accidents to solve this murder.'

Both she and Vellum preferred water-based mediums for their art, but Bob Ross was always a hoot to watch as he dispensed folksy wisdom.

Still, once Mandy went to bed that night, she started wondering what kind of conditions Reese was sleeping in, and the thought kept her awake.

Monday came far too soon. Mandy eagerly awaited the end of the customer-heavy day and Darci DeRoy's arrival at the coffee bar. She hoped she would show up. Darci was attractive and not that much older than Houston. Maybe her co-worker would find a new girl to crush on when he saw Darci.

At two thirty, Fannah left for the day. Mandy dreaded the lull from then until the usual end-of-shift rush that came a half hour later. Predictably, Houston came and stood in front of her as soon as their boss was gone.

'I think we should talk,' he said.

Mandy had been expecting him to address the night before, but not in this alpha male, arrogant tone. She deserved a respectful apology. It had been a long day, between the sleepless night and the number of gossipers who'd come to the coffee bar to talk about Reese's arrest as the word had spread through their small town of a hospital community.

'I believe I made myself clear last night,' Mandy said.

'Maybe so, but you can't treat me like this at work.' His stance encompassed the free space.

'Like what?' Mandy asked. 'I'm the lead barista. It's your job to follow my direction. You aren't even off probation yet.'

He shifted. 'Are you going to try to get me fired because I like your daughter?'

'Once again, your interest is unacceptable. You don't know my daughter,' Mandy insisted. 'And given that she looks her age, I really have to question your judgment and your general lack of sense.'

'You always talk about how mature she is.' Houston glanced up at a security camera. 'Sue me for listening.'

'More like risking arrest.' She bit down on the final consonant. 'Age of consent in this state is sixteen. It's raised to eighteen when the older partner is sixty months or more older than the younger partner. Therefore, you have no legal access to my daughter until she's eighteen, buddy. Walk away.'

'I'm new in town and just trying to make friends,' Houston claimed.

'Do you sound reasonable to yourself?' she queried. 'Because I'm sixteen years older than you and I know better.'

He attempted a smile. 'Really, I just think she's a smart girl.'

'I looked up Alaska,' Mandy said, ignoring this. 'That's where you claim to be from, right? The age of consent is sixteen there, too. As a result, there is nowhere in this country where you chasing after a fifteen-year-old is acceptable. Stay away from my house. I have a cop living in the basement and I'm not afraid to use him.'

She turned with a balletic flourish as Dr Burrell approached. 'How are you today?' she called out, grateful for the distraction.

He pushed up his glasses. 'It's a good day. We were able to send one of our young friends home with her parents after three months in the NICU.'

'Wow, that's amazing,' Mandy exclaimed. 'I mean, I know you work miracles all the time, but I'm so happy for the parents.'

'Every little life is precious,' Dr Burrell agreed. 'I have to go back in for a surgical consult. How about a couple of your famous ginger thins and a coffee?'

'Sure thing.'

Houston, stone-faced, handed her cookies from the display case while she picked up a cup for the neonatologist.

The doctor didn't seem to notice the tension between the co-workers. 'See you around, Mandy,' he said. 'Off at three thirty?'

'It's almost here,' she agreed.

'It sure puts things in perspective, right?' Mandy said when Dr Burrell was gone.

'What do you mean?' Houston asked.

'Our little problems are nothing compared with that baby being able to go home. Hospitals are incredible places.'

'Yeah,' Houston muttered. 'Don't you have cookies to make or something?'

She regarded him sourly. What was wrong with this kid? 'Did you know Coral? Like from Alaska, or did you get a massage from her?'

'You mean the woman who died? You've got to be kidding me.'

'That's not an answer.'

'Don't we have the end-of-shift rush to prepare for?' he countered.

She checked the clock. 'No, I have the end-of-shift rush to prepare for. Why don't you check the coffee urns?'

Mandy clocked out on time and grabbed her things. When she went through the side door, Darci DeRoy stood at the counter, ordering a drink.

Considering her suspicions about Houston, she watched carefully, but he didn't seem to recognize Darci. That didn't mean Houston didn't kill Coral. For all she knew, Fannah had hired a budding serial killer for the coffee bar. Stranger things had happened here before.

Darci turned around when Mandy approached and waved. 'There you are!'

'I'll grab us the sofa in the corner,' Mandy said, pointing to a spot that was out of view and earshot of the coffee bar. She walked by the staff door to the back offices, past the table where the volunteers waited to be called to assist with wheelchairs, and sank into one of the vinyl-covered but comfortable sofas. Employees loved them as much as hospital visitors.

She set her water bottle on the glass table in between the seating and pulled out her planner, along with a spare. It didn't normally come to work with her but she needed something to show Darci. She'd also brought a few pens and her tulip sticker set.

Darci came toward her, holding a coffee cup. She wore dark tights, knee-length leather boots, and a navy sweater dress. Her dark hair swung in a shiny waterfall over her shoulder.

'You have some pink in your cheeks today,' Mandy said, staying seated. She didn't feel like doing the barely-know-you hug thing with someone who was, after all, a murder suspect.

'It's such a relief that Reese was arrested,' Darci said with a happy sigh. 'We all need closure. It's been a tense few days.'

'It hasn't even been a week since Coral died,' Mandy said evenly. 'Everyone is having a terrible time.'

'Yes, my poor brother. He couldn't handle working last week, and the business can't really afford down time.'

'Small businesses are hard,' Mandy agreed. While hers had been quite successful quickly, she still had to work her day job to cover health insurance for now. 'Was the tattoo shop closed, too?'

'No, so that's good. We won't lose the rental check.'

'Were Rod and Pham close to your sister-in-law?'

'Rod likes to be close to all the ladies, if you know what I mean. Pham doesn't talk much, so it's hard to know what he thinks. He just hovers with a beer in a corner somewhere when we're socializing.'

'But he's around a lot,' Mandy confirmed. Who knew what dark thoughts might be registering in a quiet person?

'Yes. The six of us ate dinner together all the time. And our kitchen is used as the breakroom for the business for the gang. Not for classes. Then we bring stuff into the room outside of the forge. It's a good idea anyway. Some people can't handle the heat so they need a place to sit and rehydrate.'

'How is your brother coping overall?'

'Rod says he's in shock. Tom is stoic most of the time anyway, but yeah, I mean, how do you deal with your wife just going to work one day and never coming home?'

'It's the worst,' Mandy said softly. 'But I'm sorry to say that I don't buy Reese being guilty.'

Darci picked up her cup and pulled off the lid, then blew on the steaming liquid. 'No?'

Mandy shifted on the sofa to face Darci better. 'No. Sorry. I've known Reese for a while.'

'We were told there's evidence.'

'I heard that too, but I don't know what it is. The police won't say. Did you ever go to her house?'

'No. I think Coral might have once, with her portable massage table.'

'That's one thing that confuses me,' Mandy admitted. 'I feel like Reese downplayed her relationship with Coral, but she was upset about a bad massage. One of the cops told me she went to grade school with Rod. Did he ever mention that?'

'No. You still think she didn't do it?'

'No, I'm sure she didn't,' Mandy said soberly. 'There has to be another explanation. I'm hoping to talk to her soon.'

SEVEN

A hospital employee came out of the security door with his lunch bag. He took one look at Mandy and Darci spread out on the sofa and table in the lobby corner and veered toward the coffee-bar tables.

The scent of Darci's coffee wafted past Mandy's nose, making her wish she had a cup. 'You never really know people. Do you know anything about Rod? Like maybe he knew Reese from childhood?'

'No. He never said anything.'

'Neither did Reese.'

Mandy assumed Darci was about to say something damning about Reese, but instead she went on a tangent. 'When I was seven, I caught my uncle in bed with my mom.' Her flat tone belied the explosive words.

Mandy took a second to register the change of subject. 'Her brother?'

'No, brother-in-law. Anyway, I stupidly said something to my dad. I didn't get what I was tattling about, you know?'

'Sure, you were seven.'

Darci closed both hands around her cup. 'So, yeah. It had been going on under our noses for four years. I don't remember that, being a little kid, but it turned out my younger brother Glenn was only my half-brother.'

Mandy blinked. 'And first cousin?'

Darci thought about it. 'Yes, right. So anyway, my parents' marriage fell apart, my mother started drinking, and my uncle eventually got custody of my little brother. They don't interact with the family anymore.' She took another tiny sip before setting her cup down. 'But the thing was, he was the best uncle. Like, way nicer than my dad. And all the time he was screwing my mom, betraying his own brother. You just never really know about people.'

'Right,' Mandy agreed. Could this be a new suspect? 'That must have left a scar on everyone. This brother is, what, four years younger than you? Would you even recognize him if you saw him again?'

Darci pushed a lock of lank hair behind her ear. 'It depends on who he looks like these days. He'd be nineteen. If he looked like a DeRoy, I probably would.'

'Wow.' Mandy took a drink from her water bottle. 'Now that he's a young adult, I wonder if he'll come find you.'

Darci wrapped her arms around herself. 'I'm the one who told on my mum and uncle. Glenn was probably raised to hate me for breaking up the family and messing up his real father's life.'

'Wow,' Mandy repeated, then reminded herself that Coral had died, not Darci, and in Coral's place of business. The two women were not alike, so none of this old drama had anything to do with the murder.

Darci pushed her hair behind her ears again. 'Our uncle had promised Tom a new bike for his birthday but that never happened. He's nagged me about that forever.'

Mandy guessed the relationship between the siblings had been complicated for a long time. 'How is it that you guys still live together?'

'When Coral decided to take custody of Peony after she and Tom married, things were out of control. Peony had so many appointments that no one with a job could handle it alone. We all pitched in – Coral, Tom, and me. That way we could work and take care of Peony.'

'It's going to be really hard now, I suppose?' Mandy said, knowing how complex it was to parent even a healthy kid.

'No.' Darci looked thoughtful. 'Peony is much more stable. No surgeries these past couple of years, and she doesn't get sick often, so she doesn't have to stay home from school, go to the doctor all the time, you know.'

She was genuinely happy to hear that. 'That's a relief.'

'Yeah, but life is still complicated. Which is why I thought journaling might be perfect.' She glanced pointedly at Mandy's supplies.

Mandy embraced the change of subject. 'Yes. The power of downloading your thoughts to a piece of paper clears your brain and reduces your stress.'

'Really?' Darci looked hopeful.

'Oh yes,' Mandy said. 'A journal can be as simple or fancy as you like. You can use a few simple techniques every day or whenever you need. A notebook is a tool that's always there when you need it.'

'You use it as a creative outlet, though – right? I went to your website.'

'Definitely,' she agreed. 'But even with that, it can take as little or as much time as you like. A journal is very modular. You maybe saw that I sell stickers?' When Darcy nodded, she said, 'They can make your journal pretty and even faster to use. You don't even have to pick up a pen. Or maybe you want to spend the time to draw, paint, color, do calligraphy. Lots of people do.'

Darci picked up Mandy's planner and flipped through it. 'It sure is pretty, but my budget is low.'

Mandy handed her the planner she'd brought. 'I got this for free, so you can have it.' She pointed to the tulip stickers. 'And this is a gift from me. This set costs less than ten bucks and is one of my two new April designs, so you can set up everything you need for next month and give it a try.'

'Thanks,' Darci said, picking up the stickers with reverence. 'They are so beautiful. They look like little paintings.'

'Watercolor,' Mandy confirmed. 'Turned into stickers. I have to get home to make dinner, but I have a video on how to use these exact stickers to set up your month three different ways online. Just watch it with this journal, these stickers, and a pen or two and you'll figure it out right away.'

'What are the three ways?'

'It's flexible, but we focused on ideas for a student, what's best for a working mom, and what's best for a twenty-something with a job and a busy schedule. The main thing is that now you have a place for your to-do list, your random thoughts, your appointments, all of it.'

Darci nodded and set the stickers on top of the planner. 'I couldn't ask for more. Thank you. It's so strange being back here without Coral being at work, but I'm glad I made a new friend.'

'Of course,' Mandy said, though with far less enthusiasm. Darci hadn't exactly fallen off her suspect list, especially now that she understood how much stress Coral's choice to raise her sister had brought to everyone's life.

Darci changed the topic to what Mandy was planning to cook that night. Mandy managed to escape another ten minutes later.

Mandy found herself stuck in a traffic jam on the freeway and wished she'd taken another way home. Instead of making Vellum wait, she called her mother to verify she could feed her granddaughter, then pulled off the road to her favorite Indian place in the University District. She was starving.

While she ate spicy food in the fragrant red-walled restaurant, she thought over everything Darci had said about her family, and looked up the topic of 'why people kill' on her phone. She read a few articles about various killer personality types and took notes in her handy planner, then tried to figure out where her suspects might fit in.

Mandy supposed Reese could conceivably be the 'obsessive' type. She liked attention and could be pushy. Houston fitted into that category as well, and for all she knew, a number of others.

Amrik was even more of a question mark. Could he be someone overly controlled who might build into an explosion? Maybe as a spurned lover?

Peony and Darci were in her next category. Despite the sisters' closeness, Peony could be hurt and resentful by anything that took attention away from her health problems, such as Coral's job. She'd surely been traumatized by her many hospitalizations. Darci must also be a trauma victim, given her dramatic childhood. But if someone killed because of trauma, according to Mandy's reading, it was because of something major happening, not built-up resentment.

Darci could also be paranoid, though people really were talking behind the young woman's back. She'd have to research how and why paranoid people killed. Tom could be paranoid too, if he'd thought or known that Coral was having an affair. Plus the question of whether or not he'd abused Coral still hung over the murder. Could it be a simpler case of domestic violence leading to the death of the victim?

Mandy made a note on her phone. 'Affair with Amrik?'

Then she was left with Rod and Pham on her murder spread. If one of them had propositioned Coral and she had rejected them, that could be traumatic for the male ego. But for either of them to kill her, it seemed likelier it would have been in Lynnwood, not on Pill Hill. She looked back over her notes. Without knowing if Coral had been cheating on her husband, she was missing too many facts which kept her from building the right theories. Did the police have a clear picture of Coral's life by now?

Mandy went home full of tumbling thoughts and rumbling intestines. Chicken vindaloo and murder didn't seem to go well together. She picked up Vellum at her mother's and drove them both across the street, since it had begun to rain. Vellum said little.

'What's wrong?' Mandy asked as they walked into the kitchen.

'I have a lot of homework, Mom. I didn't have time to hang out with Grandma.'

'If you need to study, you can just tell her.'

'She was in a chatty mood.' Vellum dropped her hooded coat on its hook and dragged her backpack across the kitchen floor toward her bedroom.

Mandy glanced at the black streak her daughter's heavy black boots left on the floor and sighed. Her stomach gurgled. A hot toddy would be just the thing to soothe her.

She remembered a recipe for a coconut chai hot toddy. The ingredients were simple. She dropped a decaf chai teabag into a mug and turned on her coffee maker, then found some coconut milk in the refrigerator and put it in the microwave. Then she dug out some brown sugar and coconut rum from the cupboard.

The door in the hallway behind the kitchen opened and closed. Justin came in, looking ready for a workout in Husky logo sweats and some kind of high-tech body-con long-sleeved shirt.

'Going for a run?' Mandy asked.

'Time to drink?' Justin asked at the same time.

Mandy chuckled. The coffee maker gurgled and the microwave dinged. 'I decided to fight my chicken vindaloo with chai.'

Justin glanced at the stove, where Mandy had placed her leftovers since she hadn't decided whether she wanted to keep them or toss them out. 'Are you going to eat all of it?'

'That's what is left. It's all yours.'

Justin opened the plastic bag and dumped the contents into a porcelain bowl while Mandy assembled two half-size versions of her drink. She didn't want two shots of rum on a Monday night.

'Thanks. I'll meet you in the dining room,' Justin said from the microwave.

She put her violet-patterned teacups on a tray and took them in, hopeful for a murder update. They still ate in the dining room despite the table being surrounded by sticker trays, printers, and cutters, not to mention the mailing supplies.

Justin came in with his fragrant food.

'I hope your stomach is stronger than mine.'

'The rum will kill it.'

Mandy passed him a cup. 'I don't know that the food got to me as much as my dinner reading material.'

'Oh?' Justin sat down and forked up steaming rice and chicken.

'I showed Darci DeRoy a little bit about journaling after work and she told me some stories about her family. They sound pretty messed-up.'

'Oh?' he repeated, the syllable a little more forceful this time.

'At dinner I read some articles about why people kill.'

'That will give you heartburn.'

Mandy picked up her drink. The coconut smell overpowered the chai, which was probably what she really needed. Indian spices to combat Indian peppers. 'Shouldn't you be looking at the husband's family?'

'We are,' Justin said. 'You have no idea what we're doing, which is as it should be.'

'OK, well, tell me this? Was Coral having an affair with anyone? That could set off an entire chain of events.'

Justin looked at her over his teacup, his eyebrows knitted together. He took a sip of his drink. 'Mellow,' he commented. 'Not too heavy on the rum.'

'Just how I like it.'

'This is how I like it,' he said emphatically.

Her stomach fluttered, but not from indigestion this time. What did he mean? Them sitting together companionably? Surely that wasn't what was implied.

'What I like,' he continued, 'is you staying out of police business. There's a killer out there, and you're smack dab in his or her or their business.'

'Oh.' Mandy took a big gulp of her drink. 'The thing is that Darci approached me. I suppose she's technically a suspect, but she's also a young woman who needs help. Did you know that she lives with them to help with Peony?'

'I know that. I know far more than you do.'

'OK, should I be scared of Darci? She called me her friend.' She raised her eyebrows.

'Who does that just a few days after meeting someone? Especially in Seattle.'

'You don't think she's disturbed?' Mandy's stomach went queasy again.

'I'm sure she told you the story about her half-brother.'

Mandy nodded.

'And you yourself think her family is messed-up.' Justin held out his hand, palm up.

'Therefore, I shouldn't trust her?' Mandy said.

'Far be it from me to tell you who to be friends with, but I wouldn't be too friendly with anyone involved with the case right now.'

'What about Coral? It changes everything if she was having an affair.' Mandy couldn't help bringing the subject up again.

'Like with Reese?'

'No. Reese only likes Hindu men. I meant with Rod Portilla, or her boss.'

'It's an important question,' Justin agreed. 'But it's all out of my hands right now. I'm working other cases while the prosecutor's office decides if it is going to bring charges against Reese.'

'You're not still gathering evidence?'

'Other murders,' Justin explained. 'Lots going on. This morning a transient was found under a freeway overpass beaten almost to death. He is in a coma, so we can't ask him who his attackers were.'

'That's terrible.'

Justin warmed to his theme. 'There were over thirty murders in Seattle last year. All violent crimes hit a ten-year high.'

'I thought Seattle was generally so safe.' Mandy picked up her teacup and discovered it was empty. She considered a refill but knew it was a bad idea.

'Safer than the average big city,' Justin admitted. His cup was empty, too. 'Considerably so. Unfortunately, the numbers are going the wrong way.'

'I hope the arrest statistics are high as well – and, more importantly, the conviction statistics,' Mandy said. 'I doubt you have the right person – not yet. I'm going to stay on my guard, but I also feel really bad for the DeRoys.'

Mandy heard the mudroom doorbell ring. Before Justin could say anything more, she took her teacup into the kitchen and set it in the sink, then answered the door.

'Happy Monday,' Linda said with upturned lips, holding up a large plastic container between mitten-covered hands.

'Brownie night?' Mandy asked hopefully.

'You got it. Did you have a big dinner?'

Mandy patted her stomach and ushered her friend in. 'Huge. I had Indian on the way home because the traffic was so bad.'

Linda sniffed. 'And then some rum?'

'Yes. Justin and I had a toddy.'

Linda cocked her head. 'Do I smell rom—'

'Hi, Linda,' Justin said, coming in from the dining room before

she could finish her question. He set his dishes in the sink, sketched
a wave, and left the kitchen before Linda could do more than hold
up her brownie container to his back.

'—ance in the air?' she finished.

'Not in the slightest,' Mandy said. 'More like the usual superior
male lecture, although given that he is a police detective, it doesn't
really come off as mansplaining.'

'What's up?' Linda reached into Mandy's cupboard for plates,
then looked expectantly at the bottle of coconut rum until Mandy
caught the message and started to make her a toddy.

'He's cautioning me about the DeRoys; meanwhile, the police
have arrested Reese. He can't have it both ways.'

'Maybe he's trying to tell you that he doesn't think Reese did
it either.'

Mandy paused with the bottle angled over her Seattle Space
Needle souvenir shot glass. 'Oh, I get it.'

Linda tapped her nose. 'He's being subtle. I like it. Fill her up,
sweetie.'

Mandy filled the shot glass, then pulled out a fresh chai bag
and heated the water and the coconut milk. 'You're drinking double
what I did. I hope you make it across the street.'

Linda snorted. 'The brownie will sop it all up. We used to drink
whiskey toddies when I was married.' She sighed. 'George isn't
a drinker.'

'Just a lover,' Mandy teased. Their local dentist lothario hadn't
been faithful to her friend, but Linda seemed to prefer having him
to having no one at all.

She stirred in the brown sugar and took the University of
Washington glass mug into the dining room. 'I never noticed
before, but all my barware seems to have a logo on it.'

'Gifts,' Linda said, setting two plates down with brownies. She
still held a third. 'Vellum?'

A door opened and slammed shut at the sound of the name.

'She's in a very teenagery mood tonight,' Mandy whispered.

They listened to stomps through the kitchen. Vellum's face
appeared in the dining-room doorway. Linda held out the plate.
'It has veggies hidden in it.'

Vellum's expression turned thoughtful. 'Treating me like a
toddler?'

'Treating all of us like toddlers.'

She harrumphed and muttered her thanks before stomping out again with the plate.

Mandy sighed. 'It's been a long day.'

'I saw your text about Darci. Did she seem murderish?' Linda asked.

'The DeRoys have some skeletons in their closet. But that doesn't mean she or her brother have any murderous tendencies. I wish I knew whether Coral had had an affair.'

'For a motive?'

'Exactly. What was the reason she died?' She felt grumpy and overwhelmed.

'I just want to know what the police found at Reese's house.'

Mandy nodded vociferously. 'Justin won't tell me.'

'I have to think it's the murder weapon,' Linda mused.

Mandy stole a sip of Linda's drink. 'You would think. But who planted it there?'

They heard footsteps again, this time Justin's.

'Like a boomerang,' Mandy said peevishly. 'I think I need to go to bed. Usually, I have more energy than this, but the vindaloo is weighing me down.'

Justin's head appeared in the doorway. His hand appeared, holding the treats. 'Can anyone eat these brownies?'

'Go ahead,' Linda said sweetly.

Justin grunted. A minute later he reappeared, holding a fork. He stabbed it right into Linda's plastic container, then wandered past them both into the art studio.

'If you get crumbs in there, I will hurt you,' Mandy said. 'Have you heard anything more about Reese?'

'You can get on the appointment list online for the King County Jail. Also, assaulting a police officer is never a good idea,' Justin called.

Mandy and Linda looked at each other.

'You know,' he called, 'your murder spread needs some work.'

Mandy's eyes went wide. She leaped up from her chair and put her finger to her lips. Linda followed her into the art studio.

Mandy's resident cop poked his fork at her journal. 'There are more massage therapists, and also another tattoo artist works part-time in Tom's building.'

'Really? I didn't meet anyone else at the wake or whatever it was.'

'Very introverted. Hardly talked at all in the interview,' Justin said. His fork went back into the container.

Mandy saw a speck of brownie on her spread, but decided not to yell at him. 'I have seen one other massage therapist. Anyone acting jealous or anything? Are they all women?'

'Except the manager. He has three others, all with limited English skills, and then there was Coral. She was an odd hire for that bunch.'

'But Reese recommended her,' Mandy said.

'That Reese. She's mixed up in this somehow, wouldn't you say?' He gave her a superior stare.

'She'd been in Coral's house. If she wanted to kill her, why didn't she do it there? She wouldn't go to all the effort of getting her hired, just to kill her at the hospital.'

'Coral gets a new job. Coral dies.' Justin shrugged.

'Could the massage therapy service be a front for something? Drugs or whatever?' Linda queried.

Mandy's incipient headache flared into a real one. She'd been playing detective when the real police job was so complicated. She wrote 'second tattoo artist' and 'massage therapist one, two, three' on her murder spread, then slumped into her chair. 'Overwhelming. Isn't Amrik a better suspect than Reese?'

'No.' Justin handed her the brownie container. 'One bite left.'

'I think it's too late for chocolate to help me,' Mandy said mournfully. 'You can have it.'

Justin winked at Linda and grabbed the container, then whisked it out of the art studio.

'I've never seen my brownies disappear so fast,' Linda said thoughtfully. 'Why is he hanging around all of a sudden?'

Mandy shrugged. 'I think he's complicating this on purpose. We don't need more suspects; we need to know what was at Reese's house.'

'Now is the winter of our discontent,' Linda quoted.

Mandy laughed. 'Indeed, Madam Shakespeare.' She was about to say she was ready for bed when she heard the front door doorbell ring. 'What fresh madness is this?'

EIGHT

'At the front door, no less,' Linda said, turning around. 'And at this time of night?'

'Never good,' Mandy agreed, hoisting herself out of her chair. She needed to find the time to exercise the next day or her scale would report bad news.

She walked through the house, Linda trailing her. Vellum poked her head out of her bedroom. 'What's going on?'

'I'm going to find out.' Mandy yawned. The clock across from the front door read nearly nine p.m. She opened the door and immediately regretted it.

At least she had the outside light on so she could make sense of the scene. A man stood there, broad-shouldered and at least six-five. When he turned to look at her, reflective letters flashed on the vest he wore under a rain jacket. 'I-L-E-N-F?' she asked.

'Bail enforcement,' he said crisply. 'Zac Turner.' He held out a wallet and she squinted to see his photo and the words 'Bail Enforcement Agent'.

'A police detective lives here,' she warned. 'There's no one here out on bail or whatever.'

'I've got my eye on the apartment building across the street, actually,' he said.

'I don't know anyone who lives there,' she said coldly, feeling Linda's rum-scented breath on her hair.

'Me either,' Linda agreed.

'How about Reese O'Leary-Sett?' he asked abruptly. 'Know her?'

'What's this really about?' Mandy sharpened her voice.

He continued, 'Is the name Tom DeRoy familiar to you?'

'Yes. I've been over to his place a couple of times.'

He held up his phone and scrolled through something. 'What's your name?'

'Why do you need to know?' Mandy asked.

'I believe you're Amanda Meadows. You go by Mandy?'

'Yes, but how do you know that?'

'Friend of Reese?'

'That's right.'

He glanced in Linda's direction. 'Who are you?'

'None of your business,' Linda snapped.

'I'm going to get Justin,' Mandy said, starting to turn away.

His voice lost the accusatory quality. 'I've been hired by Mr DeRoy to look into the details surrounding his wife's death.'

Mandy couldn't believe it. 'Why? That's a police job.'

'The burden of proof is particularly acute in murder cases. He wants to make sure the police find the killer.'

'Does he doubt Reese did it?' Mandy asked.

'Because we do,' Linda inserted.

'Justin, there's a bail guy at the door,' Vellum said in the hallway.

Justin had come back upstairs. He came up behind Mandy and put his hand on the small of her back. 'Ladies, why don't you let me handle this?'

Mandy stepped aside and saw Justin's stern expression. She grabbed Linda's arm and pulled her into the living room as Justin stepped on to the concrete square of the porch and closed the front door. They went to Vellum's room while the men spoke outside.

Vellum had circles under her eyes. It might be from the alder trees she was allergic to, which always flared in March, or exhaustion. 'What was that about?' she asked. 'How am I supposed to finish my homework with all this drama?'

'Why don't you finish in the morning? It's almost time for bed,' Mandy told her.

'I have to read three more chapters.'

Mandy stroked her daughter's cheek. 'At breakfast. On the bus. Take a shower and get some sleep, OK?'

She and Linda went back into the kitchen as Vellum's door closed behind them. 'I'll wash your container.'

'No rush,' Linda said. 'If Tom has hired someone to nail down the case against Reese, then we for sure have to do something to help her.'

'Agreed.' Mandy yawned. 'I'll go online tomorrow and get an appointment at the jail.'

Mandy had her chance to put her resolve to help Reese to work the next day. When she went to grab her purse at her lunch break, she heard buzzing. A text popped up from Darci, asking if she was free that night.

Caution, coming from Justin, warned her off like a good angel, while her conversation with Linda, the bad angel who'd been with her the night she'd begun to uncover what had happened to her murdered cousin, replayed in her mind. Then she remembered Vellum would be displeased. Except she had a yearbook meeting after school. She didn't have to know.

I have a little time, she wrote back cautiously, then grabbed her insulated lunch sack and went to the sofa at the parking garage end of the lobby.

Tom asked me to clean out Coral's stuff, Darci texted. *He can't stand staring at her toothbrush and shampoo. Would you help me? It will make me cry.*

Oh. Mandy slumped on to the sofa. Never had she felt more like the mature, experienced woman being asked to help out a younger one with a life ritual. She couldn't even claim it would be a new experience. When her father had died, she'd helped her mother with the house, but not a week later. More like six. After the initial flurry of activity and tears had died down.

But to go through a stranger's possessions? And a murder victim's at that. She vaguely remembered offering help back at the gathering at the house. Maybe it would work out for the best, and she could learn something new about the dead woman. Love letters? A burner phone? Her computer or tablet? She might luck into something useful and she knew Linda would be horrified if she declined such an opportunity, however distasteful.

Isn't it a little soon? Mandy texted back. *It's only been a week. Has Peony thought about what she wants to keep?*

They had a fight last night. Tom suggested boxing everything up and storing it in the garage. Peony screamed to throw it all away. She was beside herself.

Wow. Maybe some family therapy? Under the circumstances, Mandy responded.

Yeah. There was a pause, then Darci texted again. *I thought we could box everything in unmarked cartons fast. Tom has to take Peony to a checkup after school. Then he'll take her to dinner.*

I couldn't even get there until around five.

We'd have until seven or so. Deal with the obvious stuff. Her clothes, the bathroom.

Are you at work? Mandy texted.

I have a client at three that will take ninety minutes. So I can't get home until close to five either.

Mandy nodded to herself and unfastened her lunch sack. She pulled out a salad-in-a-jar concoction she had whipped up in the morning. Arugula, half a can of seasoned black beans, some frozen corn and cherry tomatoes. Not exactly seasonal eating, but she happily crumbled up a small bag of ranch-flavored corn chips and then mixed it all up with a recycled spice jar's worth of balsamic vinegar and olive oil.

One of the cardiac nurses from upstairs came out of the employee door and dropped into the sofa opposite her. He nodded in approval when he saw Mandy mixing her salad.

Mandy held it up. 'Trying to stay out of your department.'

He grinned. 'Must be tough, since you're the cookie lady.'

She enjoyed the lilt of his Jamaican accent. 'Someone has to eat them.'

'Not me,' he said. 'I work too hard saving lives to risk my own.'

She nodded, wishing again she'd gotten a medical education instead of an art one. As Vellum said, you could learn art on your own. She picked up her phone and texted Darci to say she'd meet her at the house later. Then she pulled up the jail website. She found Reese's name. Visitation was only available twice a week and she'd just missed the day. The next slots were full, so she scheduled her appointment for a week ahead.

When Mandy pulled up in front of the DeRoy house, she saw Darci unloading flat boxes from her trunk. She waved, telling herself she was there for one purpose: to find something to exonerate Reese. She'd texted Linda before she'd driven here, so that someone knew where she was.

Linda promised to make her a casserole and have it over to the house at six so that there would be food when Vellum and Justin arrived home.

Mandy had pointed out that she wasn't responsible for Justin. She felt a little queasy when she considered how often they had shared food in the past few days. How often in her younger days had her friends set up housing arrangements with men they weren't involved with, then drifted into relationships or even unplanned pregnancies? At least a few times. Proximity seemed to create lust. Of course, she'd found him attractive before he moved in.

Ugh. Too many thoughts. She climbed out of the car and slipped her purse strap over her head, crossbody style, then went to help Darci with the boxes.

They took them into the house, then Darci went to the forge to get tape so they could assemble the boxes. Mandy stood in the living room, semi-familiar now. She had no idea what to look for so she went to the single bookcase to see what kind of pictures were framed. Like most families these days, they only had older shots, mostly from back before cell phones had cameras, including a wedding picture. Tom had a beard then too, but short and trimmed. Coral looked serene if not ecstatic. Mandy realized this was the first time she'd seen Coral in life. Pretty and no sign of the Goth look then. A more recent headshot of Peony was framed too – probably a school picture – and a picture of Tom with his parents. That was it. No other shots of Coral's side of the family, and nothing that would indicate the closeness of a relationship with Rod Portilla.

'Got it,' Darci called.

They taped the boxes into squares. Darci had watched Mandy's tulip 'Plan with Me' the night before, and they discussed setting up her first bullet journal.

'OK,' Darci said when they had all the boxes assembled. 'We'd better dump everything in them before Peony gets home.'

Mandy checked her phone. 'It's already close to six.'

Darci swore and grabbed two boxes. Mandy followed suit and followed her to the hallway leading off from the living room. They crowded into a small bathroom.

'How do you know what is Coral's and what is Peony's?'

'I use the other bathroom with Peony. Everything girly in here should be Coral's.'

'OK. Some of this stuff is going to leak if we just dump it into a cardboard box.'

'I'll get some grocery store bags.'

While Darci went for them, Mandy pulled the expensive shampoo and conditioner and the vanilla bath gel and razor from the tub and set them on the counter. They were all a little damp, probably from Tom's morning shower. Then she opened the medicine cabinet and the cabinet under the sink. She tossed feminine products on to the counter.

When Darci returned, she pulled Coral's items from the medicine cabinet while Mandy boxed up the rest of the bathroom.

'That didn't take long,' Darci said.

Two boxes had been filled. 'I'll take them into the living room and tape up the tops. You take the other two boxes into the bedroom and get started,' Mandy suggested.

'Yep.'

Mandy watched Darci walk down the hall to the far-left door, then returned to the living room. As soon as she was done with the tape, she returned with fresh boxes.

The bathroom hadn't been too bad, but the bedroom was very feminine. The bed had a pastel pink ruffle and matching comforter, and the four corner posts were wrapped with tulle. Decorative pillows were dumped on a chair by the bed. Mandy suspected the sheets hadn't been changed in a couple of weeks. The room had the distinctive odors of more than one person. Perfume, male sweat, and other things she didn't want to think about. No sign of the Goth style here either. Who was Coral really?

'I think you should strip the bed,' she said queasily, setting down an empty box. 'This can't be healthy.'

'Tom never does anything around the house. I don't want it to become my job to wait on him,' Darci said.

'He just lost his wife,' Mandy soothed.

But Darci had a stubborn look on her face. 'I'm not doing it.'

Mandy pulled a pair of disposable gloves from her pocket. She'd brought them just in case. With a sigh, she put them on and surveyed the room. She spotted fluffy white slippers poking out from one underside of the bed. Kneeling to grab them, her gaze went to the space between the mattress and the headboard. She saw something on the floor, back by the wall.

She grabbed the slippers and tossed them into a box, then, using her cell phone as a flashlight, she reached in. Expecting a bottle of lotion, instead she found a knife. Her hand went numb as shock hit her. She dropped her phone.

She couldn't leave it there. Gingerly, she reached for the handle and pulled it toward her. She picked up her phone.

'Oh my God,' she breathed, when she caught her first good look at the knife.

'What?' Darci dropped a handful of clothing and trotted over to her.

They both stared down at it. It looked like a chef knife to Mandy – a long, fairly straight blade, about eight inches long.

It wasn't clean.

'That's blood,' Darci whispered.

'Under the bed?' Mandy's hands trembled. She was very glad she'd worn the gloves. 'Don't touch anything else,' she warned, holding up her phone. She took a picture and sent it to Justin, then enabled her location so he'd know where she was.

'What are you doing?' Darci asked.

Mandy turned warily. 'We have to tell the police. What if this is the murder weapon?'

Darci shook her head, her eyes frantic. 'No, it can't be. Isn't that what they found at Reese's house?'

'I don't know,' Mandy said. 'The police haven't actually told me what they found.'

'They haven't told me either,' Darci said, her voice trembling. 'At least you know I didn't put it there. I had no idea.'

Mandy believed her, at least by her tone of voice and look of shock. Would someone bring a stranger into the room where a murder weapon lay if they knew it was there? 'We can't stay here.'

'We can't?' Darci asked.

'It's under Tom's bed. He knows we're here.'

'He wouldn't have killed her.' Darci paused. 'Right?'

'He's your brother. I don't know what he's capable of, but I'm waiting outside for the police,' Mandy said. 'In my locked car. I should probably put this back where I found it, but I can't risk touching it again. I suggest you go to your room for now.'

She took photos of the bed with her phone so she could explain where she'd found it. Following Darci out of the room, she zipped out of the house while Darci went to her bedroom.

Mandy got into her car, locked the doors, and called Justin. Had Tom left the murder weapon under his bed, or was someone attempting to frame him?

* * *

Mandy didn't make it home until nine. Her mother met her in the kitchen when she came home. 'Everything OK?'

'It's too soon to know if that knife I found was the murder weapon. There are questions. Was it Coral's blood? Do the wounds match the blade?'

Barbara nodded. 'I think you need to stay away from those people.'

Mandy set her purse down and slipped off her coat. 'At least I'm sure Darci is innocent now. She was a wreck. I bet no one in that household knows whom they can trust.'

'You don't have the skills to judge,' Barbara cautioned. She put a pan under the tap and filled it, then set it on the stove to boil. 'She might be a psychopath or one of those really deviant personalities.'

'A psychopath?' Vellum repeated, coming into the room.

Mandy gave her a hug. 'I'm sorry I'm leaving you alone so much.'

'It's OK. It's starting to feel less spooky around here.' Vellum forced a smile. 'Do you want some of Linda's casserole?'

'Do you remember a couple of months ago when life was normal?' Barbara asked.

'We'll get there again,' Mandy insisted. 'Food sounds really good.'

'Will Reese?' Vellum asked, going to the refrigerator.

'I don't know. I guess it depends on how long this ordeal goes on for her. I hope her parents have hired the best lawyers possible.'

'Eugenia Knight told me Reese's parents are in India.' Barbara pulled out Mandy's box of hot chocolate packets and took three.

'That's not good. Maybe I should try to figure out how to get in touch with them,' Mandy fretted.

'You're trying to solve the murder,' Vellum soothed. 'That's what she really needs.'

'I thought it was odd that Tom hired that private detective.' Mandy shivered, thinking about the knife. It had been rough-hewn, with visible defects spiraling through it, like a reject from a class in the smithy. 'Now I'm afraid he's trying to make sure Reese is successfully framed for his crime.'

'He's using the detective to build a case against Reese, probably,' Vellum agreed, setting a plate in the microwave.

'Or someone is trying to frame him,' Mandy said thoughtfully, considering her list of suspects. 'What a mess.'

Barbara clanged mugs as she set them on the counter.

'I'm going to take a bath as soon as I have eaten dinner. Are you ready for bed yet, Vellum?'

Vellum watched her grandmother pour boiling water into the mugs. 'I'll brush my teeth in here so you can have the tub.'

Mandy smiled at her. 'Thanks for understanding.'

Vellum patted her shoulder. The microwave dinged. 'There's your food. It's not your fault you found a bloody knife.'

Twenty minutes later, Mandy stepped into a bubble bath. She leaned her head against a folded towel and drank her hot chocolate. Her thoughts ran through the list of possibilities and hung on the likelihood that someone was trying to frame Tom. These people didn't have enough money to hire an expensive private investigator unless they were desperate. Maybe Tom knew he had an enemy.

Mandy also came to the conclusion that the murder was centered around Coral's home life or her husband's business, not the hospital, even though she had died there. Otherwise, the murder weapon would have been found at the hospital, maybe to frame her boss Amrik or one of her co-workers, not at the house. Of course, if Coral and Amrik were having an affair, he might have had access to the house.

But all of that was supposition. Still, she felt more relaxed when she climbed out of the tub. She stepped into the hallway, clad in her fluffy winter bathrobe, holding her empty cup.

When she went to set it in the sink, she found Justin in the kitchen. She pulled the lapels of her bathrobe together, suddenly aware of her lack of attire compared with his jeans and button-down shirt.

He turned around from his position at the sink. His cop's gaze took in every inch of her, from water-dotted feet to baby-blue velour robe to the empty mug in her hand. She felt her body warm as he perused her.

'Risk your life, then home to take a relaxing bath?' he queried.

She twisted her free hand in her damp curls. 'It never occurred to me that I'd find that knife while simply helping someone box up their dead relative's possessions.'

'Why would do you that?' he demanded.

'Because I'd been dumb enough to offer help at the memorial,' Mandy explained. 'Darci doesn't seem to have many people to turn to. She said seeing Coral's things was upsetting Peony and I can't bear to not help.'

'I think that's a great story.' He dropped the dish towel he was holding on the counter and took a step toward her.

'You don't believe me?' Her voice trembled.

'I think you were playing Nancy Drew.' His voice was low. 'I think you were hoping to find something. That knife wasn't in Coral's stuff. It was under the bed.'

'So were her slippers. I reached for them, then saw the knife. I panicked, I—'

He interrupted. 'You thought you'd be nosy.'

She didn't move, feeling pinned by his eyes on hers. Her pulse thumped. 'I didn't deliberately look under the bed. It was just there.' Her words kept tumbling out. 'I could see it.'

'What possessed you to touch it?'

She bit her lip. 'I don't know, Justin. I have an impulsive streak.'

He stared at her mouth. 'I've noticed that. I'm concerned about your long-term safety.'

'It won't happen again. Two murders this year. That's a lifetime total for anyone.'

'Not for me.'

'It's your job. I'm a barista. When people die in my workplace, it's nearly always from natural causes.'

'What about when I drop dead from the stress of dealing with you?' he asked. 'What cause is that going to be attributed to?'

Her lips parted. 'Why, Justin, I didn't know you cared.'

His eyes went smoldering. Before she knew what was happening, his face moved close to hers. She stopped breathing, caught in delicious anticipation. His mouth touched hers.

Not soft, but possessive, strong, full of shattered emotion. Instinctively, she gave in to the rawness of it. It had been so long since she'd felt someone's lips on hers.

His free hand went to her cheek. His fingertip dusted past the sensitive skin in front of her ear as he groaned softly into her mouth.

Reason resurfaced after a few sensual moments of give-and-take.

Her housemate, Detective Justin Ahola of the SPD, was kissing her! Shocked, she jerked back.

NINE

M andy and Justin stared at each other, only a breath's span apart. Her arm jolted, an involuntary muscle spasm. He must have sensed it under his fingers and pulled away.

Her face had flushed from hot to cold, as if all her blood had drained south. She spoke without thinking. 'Justin, I'm not—'

His beautiful mouth hardened into a tight white line. He whirled around and strolled out of the kitchen. In an instant, she found herself alone again, as if nothing had happened.

What was that about? They couldn't get involved.

She wandered into her art studio in a haze, then slumped into her chair, her hands clutched around the collar of her robe. She'd thought it the least sexy piece of clothing she owned. Big, bulky, blue. Nothing seductive about it. But she'd always managed to be fully dressed around him before. Somehow, she hadn't considered that he'd get home that night, considering the state of the murder case.

Her fingers went to her mouth, reliving the kiss. He hadn't meant it. They were both upset, scared even. Of course he didn't want murder coming home to where he lived. He must have thought her house the safest place in Seattle for him. It had already had its murder.

But here they were and she couldn't forget Reese, beautiful perfectionist Reese, in a nasty jail cell. She wasn't some silly adolescent to forget everything because an attractive boy had kissed her. Fuming at herself, she shoved the sexy moment into a little corner of her mind and walled it off. Then, she grabbed her planner and opened to the murder spread. Now she had a weapon. She updated the page, wishing she could highlight Darci's name to show she had an alibi, to be done with one suspect at least, but that would be bad detective work. However accidentally, she was a rather good detective.

Or at least she wanted to be, for Reese's sake. And Darci's, for that matter.

Still in a daze, Mandy went to her room and dressed, then knocked on Vellum's door and told her she was going to run over to her mother's.

Barbara let her in, an expression of confusion on her face. 'It's late. Everything OK?'

Mandy shrugged.

'One of those?' When Mandy nodded, Barbara put a hand on her shoulder and steered her into the kitchen. 'What happened?'

Mandy sat down at the kitchen table. 'Justin kissed me.'

Something clattered loudly in the sink. Mandy glanced up. Her mother had dropped her teakettle. 'I know. Crazy, right?'

'Out of the blue?' She picked up the kettle.

'Yes.' Mandy explained the entire incident while the kettle filled.

'That's too bad. I didn't expect him to be around for long, but a year might have been nice. This will probably accelerate the process.'

Mandy agreed. 'I figured he'd lick his wounds over his broken relationship and then buy a smaller house, or even a condo.'

'It seems reasonable.' Barbara set her teakettle on the stove and turned on the heat. 'You aren't likely to find the perfect match right after your divorce, so becoming involved with your tenant is unwise.'

'I know. I'm skittish enough without having someone I'm dating literally in my house. It's so uncomfortable if anything isn't perfect, and nothing is perfect.'

'I'm worried that dating your tenant might lead to Vellum's Moffat grandmother talking her into moving in with them again.'

Mandy's head snapped up. Her mother's eyes met hers. 'Yes, my dear. Vellum's already left once. I can just hear Elaine Moffat now, telling Vellum that she needs to give you and Justin some space to explore your relationship in peace.'

Mandy scowled. 'Meanwhile, Cory can't even bother to take Vellum for the weekend. He cancelled on her again.'

'Cory isn't your problem.'

'No, it's Elaine.' She shuddered involuntarily at the thought of her former mother-in-law, who possessed a large house, lots of money, and the desire to have Vellum live with her.

Barbara took a tin from the cupboard and poured loose chamomile into the infuser in her favorite teapot. 'What are you going to do?'

'Pretend it never happened. It wasn't planned or anything.' Mandy sighed.

'Now you know what's he's thinking, though.'

'Yeah, we know he likes baby-blue bathrobes.'

'Funny. I'll buy you something else,' Barbara said. 'Even if I have to drive all the way to Southcenter.'

'Sure, Mom.' Mandy looked at her hand. It had a tremor. 'Look at what the stress is doing to me.'

'Well, don't do any yoga,' her mother teased. 'What if Justin came upon you in some interesting contortion?'

Mandy giggled. 'Downward dog?'

They both laughed. When the teakettle whistled, Barbara poured water into the pot while Mandy considered how to destress herself. Maybe she needed mindful meditation after all. The hospital did have that speaker coming in. It would keep her out of the house.

'Be gentler with the cookies,' Mandy told Houston at three fifteen the next afternoon. She'd just finished baking. 'They're too warm to be handled like that. They'll break.'

Houston attempted to wink, though his other eye half closed, too. 'We get to eat them if they break, and I'm starving.'

'Don't you dare,' Mandy warned. 'If we have too much spoilage, Fannah will cancel cookies. We have to make a profit.'

'Calm down.' Houston slid a cookie into a waxed paper bag.

Mandy added it to the small pile. 'You calm down. I love doing the baking. It saves me from staring at the lobby every second of my shift.'

The bell on the counter dinged. Since Houston had gloves on, Mandy picked up the cookie bags and went to take care of the front.

'Darci!' she exclaimed when she recognized their customer. 'What brings you by again so soon?' She opened the back of the display case and added the cookies.

'What are those?'

'Chocolate chip. We never have enough.'

'That sounds good.' Darci tilted her head. 'I'm starving but I don't know if I can keep anything down.'

'Yesterday was stressful,' Mandy said sympathetically.

'It's not that. I had a doctor's appointment in the office building. I had to tell someone my news.'

'Oh?' Mandy pressed one hand against the counter. 'I hope it's good news.'

Darci grinned. 'I'm pregnant!'

She looked excited, so Mandy responded in kind. 'Congratulations!' She clasped the younger woman's hand in hers and gave it a squeeze. 'Do you have a due date yet?'

'Around Halloween,' Darci confided. 'I'm so nervous. I know all about being responsible from having to help with Peony all these years, but babies are so fragile.'

'It tends to be a blur, thanks to the sleep loss,' Mandy admitted. 'But you just take one day at a time and babies keep growing and developing.'

Darci clasped her hands together. 'I'm starting to wonder if morning sickness is just nerves.'

'No.' Mandy laughed. 'At least not for everyone. Did you want something to drink?'

'I'm not supposed to have caffeine.'

'I think we still have some ginger-blend tea bags from the holidays in the back. That might help your tummy.' She wondered who the father was, given that she hadn't seen Darci with a significant other at the wake.

'Sure,' Darci said.

Mandy dashed into the prep room, edged past Houston, and looked on the shelving units for the tea box. Luckily, it hadn't been pushed too far back yet and she found what she was looking for. When she turned around, she saw him staring at her.

'You know, that girl out there has a long-lost half-brother from Alaska,' she said, narrowing her eyes. 'Do you know her?'

He frowned. 'No. What's her name?'

'Darci DeRoy.'

He shrugged. 'I've never known anyone named DeRoy. Who were the missing brother's parents?'

'Her mother and uncle. The half-sibling would also be her first cousin.'

'Was he given up for adoption?'

'No, the uncle took him away.'

'Huh.' He went toward the prep room. 'Definitely not me then.'

As she returned to the counter, confused by Houston's cryptic response, she grabbed the rest of the cookie bags, then turned her thoughts to wondering if the father of Darci's baby was going to be involved in the pregnancy. It might bring a new player into Coral's murder, after all. She might as well focus on someone else, since Houston, determined to be irritating, wasn't giving much away.

'Here we go.' Mandy handed Darci the tea bag. 'What do you think?'

Darci studied the package. Mandy noticed a tremble in Darci's hand.

'Hey, maybe this is too much right now, but the hospital is having a meditation lecture. I was thinking about going. Do you want to come?'

'When is it?' Darci nodded and handed her the tea bag.

'This evening.' Mandy put the tea bag in a twelve-ounce cup and then slid another cup around it to hold the tea string in place. She added hot water from the special dispenser.

'I'd probably better not. That's hours from now and it's my turn to cook dinner.'

'I get it. I'll probably go home and then come back. But I don't know anything about the topic.'

'Who is the speaker?'

'Someone named Bodhi Lee.'

'That's funny.' Darci compressed her lips, then gave her head a little shake. 'I found an autographed copy of a book by him in Coral's stuff.'

'Maybe she was intending to go to the lecture,' Mandy said. 'The sign went up by lunchtime the day she died.'

Darci nodded. 'I guess so. Now I wish I could come. Maybe Peony was going to go with her.'

'I'll tell you about it afterward,' Mandy offered.

'Sure. I'll bring you the book when I'm here again so you can read it.'

'That's nice of you.' Mandy glanced at the clock. 'Oh, I need to get out of here. Shift end.'

Houston appeared in the doorway, followed by Fannah, who worked late on Wednesdays for inventory.

Mandy stepped to the side. 'OK. I'll see if Vellum wants to go with me. This Bodhi Lee must be pretty well known if he's written books.'

Darci nodded. 'Is Vellum your daughter?'

'Yes,' Houston interjected.

Darci ignored him and kept her eyes on Mandy. 'Cool name. Do you want me to wait for you?'

'Thanks, but I'll be here for another couple of minutes.'

Darci hoisted her tea, nodded at Fannah, and went in the direction of the escalator.

Mandy walked into the back room with Fannah.

'Come with me,' Fannah said, and pulled her into the prep room.

'What's up?'

'I don't want Houston on cookies,' Fannah said. 'You can have a couple of minutes to clean this up.'

'OK.' Mandy glanced around and didn't see any more mess than was usual with her own efforts. 'Any reason?'

'He eats the cookies.'

'We all eat the cookies.'

'Only the broken or burned ones.' Fannah gave her a smoldering model gaze. 'I know what happens around here. That Houston, he eats the good ones.'

'Did you have security cameras hidden back here after what happened?' Mandy asked.

'I'll never tell,' Fannah said.

'I'd worry about a lawsuit,' Mandy told her. 'What if we changed back here? Sometimes something gets spilled and we have to.'

'Then change in the bathroom.'

'That will take a lot longer. The bathroom is at the opposite end of the floor.'

'Mandy,' Fannah said in an exasperated voice. 'You do the cookies. Not Houston. Final decision.'

'No problem. I'm happy to have a little overtime.' Mandy reached for disposable gloves so she could do the clean-up. 'I have an unrelated question.'

'Yes.'

'That was Darci DeRoy. She's the sister-in-law of the massage therapist who was murdered last week.'

'Oh?'

'She's technically a suspect, despite what's happened with Reese. But she's trying to be my friend. Justin doesn't like that, though. Do you think it's strange that Darci is trying so hard to be my friend? Especially since I found Coral's body and this is where she died.'

'She's drawn back here.'

Mandy nodded. 'Exactly.'

Fannah rubbed her hand along the nape of her neck. 'I'm not surprised. It's like rubbing at a scab. Besides, people trust you.'

'They do?' Mandy asked.

'Yes, you have that kind of face.' Fannah sketched an oval in the air. 'Very open.'

'Hmm. I wish Justin trusted me when I told him that Reese couldn't have killed Coral.'

Fannah's serene expression darkened. 'You won't have heard, but Reese was formally charged with murder this morning.'

Mandy felt numb and nauseated all at the same time. She was glad she hadn't touched the cookies. 'That's horrible. Where did you hear that?'

'I ran into the office manager at the podiatrist's in the cafeteria. It stops the waiting, and Reese has a chance to have a hearing so she can post bail and return home.'

Mandy's voice broke as she spoke. 'When does that happen?'

'The article I saw said the bail hearing has been delayed until her parents are back in the US. They've been in India.'

Mandy put her hands on her stomach. 'Poor Reese. Another delay.'

'It's very tragic. That girl looks up to you, for all her arrogance.'

Mandy blinked rapidly as tears started to form. Fannah's words broke her heart. 'I can't believe she killed Coral.'

'I think anyone is capable of murder,' Fannah whispered. Her tone menaced Mandy's nervous system, leaving her flustered. 'Now, finish up your work so I can limit the overspend on wages.'

She glided out, leaving Mandy wondering what the story was behind Fannah's statement. Had she killed someone? Maybe that was how she came to emigrate from Ethiopia? Mandy had always assumed she'd left her homeland because she'd been discovered by a modeling talent agency.

'This had better be really relaxing, Mom. Couldn't we have just watched some old *Gilmore Girls* episodes or something?' Vellum complained as they crossed into the hospital on the sky bridge at seven twenty that evening.

'I don't know if that would have been just as good, but I can't stay fretting at home while Reese is in jail with a murder charge hanging over her head.'

'What are you going to do? Send waves of happiness in her direction?' Vellum snorted, then grabbed her mother's arm out of the blue.

Surprised, Mandy jerked back and they both bounced against the handrail.

'Sorry, I slipped.' Vellum glanced behind them.

Mandy saw the puddle of water glistening on the faux stone floor. 'That's not safe.'

Vellum stomped her boots until her footprints stopped leaving damp spots and they continued on. But Mandy's heart continued to pound. She'd need some effective mindful meditation to relax now for sure.

On the third floor, they found the auditorium, a space Mandy hadn't been in before. Inside, about twenty people hovered near the back, getting cups of water from a trio of the hospital's fruit water dispensers. A tinny-sounding nature soundtrack played up front.

Mandy and Vellum dispensed cups of water and went to sit in the third row. Mandy glanced at the raised front of the room. On the speaker's table was a large hourglass with sand in the lower half and a trio of books tilted upright on plastic holders. She imagined that Coral's autographed copy was one of the titles. Two men stood on stage. She recognized Jason Cho, an assistant hospital administrator. The other man must be the speaker. She noted black hair and yellow-brown skin. He wore a sleeveless pink shirt and trousers that appeared to have been based on the dhoti. The bright green patterned fabric was baggy around the knees and open on the inner shins.

When he turned, Mandy gasped and grabbed Vellum's sleeve.

'What?' Vellum glanced up and her mouth fell open.

'Houston,' they said together.

'It's like looking at an older version of him,' Mandy said. From an almost academic perspective, she'd known Houston was attractive, but too young to appeal to her. This guy was a different story. He was older than Justin, but age looked good on him, with bright white streaks of hair around his temples and laugh lines radiating from his eyes. He had a kind air.

Mandy let out a breath and relaxed into her chair.

Vellum tapped the heavy toe of her boot against the floor, sipping her fruit water. 'Are you going to take notes?'

'Good idea.' Mandy pulled out her planner.

Jason Cho leaned over the microphone on the boxy podium placed on the table. He tapped it and it gave a muffled popping sound. 'If you will all take your seats. We'd like to start our program now.' When he glanced over the audience, Mandy thought his eyes lingered on hers. She nodded and smiled, not sure if he remembered meeting her the previous month, but his gaze kept moving.

Once most of the participants were seated, Cho picked up a sheet of paper and read from it. 'The University of Seattle Hospital is pleased to welcome Bodhi Lee, owner of the Wheel Meditation Center in Homer, Alaska. Tonight's presentation is sponsored by the Integrated Medicine Department of the university. Bodhi Lee has been meditating for twenty-five years. He received training in India and has been teaching for twenty. Thousands of people have benefited from his methods, and one million copies of his books have sold around the world. Please welcome Mr Lee.'

The meditation master moved to the podium after enthusiastic applause. He clasped his hands together and smiled beatifically, reminding Mandy of a pose she'd seen in old pictures of rock stars' gurus back before she was born. When she glanced around the room, though, the audience had a definite hum of enthusiasm. Just because she was ignorant didn't mean this guy wasn't a world-class master, so she clicked her pen open to take notes.

'Chakra is the Sanskrit word for "wheel,"' the guru said in a pleasant low voice, holding just the hint of an accent, too faint to be easily recognized. 'These ever-transforming wheels of energy match our body's nerve centers. We have seven main chakras, which contain our organs, our emotions, our wellness states. We must keep our chakras healthy. If they cannot stay open, our energy cannot flow through us.

'Tonight, I will take you through a meditation to balance energy. I want you to leave here tonight feeling ready to cope with the challenges in your life. If you find this helpful, it is my hope that you will sign up for my four-part class. The university and the hospital have brought me here and have covered many of my expenses to make this possible at a reasonable price.

'My assistants are at the back of the room ready to sign you up for the class after the meditation.'

After this introduction, the guru took them through a thirty-minute meditation. When Mandy opened her eyes at the end, she couldn't believe how much time had passed. She had as much energy as if she'd drunk a sixteen-ounce double-shot Americano.

After the guru's closing remarks, the lights in the room brightened. People shuffled, smiling in an unfocused manner.

'I'm signing up,' Mandy whispered.

'This is what you want to spend your money on?' Vellum said skeptically. 'You could get this from a video online or a DVD from the library.'

'No,' Mandy disagreed. 'His voice is relaxing. You have to be able to follow the voice. Besides, it's subsidized, and maybe I can do some networking. I'll be hunting for a better job once I've been a barista for a year.'

'That's only about six weeks away.'

'I know. It's coming up fast.'

'What jobs are you going to apply for?' Vellum asked.

Mandy sighed. 'That's the problem. I have no idea – just has to be higher-paying and with health insurance. Maybe meditation will help me find clarity.'

They went to the back of the room and Mandy sacrificed her credit card to a young man who worked the day surgery desk.

She smiled at the woman signing up at the next table. 'You work in Food Services, right?'

'Yes, I do scheduling for hospital meals,' the woman said.

'I'll see you in class,' Mandy told her as the young man gave her back her credit card. In May, she might start applying for office manager and supervisor jobs at the hospital. After all, she ran a small business. It wouldn't be too much of a step up to spend her forty hours doing some kind of hospital management instead of baking cookies and slinging drinks.

Late the next morning, Mandy handed Dr Burrell one of her ginger thins and a coffee cup. 'What do you think of meditation?'

'I think it's great,' he told her. 'I wish we could get our NICU parents into a course. Especially the mothers. They could use a few minutes a day to focus on their wellbeing.'

'I attended the Bodhi Lee seminar last night and we did a body scan. I was amazed to find all these little aches and pains I never noticed.'

He nodded. 'Exactly. Our parents are so busy running to and from the hospital in addition to the rest of their lives that they don't check in with themselves. Many of these moms have just given birth, sometimes had surgery. They need to be concerned with their own health, too.'

'I signed up for the course he's doing here.' She tossed his receipt.

'Good for you. My weekly yoga class keeps me going.'

'I'll see you there tonight, Stan,' Fannah announced as she came out of the back room, followed by a sullen Houston.

The neonatologist pointed a finger at Fannah and went to fill his coffee cup.

Mandy had wondered if Fannah and the doctor were dating. That didn't matter to her. She had trouble of her own and didn't need to worry about Tristan Burrell. Justin had stayed out of her path since the kiss, but she knew she'd have to reckon with it sometime.

'Incoming,' Houston muttered in her ear as a large party came into view from the elevator bay.

Fannah had to help them with orders as a dozen people came to the counter. She handled the blender station just inside the back-room door while Mandy made drinks and Houston took the cash register and pastry display case. The somber party discussed their dying grandmother in between handing over credit cards and taking donuts and cookies. Some of them seemed sad and others were curious about the will.

The crowd seemed to attract more people, and Mandy made about twenty mochas and lattes before it died down. Houston had lost his sullen expression, and Fannah had a little smile on her face as she restocked donuts.

'All the chocolate chip cookies are gone,' she reported.

'Do you want me to make more now?' Mandy asked.

'Prep them this afternoon. I have to go to a meeting.' Fannah took off her gloves. 'When I come back, you can go to lunch.'

Mandy nodded and waited for her to head into the back room. 'What happened?' she whispered to Houston.

TEN

H ouston shrugged and gestured Mandy to move over to the coffee station, a few feet away from the back-room door. 'It's all good. Boss lady throwing her weight around. Reminded me I was still on probation and she'd better not catch me stealing food.'

'Did she tell you she had you on camera eating cookies?' Mandy asked.

Houston's eyebrows shot up. 'No, why?'

Mandy wondered about that. Fannah didn't like to fire anyone, but surely if she had evidence, she'd have announced it to Houston. Maybe she'd been misleading Mandy about cameras in the back. Either way, these days it was better to act like someone was always watching.

Mandy shrugged. 'Just wondering. She told me I was supposed to make the cookies.'

Houston smirked. 'Like that would stop me from eating them.'

Mandy stared at her co-worker, his demeanor so different from the above-it-all Bodhi Lee. 'I don't know if you heard me talking about the meditation lecture last night.'

'Not really.'

'You look a lot like the speaker. I'm less sure now, but last night Vellum and I thought Bodhi Lee could be your father.'

Houston put his hand on the counter as if to steady himself. 'You're kidding. Who is this guy?'

'He has a meditation business in Homer, Alaska.'

'Alaska?' Houston repeated. His voice lowered. 'Wow.'

'What is it with Alaska? Everyone seems to be from there. Do you think he's a long-lost relative or something?' She forced herself to tamp down her enthusiasm. 'Lots of people look alike for no apparent reason.'

Houston licked his lips. 'The thing is, I came here looking for my father. My mom always said she had a fling with a summer fisherman who was going to college in Seattle.'

At least that didn't make it sound like he could be Darci's long-lost half-brother. 'You came down here to find him? Do you have a name?'

'No, but I did one of those DNA tests they have online.'

'No name on your birth certificate?'

'No. Just a blank spot for father.'

No, he wasn't Glenn for sure. 'That led you to Seattle?'

'Yeah. I had a seven-day free membership to the DNA website and it showed I had some second cousins with grandparents who died in Seattle.'

Mandy thought. 'Second cousins means you share a great-grandparent?'

He looked confused for a moment, then his expression cleared. 'I guess. I figured that meant my grandparents had been here, too. Anyway, it seemed to match the story, but when I tried to email my cousins, they didn't respond. I found one on Facebook and it showed he worked at Boeing.'

'Isn't Alaska really big? I thought you were from Anchorage.'

'It's just a couple hundred miles from Anchorage to Homer.'

'Oh, really? That's like Portland to Seattle. I thought you had to get on a plane to go everywhere up there.'

'No, not everywhere.' Houston pulled his cell phone out of his pocket.

'You're not supposed to have that behind the counter.'

Houston rolled his eyes. 'How do you spell this guy's name?'

Mandy spelled it out.

Houston poked at his phone for a few seconds. 'I found his website.'

Mandy leaned over the phone. It wasn't hers, after all. Houston scrolled through the main page, then pulled up the 'About' page, then Bodhi's biography. 'This doesn't even say where he is from.'

'I wonder if those credentials are real. But then the hospital must have checked him out.'

'Maybe.' Houston chose the seminar page. 'Look, he taught in Anchorage last month.'

'Coral was from Alaska. And she had an autographed copy of his book in her possessions. I wonder if she went to his seminar.'

'We could call the Center.' Houston paused. 'If we cared. C'mon, Mandy, we're trying to figure out if this guy is my dad!'

'Coral was murdered and someone she might have known in Alaska just happens to be in Seattle right now,' Mandy argued.

'Coral died over a week ago. Was this guy here then?'

'That's a question for the police. I'll give them the information.'

Houston leaned on the counter. 'How are we gonna find out if he was teaching in Anchorage over twenty years ago?'

'I know he was doing meditation that long ago from the introduction. I could ask Jason Cho what he knows about Bodhi Lee.'

A couple came in through the main lobby doors and headed toward the coffee bar. Houston tucked his phone away. 'Don't worry about it. I'll sign up for this class too, and talk to him myself.'

'Brave of you,' Mandy commented, pasting on her customer service smile.

Houston walked to the espresso machine. 'Fortune favors the bold.'

'Darci,' Mandy exclaimed as Coral's sister-in-law appeared at the counter just after Fannah left that afternoon. 'Here again so soon?'

'I know, but I actually have a private client a couple of blocks from here. She's a shut-in and her daughter pays me to do her hair. Coral provided massage, so we worked as a team.'

'I see.'

'Yeah.' Darci made a face. 'I called a couple of Coral's friends but no one wants the job, so I'm going to see if Amrik can find me someone.'

'At least they're used to coming to this part of town.'

'Exactly.'

'Do you know much about Amrik? Were he and Coral close?'

Darci shrugged and pulled a book from her bag and set it on the counter. 'I barely know the guy. She didn't talk about him, if that's what you mean.'

Mandy glanced at the title. '*Chakra Meditation*,' she read aloud. 'Cool, thanks. Did Coral get this when Bodhi Lee spoke in Anchorage?'

'When was that?'

'A month ago. Did she go home to visit or anything?'

'Not in February. She did go back with Peony for Thanksgiving last year. There was some kind of family reunion with her extended family.'

Mandy made a mental note to check Bodhi Lee's schedule for last November. She flipped the book open and saw it had been published five years ago. Then she hunted for the inscription, which was a generic *Be balanced and mindful* and undated. 'What's this?' She pointed to the non-English phrase.

'I don't know. Sanskrit or something?' Darci suggested.

'Probably,' Mandy agreed. 'Thanks for this. I'll try to read it before the seminar starts.'

'Is it on Saturday?'

'No, it isn't until Monday.'

'I wondered if you'd like to attend a knife-making class. We have a beginner class on Saturday.'

Mandy shook her head. 'I can't. I used up all my discretionary budget for the meditation class.'

'It would just be for the price of materials,' Darci coaxed. 'It is an expensive class, but this is your chance to see what we do for almost nothing. We have two spots left.'

'Let me think about it, OK? If my daughter is interested, I would consider it.'

'Great! I hope we see you there.'

'Do you want something to drink?' Mandy tucked the book on the shelf under the cash register.

'No, thanks. I need to talk to Amrik.' Darci sketched a wave and walked away.

Houston appeared as soon as Darci had walked across the lobby.

New stains decorated his apron since Fannah had tasked him with cleaning the blender station. 'I heard Anchorage.'

Mandy showed him the book. 'Any idea what this inscription means?'

'Hold out the book.' Mandy complied and Houston snapped a picture. 'BRB.'

Be right back. Mandy rolled her eyes at the abbreviation. She made a vanilla latte for a nurse and handed coffee cups to a couple of the volunteers. Darci left the lobby, followed by a young woman who wore the chair massage smock.

Conveniently, Jason Cho stopped by for a tea and muffin. As Mandy handed him his cup, she said, 'I really enjoyed the seminar. What a great idea to bring in Bodhi Lee.'

'He's pretty great,' Jason agreed. 'Did you sign up for his series?'

'Yes, I'm really looking forward to it. Are you signed up?'

'Yes.' He took his muffin with a smile. 'The hospital sent senior management through the training last week. I want to do it again. You'll enjoy it. I'm meditating every day for ten minutes now.'

'That's great.' Mandy took his cash and gave him his change.

He dropped it into the charity donation box. 'See you next time.' He disappeared back into the elevator bay.

Luckily, she wasn't busy or she'd be pretty irritated by Houston's disappearance. Just after she'd sold the last of their donuts, he reappeared from the back.

'Got it,' he said. 'It's a pretty standard Sanskrit saying.'

'What does it mean?'

He handed her his phone and she read it aloud. 'Our body is love, we are eternal.'

'What do you think?' He tucked his phone away again.

Mandy pulled out the book from the shelf under the counter and considered the flowing script barred by black lines at the top. 'It's either something commonly said in the chakra or meditation world, or he and Coral were involved.'

Houston folded his arms and glanced away.

'What?' Mandy asked.

'I hate that she's dead.'

'I know, it's really sad.' Mandy tucked the book away again as customers walked toward them.

'Coral could have told me more about Bodhi. Now I'll never know what she knew.' He disappeared into the back again instead of helping her with the customers. Was he even trying to survive probation?

That night, Mandy and Vellum reached the house at the same time for once. They agreed to work on sticker orders and managed a couple of hours before Vellum went to do homework. Mandy heated some chicken noodle soup her mother had made and stashed in the freezer for flu season. They hadn't needed it then. After that, she went into the art studio, turned on the fireplace, and switched on the lamps.

She opened the window shade and sat down at the desk, then pulled her planner off the windowsill. Although she felt the need to create something new, first she needed to update her habit trackers. She ticked off the number of hours she'd slept the previous night, laughed at the blank exercise block and discovered that past Mandy had thought she might make sloppy joes with ground turkey, if she'd made it to the grocery store this week as on her to-do list. Oh, well. Sometimes her journal had all the elements of a fantasy life. She'd catch up over the weekend, especially since sloppy joes did sound delicious.

She flipped through her journal until she found her murder spread. Bodhi needed to be added, but where? He didn't fit in as a co-worker, family, lover, or neighbor as far as she knew. For now, she wrote his name on a stray piece of sticker paper and only uncovered a little bit of the sticky part so she could remove it if she needed to. She added a question mark on the left then stuck the sticker on the bottom of the paper.

She remembered her cousin's murder and knew her next step was to check alibis. Some were super easy to check on social media, as she recalled. She found a post from someone tagging the tattoo studio, indicating that Pham had been working on her tattoo at the time of the murder.

Her system last time had been yellow for 'no alibi' and pink for 'alibi.' She covered Pham's name with a pink highlight using a blush-colored Tombow marker. Reese didn't have an alibi so she received a yellow line. Now she needed to go through the rest and see what she could learn on social media.

'Two down, seven to go,' she said aloud. The police would know a lot more than she did, but dare she talk to Justin? The mere thought sent butterflies floating through her stomach. But Barbara Meadows hadn't raised any cowards. She pulled out her phone and sent Justin a text, asking for a trade of information.

Then she stared at her murder spread some more. Had Amrik been at work? Was a security camera perched over his massage empire? Houston left at five on Wednesdays. Had he still been in the hospital when she'd found Coral? It had been just after five. Maybe Fannah would know. What about Darci? Was she at her hair salon? Were Tom and Peony in the house together? Where had Rod been?

'What are you up to now?'

Mandy whirled at the sound of Justin's voice. He stood in the doorway, barefoot despite the evening chill. Water slicked back his hair and he wore an unbuttoned Henley shirt, exposing a stripe of chest. Yeah, he was mouthwatering, this guy who had kissed her.

She forced her brain to snap back into the groove. 'I know a little something, but I'd like to update my alibi list. Will you trade?'

He put his hands on his hips. 'I'm the police, Mandy. Don't make me haul you downtown.'

'Oh, c'mon. You want me to know whom I can trust, right? I'm guessing that means Darci has no alibi.' She gave him a speculative look.

Justin crossed his arms, making his shoulders look even broader. 'What do you think you know?'

'Bodhi Lee.'

'Who's that?'

She pointed her yellow Tombow at him. 'He's a meditation teacher from Alaska.'

'So?'

'Coral knew him. Does Amrik have an alibi?'

'Not yet. We don't have the manpower to get through all the surveillance tape quickly.'

'So he says he was at the hospital?'

'Yes. Why do I care about this Lee?'

'Coral had an autographed book by him in his collection. We know he led seminars in Anchorage, which is where she was from.'

'So what?'

She decided not to waste a question on Houston since Fannah must know. Going to the next name, she asked, 'Does Peony have an alibi?'

'She says she was at a prom planning committee meeting but the school couldn't verify it.'

'Why not?'

'It wasn't supervised by adults. We talked to friends of hers who confirmed she was there. Once again, why is Lee important?'

Mandy picked up the book off the desk and opened it to the inscription. 'See that Sanskrit?'

He walked in and leaned over the book. 'OK?'

'It means "Our body is love, we are eternal."'

'Huh.' Justin studied the book, then took it and flipped through the pages. 'This isn't new.'

'No, and I don't know when or where Coral met Bodhi Lee, but the hospital sponsored him to come down here to teach. You should find out when he arrived in Seattle. I attended his seminar a week after she died.'

Justin narrowed his eyes. 'A week after?'

'Jason Cho is an assistant hospital administrator. He told me that he took the seminars last week. So I don't know exactly when Bodhi Lee came into town, but it's pretty likely he was here when Coral died.'

Justin quirked his cheek. 'How do you know what the inscription means?'

'Houston Harris, my co-worker, looked it up. It didn't take him long so it must be pretty common.'

'Maybe something from the *Bhagavad Gita*,' Justin mused. 'This guy teaches meditation?'

'Based on the chakras,' Mandy agreed.

'This guy comes into town to the hospital to teach, and it happens to be where Coral is working.' He shifted. 'We have her appointment records. I don't recognize his name but I'd like to bring him in. If nothing else, he may be able to give us some background about her life in Alaska.'

'I'm happy to help,' Mandy said primly. 'How about Tom and Rod? Do they have alibis?'

'Would I have warned you away from them if they did?'

'You might have learned something new.' She paused. 'Darci

invited me to attend a knife-making class this weekend for the cost of materials. She has two spaces open. I suppose you think I shouldn't go?'

'Are you asking me to go with you?'

'No, I thought I'd take Vellum if she's interested.' Mandy watched his expression harden and realized she'd said the wrong thing. But if he was hoping she would ask him on a date, he'd be waiting for a long time. She needed his rent money. 'If you thought it was safe.'

He shrugged. 'You won't be the only students, right?'

'Right.'

He turned away and called over his shoulder. 'Do what you want, Mandy. You don't listen to me anyway.'

She leaned back in her chair. Of course she did what she wanted. He wasn't the boss of her.

He was just the police.

Mandy had a long to-do list to check off on Friday. Vellum had agreed to attend the knife-making class on Saturday, so she had a ton of work to do with Mandy's Plan so that she could take a day off from her second job. But she also had alibis to check.

When she had her morning ten-minute break, she went to the chair massage place. One of the therapists was at the front desk.

'Hi, I'd like to have a massage,' Mandy asked, nonplussed by the absence of Amrik.

'Busy schedule today,' the therapist said.

'Can I see your openings?' Mandy lifted her hands. 'I have to plan it around work so it's complicated.'

The woman handed her the schedule, which was clipped into a three-ring binder. Mandy crowed silent victory. She turned slightly and quickly flipped back ten days. Lo and behold, Amrik wasn't working when Coral died. Or at least, he had a line through his part of the schedule after two in the afternoon. She supposed he could have been on the desk.

Mandy turned back to the therapist and put her finger on the top page. 'What's your name?'

'Dhriti.'

'Such a pretty name.' Mandy found her name and discovered no line ran through her schedule for this hour even though she wasn't doing a massage. The spot was blank, though, instead of lined. 'Hmm, this is a busy day. Looks like everyone is busy when I'm free.' She handed the binder back with a smile.

'Suky called in sick,' Dhriti explained. 'Try again tomorrow.'

'Thank you.' Mandy went back across the lobby, figuring she'd sit down for the rest of her break and check her phone.

'Right lady, wrong place,' Dr Burrell said, coming from the elevator bay.

Mandy straightened. She'd almost made it to the bench along the wall. 'Hi, Stan, I'm on my break.'

'Me too. Enjoying the TGIF spirit?'

'I *am* glad it's Friday,' she agreed.

'What are your plans?'

'Vellum and I are getting crafty and taking a knife-making class in Lynnwood.'

'That's really cool.'

'I could see if you could join us,' she invited. 'I know the smithy owners.'

'Thank you, but I'm more the outdoorsy type. I have to protect my hands.'

Mandy stared at her carefully manicured fingers. 'I hadn't even thought about it. They'd better let us wear gloves. We need to look nice because we're doing art on camera.'

'You always do, Mandy.'

She blushed at the sincerity in his voice. 'Thank you. But if you are protecting your hands, how can you be outdoorsy?'

'I like places like the Arboretum. I don't go out to the back-woods and live off the land. I just like to be outside.'

'I love the Arboretum. It's a happy place for me.'

He glanced toward the glass front doors. 'We should go. It's a great time of year.'

'I agree.'

He gave her a long look, then nodded. 'You've got your phone there. Let me give you my number.'

She unlocked her screen and passed her phone over. He called his phone from hers then handed her phone back. 'There. We're all set.'

She grinned, then caught sight of the time on her phone. 'Oops. Break's over. Have to run.'

'Take care, Mandy.'

'You too.' She paused, wondering how his yoga buddy would feel about this. 'Stan.'

He grinned. She walk-trotted away. Running was never OK in the hospital. Too many people were stressed already and might panic if they saw someone running.

She was a minute late returning from break, but thankfully Fannah didn't notice. It would have been especially awkward if Fannah had seen her with the handsome doctor. Mandy still didn't know if he was dating Fannah or not. She didn't want to be part of a love triangle at work. Or anywhere else for that matter.

ELEVEN

When Mandy arrived home, she was eager to have a productive night. She found that easy, since no one was interacting with her about Coral. Texting Justin about Amrik not being on the massage business schedule that day brought no response. Not surprising, really, since the police would have known already. A couple of hours later, she tried again after she heard him coming through the backyard. She sent him a text about Tom and Rod, but, again, no response.

Vellum sat on the other end of the dining-room table, stamping the customer envelopes they had filled and passed through the postage meter.

Mandy noticed her head slumping. 'Is something wrong?' She leaned across the table and felt her daughter's forehead.

'I'm not sick, Mom, just frustrated.' She slammed the stamp on to the package.

Mandy winced but the *Thank you for your business* stamp showed clearly, and the stickers inside wouldn't have been damaged.

Vellum sniffed. A tear ran down her cheek.

'Oh, sweetie, did something happen at school? Bad test? Boy trouble?'

Vellum shook her head, her thick hair swishing around her eyes. 'Not *my* boy trouble. *Yours.*'

'What do you mean?' Mandy thought of the kiss with Justin.

'Dad won't make up our weekend. As usual.'

Mandy forced a practical note into her voice. 'If he had, we wouldn't be able to spend tomorrow playing with fire.'

'I guess.'

'It's going to be fun,' Mandy insisted. 'Get all sweaty, hit things with hammers. Come out with a knife.'

'You're not going to make me go camping next, are you?'

Vellum's tone of suspicion made Mandy laugh. 'People with two jobs don't find the time to go camping. No worries there.'

'What would you do if you started dating someone who liked camping?'

'I'm not dating,' Mandy said quickly.

Vellum looked shifty-eyed. 'You'd never ever get back together with Dad?'

'No,' Mandy said firmly. 'I could never trust him again after what's happened. You have a good relationship with his parents, and him too, basically. That's enough for me.'

'I just can't expect much,' Vellum said with downturned lips.

'At least I am more than happy to have you around,' Mandy pointed out.

Vellum touched her hand across the table. 'I know. And you can date. I'm fine with it.'

'Really?' Mandy asked.

'Yeah, I mean, if it's me that's holding you back. I'm fifteen. I get it.' Vellum gave her a lofty look.

'I don't want to know what you think you understand,' Mandy said with a laugh. 'But I'm glad I have your blessing.'

'Just not Justin,' Vellum added.

'No?'

Vellum shook her head with emphasis. 'Too close to home. It could get ugly if it didn't work out.'

'Smart girl.' Mandy pushed back from the table. 'I have dishes to do and you have homework.'

'Did we get all the orders processed?'

'Enough. We'll catch the rest after our livestream on Sunday.'

'Sounds good. What time do we have to leave tomorrow?'

'Seven thirty. Not much better than a school day.'

'No.' Vellum yawned. 'I won't stay up too late.'

Mandy kissed the top of her daughter's head and swept up the prepared envelopes for mailing.

Saturday dawned bright and early. This last weekend of March did have a true hint of spring in the air, but Mandy's feeling of sunny happiness was quickly dashed by the discovery that she was out of her favorite coffee pods. To make matters worse, her freezer contained no muffins and Linda hadn't dropped by with brownies recently. She hoped this wasn't an indication of how the day would go.

'What's wrong?' Vellum came into the kitchen, her hair wrapped in a towel.

'We're out of fun carbs,' Mandy whined. 'I guess we're having oatmeal for breakfast.'

Vellum wiped a water droplet from her neck. 'We're about to go do hard physical labor, Mom. Oatmeal is perfect.'

'Very true. Hurry up or we'll be late for our knife class.'

When they pulled up alongside the smithy in Lynnwood, they found a trio of cars already parked alongside the prefab building that held the businesses. Two men in their fifties, bellies hanging over their Carhartts, drank coffee from metal mugs in front of the entrance.

Vellum ignored them and stared at the planter outside the door. Mandy followed her gaze and saw that someone had planted pansies in it since she had last been there.

'Howdy,' said one of the men, his eyes raking down Mandy's body.

The other man nodded and kept his eyes on Mandy's face.

Mandy pulled at Vellum's arm and said hello as they passed by. She hoped Darci would be in the class at all times.

Her new friend was at the table, dressed in overalls over an army green T-shirt. She squeezed Mandy's hand. 'Thanks so much for coming today. I wanted to see a friendly face.'

Mandy smiled and pulled the cash for supplies out of her pocket and handed it over. Vellum watched the money pass hands mournfully, even though Mandy had given her all her allowance the night before.

'Are you excited?' Darci asked Vellum. 'I'm Darci, by the way.'

'Vellum. I was always curious about sculpting with metal.'

'She fell in love with the baby whale tail at the Seattle Center,' Mandy confirmed.

'That's a great sculpture,' Darci agreed. 'The skills you learn today will set you on the right path to making something like that someday.'

Vellum nodded. 'Cool.'

'Hi, Vellum!' said an enthusiastic voice.

Mandy glanced up. A water dispenser was installed next to the door to the forge. And beyond that stood Houston Harris, holding a metal water canister. Oatmeal gurgled in her stomach. 'I didn't know he was going to be here.'

Vellum squeezed her arm. 'I didn't invite him.'

'He must have heard me talking about us going and signed up.' Mandy pasted on a fake smile for her co-worker, but wondered how he could afford the class since he was apartment hunting and why he was interested in taking it at all. One day of blacksmith training at full price cost hundreds of dollars. Was he that interested in Vellum?

'It's so great to see you again,' Houston enthused. He walked up to them and stopped in arms' reach of Vellum. 'How've you been?'

Mandy saw water droplets on Houston's lips and wanted to smack them off him. 'How did you hear about this?'

'Hi. Darci invited me,' he said in a defiant tone. 'She came to the coffee bar once when you weren't around.'

Mandy wondered when that could have been. Darci seemed to hang around the hospital an awful lot, but maybe she had more private clients or had needed to see her OB/GYN.

'Hi,' said a low-energy voice.

Mandy turned to the forge door. Tom distractedly passed his hand through his hair. A streak of oil on his hand transferred to his forehead.

'Can we get everyone in here?' he called.

Mandy went to the main door and opened it to usher in the men outside. Now there were five students. Rod walked in behind the men.

'Thanks for holding the door,' he said, but without his usual warmth toward Mandy.

She nodded and darted back to Vellum, not wanting to leave her alone with Houston. The kid just irritated her.

'Well, umm, thanks for coming. Bill, you did the axe class with us last year,' Tom said, pointing in the direction of the guy with wandering eyes. 'Are the rest of you completely new to blacksmithing?'

'I went to blacksmith camp in eighth grade,' Houston volunteered. 'But we just made a trivet.'

'That's great,' Tom said half-heartedly. 'Any of the others?'

The other man shook his head, as did Mandy and Vellum.

Tom pushed open the door to the forge, his head bent forward as if it were too hard to hold it up. He led everyone around a large table. On it was a roll of butcher paper, some pencils, and a curved knife with holes poked through the tang. Plain metal, it didn't have a handle.

'Today we will learn the build on this knife. Handle making is another full-day class.' Tom shuffled his feet. 'I hope everyone can return for that session.'

Darci poked her head into the forge. Mandy glanced at her and saw the concern on Tom's sister's face. She walked in, followed by Peony and Rod, and they waited along the wall while Tom gave his initial speech.

At the scarred worktable they'd been assigned to – far away from Houston, thankfully – Mandy had fun using the ruler and drawing out the specs of a knife.

'Math,' Vellum muttered under her breath.

'But someday this will help you do the calculations for a baby whale sculpture,' Mandy whispered back.

'Tempting.' Vellum broke into a grin.

After they drew their knives, Tom went into a long speech on tools, then showed them the metal they'd be using. He gave them basic information about welding, then the rest of his team helped everyone weld their metal on to metal sticks they could hold. He assigned Mandy to Darci and Vellum to himself.

'It's either this or tongs,' Darci told Mandy as they walked to the welding station. 'This is way easier.'

'Is Tom always like this?' Mandy asked. 'He seems so distracted and he keeps looking at Peony.'

'We had a terrible night last night.'

'How come?' Mandy asked.

Darci put her mouth close to Mandy's ear and lowered her voice. 'Someone tried to abduct Peony after school on Friday.'

'What?' Mandy clapped her hand around her mouth and turned around. Only Vellum had noticed her outburst. She raised her eyebrows. Mandy shook her head and glanced at Peony, who fiddled with the dials above a small forge that wasn't heating properly. Tom went to help her.

Mandy didn't have any context to know if Peony was usually competent in the forge or if whatever happened had her frazzled. She didn't look any different from the couple of times Mandy had met her, but then both occasions had been around Coral's death – not times when she'd have been at her best.

She turned back to Darci. 'From high school?'

'Yes.' Darci's hand fluttered to her cheek. 'She's a senior.'

'That's terrible,' Mandy exclaimed. 'What exactly happened?'

Darci pulled on a welding helmet as she spoke. Metal sizzled as Darci welded a side of Mandy's bar of spring steel to a metal stick. Then she had Mandy turn it while she finished setting the welds. When they were done, she lifted up the visor. 'There was an SUV. Black. I guess they tried to haul her in, but it was so awkward because of her leg braces that a school security guard noticed and rescued her.'

'Wow,' Mandy repeated. 'I guess it's on the news and everything, huh? I didn't check my phone or turn on the TV this morning.'

Darci checked her welds and shut the visor again. Sparks flew as she gave her welds a finishing touch. 'Peony fell backward on the security guard and the kidnappers jumped into the back of the SUV and roared away.'

Convenient. 'How about security cameras? Did they get the license plate?'

Darci yawned and pulled off the helmet. 'Covered with mud.'

'Clever. Had there been any threats?'

Darci shook her head. 'Against Peony? Definitely not.'

Mandy wondered if there had been threats against anyone else. 'Was there family drama before her sister died?'

'None,' Darci said. 'But Peony says she's afraid to move out of Tom's house now. Let's get your metal up to temperature. It takes time.'

'If I were her, I wouldn't want to leave the house, much less move,' Mandy said stoutly, following her to the free furnace. She noted that the shop had five of them, so either someone had dropped out of the class, leaving a free spot for Houston, or Darci had lied about there being only two spots left. 'Was she going to move? I remember hearing fears about her being sent away because she isn't a DeRoy.'

'She's moving in June.' Darci moved a block out of the way and stuck in Mandy's spring steel.

The heat hit Mandy. She pulled off her sweater and tied it around her waist. 'I remember she turns eighteen next month.'

'In just a few weeks, yes.'

'She must feel like her life is completely falling apart.'

Darci smiled sadly at the sympathy in Mandy's voice. 'She wants to stay here with us for now. To finish school.'

'They've upped security?'

'Yes. Tom talked to the principal this morning before the class.'

'No wonder he's even more stressed.'

'Yeah,' Darci said.

'Hot metal coming through!' Rod guided Bill to an anvil with a glowing rectangle of steel, holding it with tongs.

'He didn't bother to weld,' Mandy noted.

Darci shrugged. 'He's been here before. Some guys are here every weekend learning the trade. A lot of men consider it relaxing.'

'Any women?'

'Not yet, but there are female blacksmiths, especially farriers.'

'Why?'

'Horses,' Darci said.

'Oh, sure. If you're good with your hands and like animals, it would be a good choice if you don't want to be a vet.'

'Yeah.' Darci yawned again.

'What are Peony's plans?'

'No career plans, not yet. She's not one of those kids with a lot of direction. I was the same.'

Mandy nodded her understanding. 'Me either. Which is how Vellum came to be.'

'Peony doesn't have a boyfriend yet. Or ever. She'd hoped to move into Reese's basement after graduation, but now Reese is in jail anyway.'

Mandy was taken aback. Was that what Reese had been hiding? 'Oh, I didn't know she'd been looking into that.' Or that she could afford it. Maybe she had disability payments or survivor benefits or some kind of inheritance.

Vellum waved at her from across the forge. She was waiting for her metal to heat, too.

Mandy waved back, realizing there were levels within levels of Reese's relationship to this family. Had Mandy's attempt to show Houston her basement been thwarted because Reese already had a plan involving Peony?

Mandy considered. This new information also meant that Peony, and whoever had driven her to Reese's house to check the place out, might have also been in Reese's house and could have planted the mysterious evidence that had caused her to be charged with murder.

'Peony and Reese were friends?' she qualified to Darci.

Darci led her to a water cooler along the wall and poured water into two metal canisters, then handed one to Mandy. 'No, but she'd had Coral and Peony to tea recently. The sisters were pretty bound at the hip. Coral took Peony everywhere. Who knows what Reese thought about the idea of having a teenager as her tenant?'

Mandy took a long drink. 'Where would Peony have found the money?'

Darci shrugged and wiped her mouth. 'If she'd gone out on her own, it would have changed everything for the family.'

'In a good way?'

'If Peony could handle it, sure.'

Mandy drank again. 'Do you think Reese killed Coral?'

'This isn't a TV show,' Darci said. 'I trust the police. They obviously had a good reason to arrest her.'

Mandy pursed her lips and glanced around. Tom had walked over to Peony. Sparks flew as he guided her hands to finish a weld. Flushed, Peony handed the metal rod to Houston and they walked to the forge to heat it up, far behind the others.

Mandy saw no sign that Tom was mistreating her. He'd been gentle with the girl. She decided to try to forget about the mystery and focus on learning how to make a knife. Too much danger lurked in forges, and distraction was not a good idea.

'Feel free to set Peony up with Houston,' she invited. 'After she turns eighteen. He's twenty and has been a pest with Vellum.'

Darci's head swiveled on her neck as she watched Houston's gaze trail to Vellum's station before moving back again to the welding tools. 'Yeah, I can see he has a crush on her.'

'I've told him off. I've explained the law.' Mandy shrugged. 'Vellum's a smart girl but doesn't seem to understand the five-year age difference is not OK.'

'He's cute.' Darci grinned at her.

'Then you can ask him out. You're not that much older than him.'

'Hmm,' Darci pointed at her midsection. 'Nah. Busy.'

Mandy woke up on Sunday to aches and pains in parts of her body that had never hurt before. She was used to some forearm pain and finger stiffness from over-arting, but this ache in some strange spot between her kidneys was new and her neck had never been quite this stiff before.

She rolled over in bed and reached blindly into the bedside drawer for a bottle of painkillers. When her hand moved for her water glass, her fingers brushed something that wasn't normally on the tabletop. Something metal.

Mandy groaned and pushed the light switch. After she swallowed two gel tablets, she picked up her new knife. The sleekness of the metal felt soothing under her fingers. She wasn't about to spend two hundred and fifty bucks to take a handle class, but she could wrap it in cord or something like that. At least the pain had come from making something tangible.

After getting the coffee maker going in the kitchen, she went and checked her planner. Time to turn the page to the new week. They'd do their livestream in an hour to set up the coming days with their loyal fans. For now, she checked her main March calendar, then flipped to April, only a couple of days away. *Spring Break* was written across the week and she had to get Vellum to her art camp's bus pickup in a few hours.

She went back to the kitchen, grabbed a coffee, then put a couple of slices of wholegrain toast into the toaster. Finally, she banged on Vellum's door. 'Are you packed for camp?'

A muffled thump resounded through the door, then Vellum poked her head out. 'Are you taking a shower?'

Mandy chuckled at the bed-head tousle of Vellum's hair. 'Do you need it first?'

'Yes, my hair takes hours to dry.'

'Go ahead. I'll eat and set up for our livestream, then jump in myself.'

'OK. I'm basically packed. I still can't believe Grandma paid for camp.'

'Otherwise, you would have had to go as a counselor instead of a camper.'

'Yeah, I could maybe do that next year. But the art teacher is really good, like art-in-galleries good, and I wanted to work with him again.'

'Makes sense to me as long as you don't develop a crush on him.'

'Wouldn't matter.' Vellum pushed hair out of her face. 'He's gay.'

'I'm glad to hear it,' Mandy told her. 'Enjoy the shower. What do you want for breakfast?'

'Oatmeal.'

'Not toast?' Mandy asked hopefully.

Vellum raised her eyebrows.

'Fine.' Mandy stomped back to the kitchen and started the fancy oatmeal. Why she so resented making it she didn't know. Maybe because it was Cory's favorite breakfast too, but that was too much insight for a Sunday morning.

The day passed in a flash. The livestream went well, with new sticker orders pouring in from the sixty people who'd joined in. The printers and cutters clacked away in the dining room as Mandy quickly made rice and stir-fry for lunch, then packed Vellum up and bundled her to the bus pickup in a high school parking lot.

By three thirty, she was back home. Instead of going straight to her sticker assembly line, she stopped in at Linda's. Her friend gave her a cup of tea, then hurried her out the door because she had a date with George Lowry for an early dinner.

Mandy felt dangerous with a quiet night and a container of fresh brownies. She resolutely left them in the mudroom for now and went to sort out her orders. Brownies would make a nice reward for later.

After she assembled about eighty orders, her business was caught up for the day. She made herself a last cup of coffee and settled herself on the sofa in the living room with the brownies and her journal. Time to update her to-do list for the week.

At that moment, Justin came to mind. If he ate half the brownies, she wouldn't feel so guilty, but then she'd have to interact with him, and he would frustrate her by not sharing information. Not to mention that kiss.

Back to more important subjects. He'd know about the kidnapping drama by now. Surely the school would have reported it. She wanted information he wouldn't share. But she knew of someone who might.

She opened the back of her journal and tilted out the collection of business cards in the rear pocket until she found the one for Zac Turner.

It might be Sunday afternoon, but bounty hunters were unlikely to work conventional schedules. She typed his number into her phone and dialed, then touched the speaker button. As the phone rang, she slid the assorted cards back into place and then flipped back to her murder spread.

'Turner.'

She blinked. He'd answered. 'Uh, hi? This is Mandy Meadows. You came to my house regarding Coral Le Charme's death.'

'You're the friend of Reese O'Leary-Sett, right?'

'Yes. I live on the other side of Roosevelt.'

'Yeah, I got you now.' She heard pages flipping. 'Brunette, curly hair.'

'Yes,' she confirmed.

'What can I do for you?'

'I was at the forge yesterday and the household seemed really unsettled. Did you hear about the kidnapping attempt?'

'Yes, of course.'

'I was just wondering if that was related to the murder. After all, Reese didn't do that.'

'No. Anything else?' His attention seemed elsewhere.

'Yes.' She tapped her finger on her yellow highlighted names. The ones with no alibis. 'I don't have alibis for Coral's husband, Tom, or his business partner, Rod, or his sister, for that matter. Do you have alibis for them? And then there are the hospital people. I haven't seen you around USea.'

'Don't you live with a cop? Trying to do his job for him?'

'No, I'm trying to help my friend. I'm the only one in her corner, it seems.'

'Have you eaten dinner yet?'

She stared at the brownies in her lap, confused by his question. 'No.'

'I haven't eaten either. Why don't you meet me at Joey Kitchen in the University Village in half an hour? We can trade information.'

Mandy sighed. She didn't want to go out. But it was for Reese. She'd have wanted Reese to do it for her if the tables were turned. 'Sure, see you soon.'

TWELVE

Mandy changed from sweats to a black pencil skirt, figuring her navy top suited her well enough for dinner with a bounty hunter, and dashed out the door. She had trouble finding parking, very common at the University Village, and arrived at Joey Kitchen ten minutes late.

A server led her to Zac's booth. He slid out and stood as she arrived. Up close, without Justin to back her, he seemed far larger, and without a cap he appeared younger, with buzzed brown hair, the kind of guy who would have looked at home on a high school football field, a coach's whistle around his thick neck.

He held out his hand and shook hers, looking right into her eyes. Was this a business meeting or a date?

'What would you like to drink?' the server asked.

Mandy had downed her coffee before she left. 'Just water, please.' She sat across from Zac. He already had a hummus platter in front of him.

When he saw her glance at it, he moved it into the center of the table. 'It's excellent. Have some.'

She took a pita chip and slid it through a combination of tzatziki sauce and hummus, then took a bite. 'That is good, but I don't think you invited me here to share a meal.'

He shrugged. 'We have to eat, right? This isn't far from your home.'

'Not at all. Do you live around here?'

'No, I'm north of you. But I was following up on some details locally.'

Another server appeared. Mandy opened the menu and ordered a fish dish. As soon as the server vanished, she folded her hands on the table and leaned forward. 'Anything I should know?'

He nodded. 'Look, the DeRoys think you're a really nice lady, and I can tell you care about your friend. So I thought you ought to know that Reese didn't murder Coral.'

Mandy's stomach seemed to leap into her throat and stay there. *Thank you.* She coiled her fingers together. 'Can you get her out? I mean, tell the police what you know?'

'They don't care what I think, but eventually the truth will reveal itself.' He stabbed a chip into the hummus and leaned back. 'I hope your friend is a tough chick. Jail isn't fun.'

'So far I haven't seen her. I have an appointment at the jail next week. Was the kidnapping attempt taking place while Reese is in jail proof of her innocence or do you have more evidence?'

Zac swallowed and reached for another chip. 'Yeah, the kidnapping attempt. When multiple dramas are happening with the same family, you know it's all related. I suspect Coral was murdered to expose Peony. One of her caregivers is dead, the primary one. The entire family might be in danger.'

'Wow, that's scary.' She'd taken her daughter to the forge. 'I have wondered why Darci keeps coming to the hospital. I know she's had some business there, but still, it's a long way to come.'

'Most of the best doctors around here practice on Pill Hill.'

'True, but not all of them. There's the University of Washington Medical Center, and Seattle Children's Hospital – all kinds of places that are closer to Lynnwood.'

He shrugged and grabbed another pita. How much fuel did he need to keep that large, muscle-bound body going? She hoped bounty hunting paid well.

'Have you had any other insights during your investigation? Like developing a suspect?' She enunciated the last word.

He kept his gaze on his platter. 'I can't say.'

She snagged another chip. 'I've wondered about Coral and

Peony's parents. I know they didn't come to the memorial party. I didn't see pictures of parents in their house.'

'Yeah, I don't think they're close, but I also don't think it's unusual to send kids out of the small communities in Alaska when you can. Peony is probably getting much better medical care, even education, here.'

'I don't doubt it,' Mandy agreed. A server set down a water glass in front of her and then departed. 'I didn't question that at all. I just wondered why there weren't any family photos or Alaska memorabilia or anything, now that I think about it.'

The bounty hunter shrugged and slid the last pita chip through the tzatziki sauce. Mandy's stomach rumbled gently in protest. She hoped their main courses arrived soon.

Disheartened, Mandy considered that Zac didn't seem to have an inquisitive enough mind to solve a murder. Nonetheless, she had him in front of her, so she continued to press him. 'OK, so you agree the parents are alive. Have you questioned them about enemies Coral might have had in Alaska? Stalkers?'

'No, I don't have their contact information.'

'What about Tom? He's not from Alaska, but what does he know about their lives there?'

'He was up there as a visiting blacksmith instructor five years ago. The course was in Kodiak. That's when he met Coral. She came down to see him and they married in Las Vegas – kind of a whirlwind deal. About a year later she took custody of Peony. So they had her three or four years before Coral's murder.'

'OK. Does Tom not have any answers?'

'Rod described Coral as the type of person who leaves her past behind her.'

'Tom was only ever in her hometown that one week?'

Zac nodded. 'That's my understanding.'

Mandy paused her line of questioning as their food arrived. She took a couple of fortifying bites of fish, then questioned on, not knowing if Zac would take off as soon as he finished shoveling his food into his mouth. 'Did her parents ever come down here?'

Zac cut his steak into precise bites. 'It hasn't come up. I really don't know anything about the Alaska thing.'

'Have you run across Bodhi Lee yet? I gave the name to the

police.' She explained how she knew he had met Coral and the timeline.

Zac drained his beer. 'Wow, you are quite the amateur detective, aren't you? Ready to change careers?'

'Not yet. So, do you know about him?'

He shook his head. 'Sorry, no. I'll ask Tom but I don't imagine he'll know anything. I did consider the Le Charmes still up in Alaska, but Tom is certain that his in-laws aren't behind what's going on.'

'Why not?' She was glad the subject had come up, at least.

'Because Coral took custody of Peony a few years ago. Peony is almost an adult now. They've never fought custody. The documents are in order.'

'What was the story?'

'Once Coral was settled down here, Peony's doctor in Kodiak wrote an order to have her receive intensive pool, equine, and speech therapy in Seattle. Eventually, Coral went to court for guardianship due to the inability of their parents to get quality medical care on a small island.'

'Did they fight the guardianship?'

'No. And when Tom went to their lawyer to see about Coral's will, he suggested that Peony file for emancipation since she is almost eighteen anyway.'

'No problem with her parents?'

'No.'

Mandy took another bite. 'I expect they just want the best for her, but I'm surprised they haven't at least come to Seattle.'

'I don't imagine they have much money. Coral and Tom don't either.'

'They'd have been in a much tougher place without Tom's inheritance.'

'You mean the land?' He glanced up.

'Yes.'

Zac spread blue-cheese butter over a slice of sirloin. 'There's no family drama here, Mandy. We have to rule out the hospital, given the kidnapping.'

'Peony is very attractive. Could some wannabe boyfriend of hers have killed Coral because she wasn't letting Peony date?'

'I'm looking into exactly that. Peony doesn't drive and I believe with all her appointments the family wouldn't have been inclined to taxi her around so she can socialize.'

'There's always the bus,' Mandy murmured, feeling sorry for this isolated young woman.

Zac spread more butter on his steak. 'I appreciate this information about Bodhi Lee. Given the absence of Alaskans in their daily life, I hadn't considered someone from the Le Charmes' distant past being involved.'

She didn't have the sense he knew much of anything, so she moved on to the next topic troubling her. 'How about those bizarre tattoos Coral had? Did she get them down here or in Alaska?'

He licked butter off his lower lip. 'I don't know.'

She leaned toward him again. 'Tattoos are normal, but bullseyes like that? Like her body was a target for something? I don't like it. I remember reading an article once about women being forced to get tattoos in domestic violence situations, like "property of" tattoos or their partner's names, that kind of thing. Do you think the tattoos could be something like that?' She leaned back.

'She lived next door to a tattoo parlor.'

She made a circle with her finger. 'Right, but who gets tattoos that look like targets?'

'Maybe something tribal?'

'Was she Native? Or part Native? Are those tattoos Inuit iconography?'

'I have no idea,' Zac said.

'What *do* you know?' Mandy asked, frustrated. 'You sounded so certain. Whoever killed Coral must have had access to Reese's house. Or the evidence the police have is bad.'

Zac didn't respond. 'I like this wannabe boyfriend idea. Do you think Reese could have had some kid mowing her lawn or doing work of some kind?'

Mandy had no idea. She took the time to take a couple of bites of her tuna before she continued. 'Reese was being very cagey about the entire situation. I'm flummoxed. I have no idea what was really going on or who she might know. She'd have the money to get a gardener, I guess.'

'The trail is going cold,' Zac said, looking mournfully at his plate, already empty of meat. 'It's closing in on two weeks since Coral died.'

Mandy's appetite disappeared. 'I know. But, Zac, if you have evidence that would get an innocent woman out of jail, it's your duty to free her. We can't help Coral anymore, but Reese needs us. Peony likes her, so proving Reese is innocent will help Peony, too.'

Zac licked his lips. 'Nice family. But you know how the cops are. Everything is going to have to be wrapped up in a perfect little bow in order to change their minds.'

'What should I ask Reese when I see her?'

'If she was being cagey before, I doubt she'd reveal all now. She's probably protecting someone.' He shrugged. 'Just keep doing what you're doing. The killer is on the outside still.'

Mandy knew Zac hadn't meant anything with his offhand 'nice family' remark about the DeRoy/Le Charme family. Nice families didn't have domestic violence or forced tattoos, or knives under their beds. If, indeed, that was the case here. She could only be sure about the knife.

When she walked into her empty house later that evening, she had the urge to stare at the television and fork brownies into her mouth, but she couldn't give in to stress eating. She'd hoped the professional had answers, but Zac didn't seem to, and her plea that helping Reese would also help Peony didn't move him.

Instead, she found Coral's autographed Bodhi Lee book in her bag and decided to read it. Relaxing on to the living-room sofa, she opened the book. She knew basically nothing about chakras and, being the businesswoman she was, she couldn't read through the descriptions without visualizing chakra journal spreads.

She learned about the seven chakras and how each one and its functioning was supposed to be related to body parts and behavior. Nothing really clicked until she read the lines 'Chakras are the windows to your soul. Each chakra is like a bullseye, telling a practitioner, "This is where your client's body is out of balance!"'

Oh. Mandy leaned back and closed her eyes, remembering the cluster of small dark tattoos around Coral's abdomen. Could someone doing chakra work have told her to get tattoos there? She opened her eyes and looked at the chakra book. From navel to pubic bone was the womb or sacral chakra, *svadhisthana*. Maybe

Coral had dealt with infertility or some kind of other pelvic issue and the tattoos were meant to help cure it.

Either way, she was suspicious. Could the tattoos have been something to do with Bodhi's practices rather than a sign of abuse?

Darci had said Coral wasn't abused. So had Zac Turner. But that opinion wasn't universal. Amrik had said otherwise. Had Coral lied to Amrik just to get the job? To Reese? Or was Amrik lying?

Maybe she'd turned to lies because of her terrible massage skills. But that thought led Mandy back to her friend, who never would have tolerated an incompetent massage therapist more than once.

She really wanted to talk to someone about this. But Vellum was gone and Reese was locked away. Justin wasn't home. She decided to walk over to Linda's and see if she was home from her movie date with George.

She took the closed brownie container into the kitchen, transferring her square of gooey chocolate goodness to another container. Then she washed Linda's dish.

She pulled her coat on and pushed her feet into her fluffy slipper-slides to go over to Linda's. If George wasn't there, she'd have her bestie's ear for a conversation about Bodhi Lee's book.

But just as she'd picked up Linda's container, someone knocked at the back door.

Linda must be coming to see her! Mandy slipped off her coat and went to the back door. When she flipped on the light, though, she didn't see her friend. It was her ex-husband.

She opened the back door with a frown. Cory had lost his show-up-whenever privileges when they divorced.

'Vellum went to camp this afternoon, remember? It's spring break.'

'I know.' He shoved a bunch of daffodils wrapped in florist paper into her arms.

The yellow spring flowers were cheerful enough, but didn't match her ex's downcast expression.

'I don't want you showing up here,' Mandy said, not stepping back. 'It just gives your mother more ammunition for her absurd claim that I'm to blame for the end of our marriage.'

'Just trying to be nice,' Cory said, giving her a weak imitation of his dimpled smile.

At thirty-eight, Cory was still a handsome man. Despite refusing to work since the divorce, he still kept his thick blond hair in an executive cut. He had plenty of time to stay fit, logging hours on the tennis court or swimming at his father's pricey club in downtown Seattle. His grandmothers' checks and his father's credit card kept his clothes on point, and his mother housed him in a basement suite in her house.

Her voice rose. 'Don't try to be nice to me; be nice to your daughter. Like don't cancel your weekends with her.'

'Shouting at me outside does no good, Mandy. I need to talk to you.'

Mandy attempted to stare him down, but he kept that weak smile in place and didn't budge. A little wave of nerves set her belly tingling. But this was Cory. He wasn't dangerous, at least not to her physical health, unless you counted working two jobs because he wouldn't pay his child support.

'Let me in,' he said. 'It's getting cold out and we have nosy neighbors.'

'*I* have nosy neighbors. Not you. You have no claim on this property anymore.'

'Fine,' he snapped, then forced that smile back on his face. 'How about a cup of your famous coffee?'

'What do you want, Cory? I'm not interested in socializing.' Mandy shivered. It was almost April. In a couple of weeks the temperature would start to rise.

'It's important.' He put his hand out, palm up. 'Please.'

She knew him well enough to recognize he thought he had something important to impart. With a sigh, she stepped into the warmth of the kitchen. He followed. Ignoring him, she decided to make him four ounces of coffee and herself none, to make it clear she wanted him gone.

He waited patiently for a minute, then, as the coffee started to gurgle into the cup, he asked, 'Can anyone eat these brownies? I'm sure you're on a diet.'

She turned to him with narrowed eyes. 'Oddly enough, I haven't needed to diet since I kicked you out. My emotional eating is much reduced, thank you.'

His jaw worked as he stabbed a fork into the brownie container, which he'd already opened when her back was turned. He chewed and swallowed. 'Linda?'

'Of course.'

'Thought so. She always uses the dark chocolate chips.'

She grabbed the teacup from the coffee maker and set it in front of him.

'Aren't we going to sit down?'

'You won't be here that long, unless you have a check with backdated child support for me?'

He drank half his coffee in one long gulp, characteristically ignoring the question. Finally, he said, 'I have bad news.'

'Gee, how unusual,' Mandy snapped. She turned off the coffee maker, then leaned against the refrigerator, a full four feet away from him.

He cleared his throat. 'My father had a stroke on Friday.'

Mandy's jaw loosened. What could she say to that? 'Did he make it?' As soon as she said that, she knew she should have made sympathetic noises, but the senior Moffat male had never been more than a distant figure to her, long divorced from Cory's mother and a high-powered workaholic lawyer in a firm downtown. He hadn't instilled his son with his own work ethic; instead, Cory had been weakened by an open credit card and an inherited urge to philander.

'Yes. He paged his secretary and she came in and recognized the symptoms immediately. EMTs got to him in time. He's still in the hospital. It was bad enough that it will be a long road back.'

'That's terrible. He's what, sixty-five?'

'Sixty-six.' Cory drank more coffee. 'I guess his current lifestyle is done for. No more seventy-hour weeks, no more major trials.'

'It happens to everyone in the end.'

'Yeah. It just seems too soon. I mean, he's fit. High blood pressure, but who doesn't have that over forty? Anyway, sitting in that hospital these last three days has got me thinking.'

Mandy's breath caught. Was she finally going to get Vellum's support check?

But Cory opened his mouth again, and her hopes were dashed. 'The situation has made me realize that my father poisoned my thoughts on marriage.' Nothing but blather from her ex as usual.

'They got divorced when you were young.'

'Exactly. I don't want Vellum to repeat the family curse.'

'Then treat her well enough that she respects men,' Mandy suggested. 'Act like a grown-up.'

'I want to come back,' Cory said. 'When she sees us as a unit, it will repair the damage.'

Before Mandy could react, he crossed the kitchen floor and wrapped his arms around her waist. She tilted her upper body away from him, but he nuzzled in, his lips grazing her neck.

'Stop it,' she squeaked, as his tongue tickled her sensitive skin. 'I don't want you touching me.'

His lips moved to her ear. She pushed away, stumbling back. Then her foot caught against something.

She whipped around to see Justin. The back door was open and his cheeks were ruddy with cold.

'I see you're busy, but you think you could take it somewhere else so I could get into the refrigerator?' he asked politely.

She'd never heard quite that tone from him before. 'Go home, Cory,' she managed to say. 'I'm sorry about your father, but you aren't welcome here until Vellum returns.'

Cory's jaw moved, then he went and picked up the bouquet again and shoved it into her hands. Then he smiled, as if she'd never pushed him away, kissed her cheek, sketched a wave at Justin, and went out the back door.

'I'm so glad you walked in when you did.' Mandy, feeling numb, let the daffodils fall to the floor.

'Were you afraid he was going to force himself on you?' Justin asked in a level tone.

She shuddered. 'He already was. Kissing me.'

'Do you need a restraining order?' he suggested.

She stepped away from the refrigerator. Her foot slipped on the flowers, tearing delicate yellow petals away from the center of the flower. 'I would never go back to my cheating ex,' she said. 'He just needs to understand that.'

'You didn't answer my question.'

After a pause, she managed, 'The situation is awkward to say the least.'

'Why?'

The doorbell rang again. Mandy whirled around. 'Cory wouldn't dare come in again!'

THIRTEEN

J ustin stomped to the back door just as Mandy's phone rang. Absentmindedly, she answered as she followed Justin to see who was on the porch.

'Hi, Mandy, it's Darci!' said her caller. 'What a weekend! I only just now could call. How did you like the class?'

Justin opened the door. Cory stood on the tiny porch landing. He craned his neck, glancing over Justin's Viking build at Mandy. She couldn't believe he'd stayed on her property.

'When is Vellum coming home?' Cory asked loudly.

'I'll call you back,' Mandy said into the phone and hung up.

'Well?' her ex demanded.

Justin didn't budge.

'Friday,' Mandy said, over Justin's shoulder. 'It's a five-night art camp.'

Cory snorted. 'Sounds expensive.'

'Your mother paid for it.'

All three of them stilled as the atmosphere hushed. Mandy didn't know why. Suddenly, splattering noises sounded on the roof. Thick drops of rain pelted down. Cory pulled up the collar of his coat.

'Go home, Cory. I'm sorry about your father.' She whirled away ahead of Justin, who shut the door in Cory's face and locked it, then, as he passed through the mudroom, shut and locked that door, too.

'What happened to the father?' Justin asked.

'Stroke. In the hospital.'

'Is he going to recover?'

Mandy dropped her phone to the counter. 'It didn't sound like it – not completely. He's just about retirement age, but had no intention of leaving his law practice. Might have to now, though.'

Justin nodded. 'Your ex is having a weak moment and turned to you for comfort. Don't let yourself get weak along with him, unless you really want him back.'

Mandy crossed her arms over her chest. 'You saw what was happening. I didn't want him touching me.'

'But you let him in the house. With flowers. And you made him coffee?'

'I was being naive.' She tried to explain. 'He's so dialed out of Vellum's life. I actually thought he'd brought the flowers for her, to apologize for missing their last weekend together. He didn't even know she'd gone to camp.'

'Take them at the door and shut it,' Justin advised. 'That guy thinks he owns you.'

'He doesn't,' Mandy said flatly.

'You're so guarded because of his baloney,' Justin said in an equally deadpan voice, 'that you can't give decent guys a chance. Think about it.'

He gave her a level stare, grabbed a banana from the fruit bowl, and left the room.

Mandy stared at his back. Just because she had ended their kiss didn't mean she was guarded. Didn't he get that she specifically didn't want to date *him*? She ran her fingers through her hair, snagging on tangled curls. Admittedly, she didn't want to date anyone, but that was her choice and not because she was pining over her lost marriage. Her attraction to him frustrated her, but her good sense prevented her from considering the flirtation wise.

She glanced at her phone. *Right.* She needed to call Darci. Hitting redial, she resolved to spend the rest of her evening quietly.

'Everything OK?' Darci asked.

'Drama with the ex,' Mandy explained. 'His father had a stroke and he's feeling lonely.'

'That's too bad,' Darci said. 'I hope you aren't hooking up with him. That never ends well.'

'Definitely not. We only just finalized the divorce earlier this year.'

'I have just the thing to take your mind off your problems.'

'Oh?' Mandy asked cautiously.

'Tom said I could offer you a ten percent discount on next week's knife-handle class. Isn't that great? You can make your blades functional.'

These people were clueless. 'The first class was fun, but knife-making is too expensive of a hobby for us.' She couldn't imagine paying over four hundred bucks so she and Vellum could finish their blades. Not to mention Vellum probably couldn't keep up with her spring break reading schedule at camp and would have her nose buried in the classics all weekend.

'Maybe I can do fifteen percent,' Darci offered.

'We're actually committed on Saturday anyway,' Mandy said. 'We have to do a special livestream on Saturday morning. Usually we do them on Sundays, but enough of our followers asked us to do the set-up on Saturday that we're giving it a try. We always sell a lot of product after them so I can't cancel it.'

'I totally get it. Maybe you'll make enough that you can do the class next month!'

Darci had an answer for everything. Mandy took the coward's way out. 'You never know.'

'I hope you'll consider it, especially for Vellum. We need more female bladesmiths.'

'It's a great way to work frustrations out,' Mandy said, though the last thing she needed for herself was another work-hobby, especially one that didn't pay very well.

'You're so right.'

'But Vellum has a pretty clear career path mapped out for herself. She isn't following in my footsteps either.'

'She's only fifteen. You never know,' Darci said in a singsong voice.

'True. Is Peony planning on being a blacksmith?'

'I doubt it. It takes a lot of therapy to keep her at the level she's at.'

'I saw she needed leg braces.'

'Yes, and she's come a long way. I'm so glad Coral saw that and persuaded the family to allow Peony to come from Alaska to the lower forty-eight for treatment.'

'I don't know much about Kodiak.'

'Only a few thousand people there. A fair amount of tourist trade – hunting and fishing and all that. Summer work for a farrier. I've never even been there, but my brother went one summer.'

'I've never been to Alaska either. My parents did a cruise years ago.' Mandy stretched her neck from side to side. 'I need to get going, but thanks again for arranging the first class. It was hard work but we enjoyed learning to make the knives and, who knows,

Vellum may want to sculpt in metal as a hobby someday.' She hung up the phone.

As much as she didn't want to go there, she needed to track down Justin.

She checked the laundry baskets and combined the bedroom and bathroom laundry, then went downstairs with it, figuring it created an excuse to be down in Justin's domain.

When she reached the bottom of the steps with her basket, she heard a car start. She dropped her basket by the washer and went to Justin's sitting-room door. It was slightly ajar and when she peered in, no one was there.

His bedroom door was closed. She knocked tentatively, but there was no answer. He must have left again.

As much as she wanted to talk to him about Zac's insistence that Reese was innocent, she had a bad feeling she and Justin would have just battled over Cory again.

He said she was closed-off. His kiss had taken her by surprise. It didn't matter that she found him attractive and he probably knew it. She needed to wait out his crush on her, and then maybe they could build an actual friendship.

For now, the laundry called, and the bathtub. Monday was just around the bend and it was April Fool's Day. She wondered if she'd get the merry kind of prank, or something more sinister.

The house felt terribly quiet on Monday morning with Vellum gone. With the absence of tenant noises, Mandy assumed that Justin had woken up even earlier than she had and was gone again, or he'd never come home the night before.

The coffee bar at work, in contrast, kept crazy busy. Apparently, everyone wanted to caffeinate up in order to perpetrate or cope with pranks.

Houston kept trying to offer hugs to the customers. A couple of the nurses accepted, giggling. The buzzer he wore on his hand shocked his unfortunate hug recipients. Fannah soon caught him and stopped his prank. Mandy had to admit the nurses thought it was good fun, though, and one of them slipped Houston her number.

'Don't make me tell Fannah,' Mandy warned after lunch, when he eyed a young administrative assistant in Accounting with a speculative gleam. 'Though honestly I wouldn't have to. I still remember the horrifying shriek Shamika let loose when she dropped her blueberry fritter on the floor one time. Girl can scream.'

'Hmm.' Houston rubbed his chin. 'Is she single?'

Shamika ordered an ice-blended mocha at the counter.

'How's your daughter?' Mandy asked pointedly. 'In preschool yet?'

'Next year,' Shamika said. 'My sister takes care of everybody's kids, but the preschool is just across the street from her.'

'That makes it easier,' Mandy agreed, while Houston clattered dishes in the sink behind her. 'What's your husband up to these days?'

'He's training in mixed martial arts,' Shamika said proudly.

A crash behind Mandy startled her. She dropped Shamika's receipt. 'Sorry.'

'No worries. See you later.'

'Houston, are you going to fix the drink?' Mandy glanced over her shoulder. Houston glared at her and shrugged, then went to make the ice-blended mocha.

Mandy wore her smile until her next customer walked across the lobby.

She wasn't used to seeing Amrik from the massage business on her side of the floor. His entire face seemed to have developed a sag, even his cheekbones. With slumped shoulders and a generally hunched posture, he looked like someone who had slept badly – for a week or more.

'Hi, Amrik.' Mandy put her hand on the counter, holding back the motherly instinct to squeeze his hand. 'What can I get you?'

'Coffee,' he croaked.

He'd claimed he never drank it. Was he a liar? 'Want a cookie or pastry with that?'

He rubbed at his eyes. 'I had to take a break between clients.'

'Are you OK? You look exhausted.'

He licked his lips. 'I'm just so worried.'

She nodded and rang up a large coffee, then grabbed him a cup. When he didn't expand, she asked, 'About what?'

He leaned his head over the counter and whispered, 'Reese and I had a whirlwind romance.'

'No!' Mandy gasped. 'I knew something was going on with her. This must be part of it. She was being very secretive.' She had so many questions. Did Reese's parents know? How long had it been going on? Was it serious?

He smiled wanly. 'I was sleeping over every night. Best sleep of my life. Then the police arrested her and it was back to life as usual – well, for me at least.'

'Except you're heartsick,' Mandy diagnosed. Every night? She had to admit that while she saw Reese regularly, it wasn't at her home.

He nodded.

She swirled her finger in the air to send him toward the coffee urns. They both walked that way, him around the counter and her behind. Houston had slunk off to lick his wounds in the back, so they were alone.

Up close, the normally golden undertones of his dark skin had gone ashy. 'Do you love her?' Mandy whispered.

He nodded.

'You must not think she killed Coral?' She tried to sound delicate.

'Never,' he said stoutly. 'I know what the police found and it didn't belong to Reese.'

Someone who knew! 'What was it?'

His eyes opened in alarm. Had she shouted her question? Mandy saw the bloodshot streaks of red in the whites. When he lifted his cup, his hand trembled.

Mandy heard footsteps behind her and raised her voice. 'I'm sorry to hear you aren't feeling well, Amrik. I'll just dispense this for you, shall I? French roast or light?'

'Light,' he croaked. 'I'm not much of a coffee drinker.'

She pushed down on the lever. 'We have regular French vanilla and hazelnut if you'd like flavoring.'

'Anything dairy-free?'

She nodded and opened a tiny tub of the regular flavor, which didn't have cow's milk or byproducts in it, and dumped it in. 'There you go. I hope you feel better tomorrow.'

'Not until – well, you know,' he managed.

She lowered her voice. 'Please tell the police the truth. We need to free Reese.'

He coughed and nodded. She grabbed the coffee out of his hand before he could spill it and snapped on a lid and a cup holder.

'There you go,' she said soothingly. 'Feel better now.' When she turned around, Fannah had a hand on her hip. Her other hand was pointing toward the cash register, below where the waiting line of customers could see.

'Where did they come from?' Mandy asked. 'No one was here just a minute ago.'

'Seminar for visiting specialists,' Fannah said. 'Hop to it.'

Mandy pasted on her fakest smile and went to take orders. Houston kept busy with the blender in the back while Fannah worked the espresso machine. Once the rush was over, Fannah sent her to make cookies. She never got her afternoon break, and by the time her shift was over and she could get over to the massage part of the lobby, Amrik had left for the day.

Frustrated, she called Linda and asked her if she wanted to meet at a cupcake place nearby that Linda had been dying to try. Linda agreed. Mandy sped around the sky bridge circuit for twenty minutes, in the vain attempt to burn off a few calories in anticipation of her treat, then walked the two blocks to the Two Hares Cupcakery. She had an hour before her first meditation class started.

Linda was already seated at a small table in front of the picture window. Mandy waved and rushed in.

'How did you get here so fast?' she asked.

'I wasn't home when you called. The animal shelter asked me to take a potted plant to a funeral home because one of their main benefactors just died.'

'Uh-oh.' Mandy knew the animal shelter was close to her friend's heart. 'Is that going to cause trouble with their operating expenses?'

Linda tugged Mandy's purse from her arm and gestured to the chair. 'I ordered for both of us when I came in. Sit.'

Mandy followed orders, then peeled off her coat. All that exercise had her feeling flushed.

'Anyway,' Linda continued, 'we're hoping the woman left a bequest in her will. No guarantees, of course. She had three kids, five grandkids, and a great-grandbaby.'

'Fingers crossed.' Mandy looked up and saw an employee heading toward them with a tray. On it were two drinks in paper cups and a trio of cupcakes.

'Here we are,' the employee cooed, her long, straight black

ponytail sliding from one shoulder to the other. 'Lemon meringue, Vietnamese coffee, and peanut butter cup.'

'Holy cow,' Mandy muttered. 'I needed a three-hour walk, not twenty minutes.'

Linda nodded her thanks to the petite woman. 'I wondered why you took so long. I thought you'd be here before me.'

'I thought you were coming from home, so I walked the sky bridges first.'

Linda shook her head. 'So fitness-oriented.'

Mandy snorted as Linda grinned. 'Not exactly. I've been so busy at home that I've had no chance to just sit on the couch and pig out on brownies. But now we're going to sit here and relax and ingest all the calories.'

'Life is too short to worry about calories,' Linda said.

'You're probably right.' Mandy opened her bag and pulled out her sketchbook and a small metal case of watercolor pencils.

'Too pretty not to draw?'

'Exactly. I can get an entire process video out of these pretties.'

'I'll take your photos,' Linda offered.

'Thanks.' Mandy opened her sketchbook and chose yellow, black, and brown pencils, while Linda fussed with the display and snapped shots with her phone.

'I think that's good.' Mandy liked her angle on the cupcakes, with all three in a diagonal, mouthwatering display. Linda wouldn't be able to keep her hands off them for long. 'Which one do you want?'

'I thought we'd cut them all in two.'

Mandy nodded agreement. 'Which one do you want first?'

'Hmm.' Linda bit her lip. 'Peanut butter, I guess.'

'Got it.' Mandy put pen to paper.

'Why are you using watercolor pencils instead of regular colored pencils?'

'For one thing, I could use a little water and turn the pencil marks into a fluid wash. But mostly I do it when I don't want pencil marks to show under my artwork. The watercolor pencil will dissolve when I do the painting.'

'That's cool. Do you want me to film you sketching?'

'No, I'll do it under camera later. I'll just get my impressions down so we can eat.'

'I like the cupcake papers,' Linda exclaimed, watching as the cupcake took form under Mandy's pencils.

'Gorgeous,' Mandy agreed, adding lines to make the gold-threaded red wrapper folds pop. 'I'm going to have fun figuring out how to make them look realistic. The baking process faded the colors so much.'

Linda went to the counter and spoke to the employee, then returned. As Mandy's pencil moved to the next shape, Linda grabbed their plastic knife and sliced neatly through the middle.

'Stop!' Mandy called, distracted by the puddle of gooey peanut butter mousse oozing from the cupcake's center. 'Take a picture, please.'

'Let it never be said that I found a dessert too pretty to eat,' Linda grumbled good-naturedly, snapping a few pics. 'OK, all done. I'm going in.'

Mandy laughed and did quick two-minute sketches of the other cupcakes. The lemon one had a formed oval of lemon curd in the center, and the coffee one had a fully molten core, just like the peanut butter. 'Do they taste as good as they look?'

Linda took experimental bites of all three. 'The lemon is the best, actually. Peanut butter isn't quite up to snuff.'

'That's too bad.' Mandy slid the lemon half on to her plate. She let it sit there while she drank Earl Grey tea.

The employee returned and handed Linda a piece of paper.

'Oh, it's a fresh cupcake wrapper. How lovely.' Mandy leaned over the table.

'Vietnamese design,' the employee said. 'You paint?'

Mandy explained and gave the woman her Mandy's Plan business card. 'I teach classes if you're interested.'

'Yes,' she said. 'I'm Cam. Can I give you my email?'

'Yes.' Mandy wrote down the email. 'I'll send you some information.'

'Catch me up,' Linda invited, when Cam had returned to the counter. 'I feel out of the loop.'

'I know Reese's secret now. Or at least one of them.'

Linda wiped a bit of lemon frosting off her upper lip with her finger. 'What is it?'

'She has a boyfriend. Amrik Kurmi, Coral's boss.'

'Oh,' Linda breathed. 'That's how she got Coral the job.'

Mandy forked up a triangle of cupcake. 'I don't know the timeline. But Amrik has his own secrets. He says that what the cops found that got her arrested wasn't Reese's.'

'Oh, Lordy, Lordy, Lordy,' Linda said. 'Did he basically tell you he was the killer?'

'Obviously not, but he knows more than the police do. And then there's that blasted bounty hunter, who I thought knew something, but no facts emerged from his mouth when we had dinner.'

Linda's mouth slackened. 'Mandy Meadows went on a date?'

'No, it was business. Reese business,' Mandy insisted. 'Meanwhile, Justin is never home and is barely speaking to me.'

'It's been nearly a week since that kiss. He can hold a grudge, that man,' Linda said.

'I'm sure he's working hard, rather than ignoring me. Well, maybe. We've had a lot of murders in Seattle recently.' Mandy cut off another hunk of cupcake and let it soothe her taste buds.

Her phone rang. 'Cory,' she muttered. 'I didn't tell you about that disaster.'

'You texted me about his father.'

'He made moves on me, and Justin caught the floor show.' Mandy sighed and answered the phone, trying to inject sympathy into her voice. 'How is your father doing?'

'He's improving,' Cory said in a sulky tone.

'That's great. Why don't you text Vellum with the good news? She really wants to hear from you.'

'I'm not going to text her at camp,' Cory said.

'Why not? I don't think the reception is that great, but she'll probably get the message at some point.'

He ignored her suggestion as if he hadn't heard it. 'Why don't we have dinner and talk about the other night?'

'We have nothing to talk about, Cory. I told you at the time I wasn't interested in reconnecting.'

'It wasn't a moment. Mandy, I know I'm the love of your life. You need to give me a second chance. We all make mistakes.'

'You're only the love of my life because I haven't dated anyone better yet,' Mandy snapped.

Linda's fork clattered to the table, her frosting-colored lips forming an 'O.'

Mandy saw her expression and checked herself before anyone

else listened in. 'Look, Cory, I have a class to get to. I'm trying to learn how to relax. If you want me to like you better, pay your child support.' She disconnected the phone and sat back. 'Am I a broken record or not? Sorry.'

Linda shook her head. 'He's a louse, hun. Has he taken you back to court to get the payment lowered yet?'

'No. Even before his stroke, his father was probably feeling too unwell to file.'

'Or maybe he doesn't agree with his son's bad behavior,' Linda suggested.

'I wonder how Reese's parents are going to feel about their daughter's drama,' Mandy said. 'When do they return to the US?'

'Do they know Reese has a boyfriend?'

Mandy frowned. 'I don't know. I would have thought she'd have been oozing enthusiasm all over the hospital complex. I can ask at my appointment to see her tomorrow after work.'

'Perhaps Amrik isn't Hindu.'

'Maybe,' Mandy said. 'I wouldn't want to ask him. I appreciate that he's starting to confide in me, though, and I hope he takes what he knows to the police – and, of course, that he didn't kill Coral himself.'

'Yeah, you'd think he'd want his girlfriend home and safe.'

'Not if *he* killed Coral.' Mandy's gaze met Linda's.

Her friend shuddered. 'Tell Justin what happened and stay away from the guy.'

'Yeah. I mean, why would he have killed her? To get one girl-friend out of the way so he could have his new one?' Mandy's phone rang again. Her ex's name popped up again. She pressed the silence button and hung up.

'Good for you,' Linda praised. 'Reese would have been a better catch than a married massage therapist.'

'You're right.' Mandy rubbed her hands together and put her warmed palms over her eyes. 'I hate it when Vellum isn't home. I always feel like I have too much free time and trouble finds me.'

Linda chuckled. 'Get used to it. She's halfway through her teens already.'

'You and I can grow old together, right?'

'Sure. We'll toss a coin to see which house we sell and which one we keep,' Linda said.

Mandy nodded. 'Very sensible. I'm glad to have my life sorted out. Now, back to Reese's.' She picked up her phone again and texted Justin. 'I'm telling Justin to re-interview Amrik.'

'It's just neighborly,' Linda agreed. 'You gave him time to go to the police himself, but it's too important not to follow up on yourself.'

Mandy set down her phone. 'I just wish I knew what Amrik knew.'

FOURTEEN

The meditation class met in a luxurious conference room near the cafeteria, smaller than the auditorium. Mandy breathed in food smells wafting down the hall. Not that she needed dinner. She'd eaten a third of each of the luscious cupcakes and felt completely stuffed.

Houston stood just inside the room. 'You look green. You OK?'

'Charming greeting,' Mandy said to him as she passed by.

'I could try to record the class on my phone if you're too sick to be here,' Houston said, following her.

'I'm not sick. I just ate too much sugar too fast.'

'Are you diabetic?'

'I don't think you should be asking me such personal questions.' Mandy sank into a chair and pressed her hand to her stomach out of sight of the other employees in the room.

Houston took the next chair and swiveled to her. 'Why not? You know a lot about me.'

Mandy half closed her eyes. 'I don't know much of anything and I'm perfectly content with that.'

'Why don't you like me?' Houston asked in a plaintive voice that dropped his age about five years.

'Act your age,' Mandy snapped, then stopped talking when Bodhi Lee glided into the room, followed by two women Mandy recognized as working in the surgical intensive care unit. Both of them radiated an air of such serenity and polish that Mandy figured they had been meditating for a decade already.

Jason Cho arrived and took the chair next to Mandy. The room filled to capacity, with all the chairs taken by mostly administrative staff, two-thirds female.

'If we'd sold one more seat, we'd have needed to find a different room,' Jason said in Mandy's ear. 'This is perfect. Twenty people.'

'I'm looking forward to it.'

Jason moved his gaze toward the front of the room. Mandy thought his look at Bodhi had hunger in it.

'Is he gay?' Mandy whispered to Jason.

'Bodhi? I doubt it.' Jason sighed. 'I wish.'

'Maybe you could ask him to coffee after.'

'He's gorgeous, but I like to date people my age.'

'I get that,' Mandy said. 'You're younger than me, right?'

'I'm thirty. Why, do you know anyone?' His gaze settled on Houston for a moment.

'He looks like Bodhi, right?' Mandy said.

At that, Houston turned to them and leaned in front of Mandy. 'What do you think?'

Jason stared at the barista. 'Yeah, I guess. Your skin isn't as dark but your features are about the same. Bodhi is shorter than you are.'

'My mother is white and tall,' Houston said. 'So that would account for it.'

'Are you related?'

Houston shrugged. 'Dunno. I'm here to find out.'

'I don't even know his ethnicity.'

'Alaska Native maybe?' Mandy said. 'Or Indian – from India, that is – given the chakras and meditation.'

'I'd expect him to do herbology if he was Inuit,' Houston said.

'You did a DNA test, didn't you?' Mandy asked. 'That might tell you your ethnicity.'

Houston shifted his shoulders. 'I didn't really understand it. I was Northern European, Russian, something I didn't even comprehend, and Indigenous American.'

'Do you know something specific that made you spend this much money to get close to Bodhi Lee?' Mandy asked.

Before Houston could answer, Bodhi stepped up to the podium, his lips curved in a beatific smile. Mandy glanced around and saw nearly every woman smile in response. He gave his introductory lecture again, then started a meditation session.

'Take a deep breath through your nose,' Bodhi said. 'Then again.'

Mandy obeyed. After all, she wasn't here to crush on the guy, or ask if he'd been Houston's sperm donor. She was there to relax.

'A soft gaze,' Bodhi directed, 'then another deep breath, before you gently close your eyes.'

He led them through what Mandy later realized was a full half-hour meditation. Bodhi spoke in a rhythmic voice about each chakra and what it represented, sending them through their body, checking the wellbeing of each center.

After they opened their eyes at the end of the meditation, Bodhi asked each of his students which chakra seemed tense. When it was Mandy's turn, she shrugged.

'The root chakra, I guess. I thought these chairs would be more comfortable.'

Jason tittered, but the female followers looked horrified.

'Seriously, though, I probably just need to stretch,' Mandy said. 'Long day.'

Bodhi nodded. 'Stay for a couple of minutes at the end,' he invited. 'I have a special mudra for you.'

'I'd like a special mudra, too,' said a cardiac nurse.

'I'm happy to stay late,' added her friend.

'Umm, I'll just stretch. Like I said, it's the chair,' Mandy said, embarrassed to be singled out.

Bodhi regarded her coolly, ignoring the others. 'Aggression,' he said calmly. 'Poor decision making. Back pain. These are all common indicators of root chakra blockage, along with constipation and weight gain.'

Feeling insulted, Mandy bristled. 'Not my problems, thanks.'

'Stay behind.' Bodhi's serene gaze scanned the room. 'Let us discuss the process of opening your third eye. Meditation is, of course, key . . .'

The cardiac employees gave Mandy a dirty look. She widened her eyes at them. It hadn't occurred to her that he was only looking for one response to focus on. But no one else had said root chakra and maybe he wanted to lecture on the first chakra tonight.

He talked about the third eye for another twenty minutes. 'Now,

I am going to give you some homework. It is clear tonight. Leave your curtains open and rest under the moonlight. Keep a journal next to your bed and write your dreams down in the morning, before you forget them.'

'Anything else?' asked the cardiac nurse.

Bodhi nodded. 'Find one symbol before our next class that speaks to you and bring a representation of it to our next class.'

Mandy sighed. She wondered if the USea Coffee Bar logo would do. Probably not. She'd need to look for something catchy and relevant, like a Sanskrit phrase.

Jason wrote everything down in a small notebook that had a loophole for a tiny pen. She'd had a sketchbook like that once, perfect for painting one perfect tiny flower per page. Vellum, still in grade school at the time, had taken it over, drawing smiling barnyard animals on each one.

Houston nudged her. She returned her attention to Bodhi, who walked them through a final blessing.

'Teacher's pet,' he said when people started to rise. 'Can I stay with you?'

'Sure.' Mandy suppressed a yawn. 'Let's get this over with.'

'Didn't you enjoy the class?' Jason asked. 'I found it very helpful.'

'I had a great time.' Mandy checked her phone. It was only six in the evening but it felt later. 'The meditation was very relaxing.'

'Ah, Miss Root Chakra,' Bodhi Lee said, appraising her with a quick full sweep of her body.

Houston put his hand on her shoulder possessively. She shook it off. What did he think – that she was his future mother-in-law or something?

'That's me,' Mandy said, hoping that shaking off Houston hadn't come off as aggressive. After all, he was the pushy one.

'Back pain?' His eyes swept her pelvic region again.

She told herself he was like a doctor, looking at her for diagnostic reasons. No discomfort on her part necessary. 'I tend to hunch because I lean over the cash register at work and do art at home.'

'Are you familiar with tadasana?'

'It sounds like a tasty snack,' Mandy joked. 'Maybe something with hummus?'

Bodhi blinked slowly. 'Humor is your defense, eh? Does your back ache right now?'

'The chairs were uncomfortable,' Mandy retorted.

'Set down your bags,' Bodhi instructed. 'Now, both of you, take off your shoes and stand in front of me in a relaxed posture.'

Houston shrugged as Mandy set down her bags. The class was expensive, so she might as well get her money's worth. She did as he instructed. When she pulled off her tennis shoes, she almost groaned with relief.

Bodhi shook his head when he saw how they stood. 'First of all, slide your big toes together. Then, let your ankles fall apart slightly.'

Mandy moved her feet into position.

Bodhi continued. 'Now, move your balance toward the front of your feet.'

She obeyed, immediately feeling a shift in her body.

'Excellent,' Bodhi praised.

Jason darted next to Mandy, his shoes off. She held back a giggle. Obviously, the administrator didn't want to miss any instruction.

'Now, we move into the pelvic region. I want you to neutralize the area, by pulling your thigh bones toward your tail bone, releasing there.'

Mandy followed the instructions easily, having done yoga classes for a few months when Vellum was in middle school.

Bodhi continued. 'Now, the shoulders. Draw them back in alignment with your body.' He clucked at Houston and pressed down on his left shoulder.

Before Mandy could react, he tapped the left side of her rear. 'Relax,' he whispered intimately. Finally, he looked up and down Jason and nodded without saying anything.

Bodhi returned his gaze to Mandy. 'Prana mudra should be done for fifteen minutes a day in this pose.' He took her hand and folded her ring and pinky fingers toward her palm, then touched her thumb to them. 'Leave the other two fingers erect, like so.' He did the motion with his own hands.

'That's a stretch,' Mandy commented. She could stand like this for fifteen minutes, but not with her hands contorted like that.

'Do this in the morning before work,' he said. 'I'll look forward to a report tomorrow night in class.'

Jason nodded. 'Thank you. I could use help for back pain, too.'
Bodhi's gaze slid back to Houston. 'How do you feel?'
'Off balance.'
'Quite the opposite. This is balance. Stop cocking your hips and stand like this.' Bodhi's eyelids half closed as his gaze moved to Mandy. 'Think of your hips as a bowl of water. In your new position, the water will not spill. If you leave your neutral position, you will have an accident.'

Mandy's eyes widened. 'What an image.' Her fingers started to shake from the effort of holding the mudra. 'Can we relax now?'

'That wasn't even two minutes,' the instructor said acerbically. He turned, went to the table, and started stacking his laminated diagrams together.

Mandy stretched her fingers then followed him up the step on to the platform. 'Thank you for the help. You know, I think we have a mutual friend. Coral Le Charme?'

'That name sounds familiar,' he said.

'I think she might have been a student of yours. She lived on Kodiak Island at one time.'

'I don't recall.'

She persisted. 'Maybe somewhere else in Alaska?'

'Ah, now I remember. It was Anchorage,' Bodhi said. With his diagrams put away, he straightened into tadasana. 'She took a class there and arranged for me to teach classes in Kodiak in conjunction with a tourist company.'

Mandy pressed her hands into the table and leaned in. 'You knew her well?'

'She only asked to be allowed to attend the classes when I visited. A finder's fee of sorts.'

'She must have been really into meditation?'

Bodhi mimicked her position. 'It's Mandy, isn't it?'

'Yes.'

His gaze, soft and untroubled, captured her own. She wanted to look away but he mesmerized her. 'She was troubled, poor girl. I expect she desired to slow down the processes of her mind.'

'What process created trouble?'

'She was a pathological liar.' He nodded.

She found herself nodding back. 'For instance?'

'For instance,' he echoed, 'she claimed to be six years younger than her real age.'

'How old was she?' Mandy gasped.

'She claimed twenty-six but is really thirty-two.'

'Was,' Mandy corrected, wondering why he knew such a detail when he claimed only a vague familiarity with her. 'She's been dead for two weeks tomorrow.'

'Dead?' he asked, his brow furrowing.

She had no idea if his shock was genuine or feigned. 'Yes, she died right here on the hospital property.'

'Very sad,' Bodhi said softly.

'You were here in Seattle at the time,' Mandy pointed out. 'Did you talk to her here?'

His voice went flat. 'No.'

'She was working in the chair massage business here in the hospital,' Mandy prompted. 'Did you get a massage?'

'No,' Bodhi said. 'A massage from an unsettled spirit does nothing good for the body.'

Mandy felt as if she was swaying, so she tightened her hold on the table. 'I know she wasn't doing a good job.'

'Poor woman,' Bodhi said. 'She didn't keep up her meditation practice.' He released the desk. 'Go home, get a good night's sleep, and wake up early enough tomorrow to do your mudra practice.'

'Very well,' Mandy said. 'But I expect I'll have more questions about Coral's history. I'm friendly with her family.'

'I don't think I will have any useful answers for you,' he said, unruffled. 'I know nothing of her life here.'

Mandy turned around. Jason straightened chairs. Houston simply stared at Bodhi, his hands shoved into his trouser pockets. She raised her eyebrows at him and he shrugged. Apparently, he wasn't going to confront Bodhi tonight with any questions about his parentage, but they had three more classes to go. Maybe he wanted to think about how he would approach the meditation master, though he didn't seem the hang-back-and-consider type.

She went back to her chair, which Jason hadn't touched, and grabbed her possessions.

'Going home?' Jason asked.

'Yes, I've been neglecting my second job today.'

'I heard you do calligraphy. Wedding invitations?'

'I have, but primarily I focus on journaling. I make stickers, teach classes, all that kind of stuff.'

'Huh. It's tough work having a side hustle, but everyone seems to these days,' Jason said.

She pushed her chair in his direction and he grabbed it and pushed it against the wall.

'Help me with the table?' he asked.

'I should probably get a side hustle, too,' Houston said, following them to the table against the wall. 'Or finish up my associate's degree.'

'What were you studying?' Mandy grabbed one side and they took the others.

'Human resources.' He made a face. 'Not very exciting.'

'You like working with people.' Mandy stumbled a little as she walked backward, pulling the table.

'Yeah.' He sighed. 'I haven't really figured it out.'

'There's nothing wrong with being a barista.'

'I don't want to be a bartender,' he confided. 'But it pays a lot better. When I turn twenty-one, I'll have to think about it.'

'Finish your degree,' Jason advised. 'There are great colleges in Seattle. Better opportunities than service jobs.'

'Maybe I'll turn into someone you'd be happy to see dating Vellum?' he asked hopefully.

'Not for at least three years,' she said firmly. 'Focus on your education.'

'What's with the three years?' Jason asked. He nodded at Bodhi as the teacher walked out of the room without glancing at them.

'My daughter is fifteen.'

'Really?' Jason's eyes slid to the side, then he looked at her face. 'You must have been young.'

'That's why I didn't finish college,' Mandy said. 'Never did go back.'

'We could go back to college together,' Houston suggested. 'But first, I'm going to figure out who my father is.'

'Is it so important?' Mandy asked, amused at the idea of going to school with this kid.

He hunched his shoulders. 'Yeah. Maybe it shouldn't matter,

but it does.' They slid the table into place, then pulled it apart to add the leaf that had been against the wall.

'Don't you have a Facilities department?' Houston asked.

'We don't want to pay overtime. I'm on salary,' Jason explained.

'I'm not,' Houston groused.

'I'm going to grab a snack in the cafeteria before I leave,' Mandy said, hoisting her bag. Her appetite had returned. 'See you tomorrow.'

'What about Vellum?' Houston asked.

'She's away.' Mandy put her hand on her bag. 'And the special today is that jackfruit curry they started making.'

Houston winced. 'That doesn't sound good.'

'It is, though. See you tomorrow.'

He shrugged. 'I'll come with you.'

Jason nodded and followed them. 'I haven't tried it either.' He flipped off the light.

'What about the chairs?' Mandy asked.

'Anyone can pull a chair to a table.' He put his hand over his mouth, suppressing a yawn. 'Note to self, don't get up early to work out on class days.'

'Yeah, especially if you're supposed to get up early to meditate.'

Jason's mouth tilted sideways. 'Are you going to do it?'

Mandy led them around the corner to the cafeteria, then grabbed a tray. They lined up behind her. 'I want to get my money's worth.' She made her order, then went to grab a glass of fruited water.

They ended up deciding to eat dinner there and spent a surprisingly comfortable half hour attempting to explain Seattle culture to Houston. Jason had grown up in West Seattle, so he had a slightly different perspective from north-end-raised Mandy.

'I have work to do,' Mandy said, when Jason took a break from explaining the history of stadiums in the city. 'But dinner was fun. See you tomorrow.'

They waved at her, then bent their heads together again. Maybe she'd initiated a bromance. They both seemed lonely and it would be good for unfocused Houston to have a mentor.

Mandy arrived home well after dark and drove up to her unused garage. Justin was home for once, his car parked in the wide area of the long driveway. Light radiated from the kitchen.

'Hey,' Mandy called when she pushed open the mudroom door. Justin was at the stove, dressed in jeans and moccasins, his long-sleeved shirt hanging loosely over his fit body. 'Turkey chili. Want some?'

'Smells good.' Mandy set her purse on the counter and pulled off her coat. 'But I had jackfruit curry with a couple of co-workers after our meditation class.'

A pause hung in the air before he said, 'Thought you might be on a date.'

'No,' she said in her most level tone. 'I don't date. I ate with that kid who's been chasing Vellum, and the other co-worker is gay.'

'No Cory?' he asked in a casual tone.

The mere suggestion irritated her. 'He called, but I told him to share his updates with Vellum, not me. I'm sorry his father is ill, but he never showed me much kindness.'

Justin set his spoon in the rest and turned to her. 'Is he good to Vellum?'

She shrugged. 'He was going to pay her college tuition.'

His gaze flicked to her lips, then back to her eyes. 'She's the only grandchild?'

'No, but it's not a close family.' She ignored his perusal of her, and her own pleasured tinge of female awareness, and walked past him to the coffee machine. 'I'm going to have some hot chocolate and work on orders.'

'You work too hard,' he commented.

'Two jobs,' she reminded him. 'You work too hard, too. I hardly ever see you around.'

He set the lid over his chili and turned down the heat. 'You need to find time for fun.'

Feeling her nerves amp up with frustration, she pressed the button to run a water-only cycle on her coffee maker. 'Justin, I can't date right now. That's the kind of fun I don't have time for.'

Justin smoothed his hand over his jaw. 'Are you sure your ex isn't a factor?'

She put her hands on her hips. 'Linda told you my divorce story. Yes, he's made a couple of attempts to return. But I said no. That's why his mother claims the divorce is my fault. But why should I forgive his infidelity?'

Justin rinsed out the sink. 'Plus, he's been a jerk since. About the money.'

'Yeah, his true colors have shown.'

'Is he making you nervous?'

She shoved in a hot chocolate pod, the sore subject making her movements jerky. 'I didn't like how he behaved last night. Or on the phone today.'

His jaw worked. 'I didn't either. Some guys never stop seeing their exes as property.'

'At first I thought it was just the house he couldn't let go of.' Mandy watched soft-brown liquid drip into her cup, breathing in the chocolate as if it had the power to calm her.

'Some guys,' Justin said again. 'Listen, I have news.'

'About what?' she asked.

'Reese. She's been released.'

Mandy's face went slack. She turned around slowly. They'd been wasting time talking about Cory when he had this kind of news? 'What? On bail? Are her parents back?'

'Released as in the charges have been dropped.'

'Yasss,' Mandy breathed. 'That's so great! Is she home?'

'I don't know. Another thing – that knife you and Darci found didn't have Coral's blood on it, just Tom's.'

Mandy tried to focus past the wonderful news about Reese. 'You're saying it wasn't the murder weapon?'

'No. The shape of the blade was wrong for her wounds. It was a good catch, though you shouldn't have been in that house.'

'Wow.' Mandy snatched her mug. 'Why was the knife there, then?'

'Mr DeRoy claimed it was part of a Santeria ritual.' Justin shrugged. 'As long as he isn't breaking the law with inhumane animal treatment.'

'Thanks for telling me. I need to check orders, then I'm going to go over to Reese's. No, wait, I'll need to bring something.' She pulled her phone from her purse and texted Linda, suggesting she make some brownies.

After that, she took a sip of her drink, burning her tongue in the process, then rummaged around in the wine rack in a cupboard until she found a decent Chardonnay. 'This will work.' She set it on the counter.

'I really don't know if she's gone home,' he commented.

'Maybe she's with Amrik. He's her boyfriend.'

'I know.'

'OK.' She glanced at him, but he didn't follow up. 'Something I should know?'

'That's all the news.' He turned back to the stove.

She stared at his back and let sarcasm edge into her voice. 'Thanks for the update. Enjoy your chili.'

His only response was a grunt. Wanting to growl herself, she went into the dining room and turned on the lights, then set her mug on a coaster and turned on her computer to check orders. Making people wait for what they wanted to pay for was bad business.

While her computer loaded, she dashed into her art studio and updated her murder spreadsheet. She kept the word 'knife' on her weapon list, but wrote 'Tom's knife' under the first word, then crossed out the new line to show it had been considered and rejected as the murder weapon.

After that, she read a text from Linda, saying that brownies were going into the oven and she'd meet Mandy on the corner between their houses in forty minutes to walk them over to Reese's house. Next, she texted Darci.

When her computer's hum settled down into working rhythm, she checked her orders and started fulfilling them. She could get through quite a bit in forty minutes.

Her phone buzzed again with a response from Darci. She typed back with an update on Reese and a mention of her meditation class. Ten minutes later, she had a response back.

Don't trust Bodhi Lee.

Mandy quickly texted her to ask what Darci knew, but by the time she had to go meet Linda, Darci hadn't offered an explanation.

FIFTEEN

'Hey, no April showers,' Linda called from the street corner next to her house. 'It's about time the weather changed.' Mandy adjusted the handles of her carrier bag. She had wine she'd thrown in at the last minute. 'What would you want for comfort food if you'd just been released from a holding cell?'

'Something I could eat in the bathtub,' Linda said.

Mandy followed her across the street. 'I'd have to leave the door open. The bathroom might feel too much like a cell.'

'I think I'd prefer it that way. At least in your cell you aren't exposed to the entire prison population.'

'Yeah, maybe being alone trumps confined spaces.' Mandy shivered as they walked up the street. 'She might not even be home.'

'Then we'll leave our offerings on the porch. Poor kid,' Linda said.

'Yeah. At least we were right all along. She didn't kill Coral.'

'Why did they release her?' Linda asked.

'Not sure. Justin isn't my biggest fan right now, but I doubt he'd tell me much even if we were dating.'

'I have a feeling your Detective Ahola is too good at his job for that,' Linda agreed. 'Let him do his job and we'll do ours.'

'There's a light on,' Mandy said as they came abreast of Reese's house.

'That's a good sign.'

'Or a bad one. After something like this, I don't know if I'd go home or go to my mother's house for comfort.'

'Or mine,' Linda said. 'You're right. And what about Amrik? He's her boyfriend.'

'Justin was close-mouthed.' They went up the porch steps and knocked.

'It's Mandy,' she called through the door. Listening intently, she heard nothing, then a door shut deep in the house. 'I think she's there.'

'You might need to ring the doorbell,' Linda said. 'I wonder when she came home.'

'We can always leave the brownies and I can send her a text,' Mandy fretted. 'We should probably do that.'

'We don't want pets to get at the brownies.'

Mandy glanced at Linda's treats. 'You wrapped them in foil.'

'I was out of containers.' Linda grinned sheepishly. 'They're piling up at the animal shelter.'

Metal rasped against metal, then the door opened a couple of inches, secured by a chain. Mandy whipped around. 'Reese, it's us.'

Undereye circles marred Reese's normally flawless face. Her hair was wrapped in a towel turban and she wore a blue fleece sweater and pants.

'You poor thing,' Linda cooed. 'Welcome home.'

Reese's upper lip twitched. Before Mandy could speak, the door shut in their faces, but she heard the metal against metal again, then the door opened wide.

'How did you know I was home?' Reese's lips trembled.

'Justin told me you'd been released,' Mandy said, touching her friend's arm.

'We brought warm brownies,' Linda announced.

They walked in, then Reese locked the door behind them and put on the chain again.

'What got you out of there?' Mandy asked. She and Reese exchanged an awkward hug, then Reese stepped back. 'We've been doing what we could to find the real killer. I had an appointment to see you tomorrow. I'm sorry it was taking so long.'

Reese's arms hung loosely at her side as if she didn't have the energy to move. Her head was at an angle, as if it was stuck there. 'It's OK.'

'Prison bunks must be hard on the body,' Linda said.

Reese winced. 'I don't know what I did to deserve this, but I can't go back there. It's a good thing I'm innocent.'

'Sit,' Mandy urged, hearing the rasp in Reese's voice. 'I'll make you some tea.'

Linda handed her the brownies and gently took Reese by the arm. Mandy dashed into the kitchen and found Reese's cat drinking from her water dish. Her food dish looked freshly emptied. Bits of moist food clung to the edges.

'Glad to see you made it through, kitty.' Mandy searched Reese's extensive tea supply and chose a jasmine-scented green tea, which brewed much faster than black.

Thanks to Reese's quick-boil kettle, she was back in the living room with a fresh pot of tea and cylindrical handle-less cups on a tray in just five minutes. Then she dashed back to retrieve napkins for the brownies. Reese looked doubtfully at the sticky brown treats in relation to her pristine white sofa.

'I'm sorry.' Reese passed a hand over her forehead. 'We should have gone into the dining room. 'I didn't think.'

'It's OK, sweetie.' Linda patted Reese's pajama-covered leg. 'You've had an ordeal. We won't stay.'

'After the last eight days I'm not used to being alone,' Reese said. 'Have you talked to anyone at the hospital? Do I still have a job?'

'The first day after, you know, I did see a couple of your co-workers, but not after that,' Mandy admitted.

'Oh, well.' Reese sighed.

'Justin didn't tell me how you came to be released.' Mandy took a sip of tea. 'I'd been feeding him every bit of doubt I could, but I don't think anything I said helped. What happened?'

'You did help, from what my lawyer told me,' Reese said.

'That's good to hear.'

Reese cleared her throat with a tiny cough. 'I was released after Amrik confessed he murdered Coral.'

Linda's jaw dropped. Mandy put her cup on the tray and her hand on Linda's shoulder, leaning into her. 'I told him to tell the police what he was hinting at to me about what was found in your house. That sure wasn't what I expected.'

Reese's lips trembled. She set her cup down. 'The police found needles in my house.'

'Why was that important?' Linda asked. She bent down and refilled Reese's cup with hot tea, then handed it back to her.

'They were the same brand as we use at work for steroid injections.'

'But Coral was stabbed,' Mandy protested.

Reese's free hand opened then closed. Her voice shook. 'My lawyer said Coral had been injected with an opiate and the chemical profile of the adulterants in the solution matched what was in her body. The syringe was full – the one they found in my house.'

'You're saying they found opiates in a syringe in your house?' Mandy asked, heartsick.

Reese nodded.

Mandy felt too nauseated to eat brownies. She set her napkin on the tray. 'Amrik stole them from your office or something?'

'No, I can't believe that. Someone took the syringe, but the opiates didn't come from the podiatry office,' Reese said. 'I was framed.'

'By Amrik?' Linda asked.

'No. Amrik didn't kill Coral,' Reese insisted. 'He's a good man. Mandy, you must have talked him into confessing.'

'No, not confessing.' Mandy rubbed her twitching eye. 'I just asked him to tell the police what he knew. This is such a shock.'

Reese's head dropped into her free hand. Her voice came out muffled through her thick hair. 'I wanted a tenant to earn money to pay for my wedding because my parents wouldn't support my marrying him.'

'How come?'

Reese sniffed. 'My father thinks our romance happened too quickly. He wanted an engineer, or doctor, or good barrister to marry his angel.' She mimicked her father's accent. 'Not someone who has some strange massage chair business.'

'Oh, goodness,' Linda breathed.

Reese nodded. 'They aren't supportive. I have to pay for the wedding myself.'

'You were still single on Valentine's Day. We spent it together,' Mandy said, shocked by the speed of the romance. When had all this happened and how had she missed it?

'Sometimes you just know,' Reese said. 'We met at the end of January and a couple of weeks after that he sat with me in the cafeteria on a day I'd forgotten my lunch. He asked me out. It must have been just after Valentine's Day when we had dinner.'

'And then he proposed?' Mandy prompted.

'The night before the murder. That's why I was so upset when Coral hurt me. I was happy, just floating on air like a butterfly. I went to say hello to Amrik but he wasn't there, so I took Coral's open appointment to be kind, and she threw my neck completely out of whack.'

'You weren't wearing a ring.'

Reese drained her second cup. 'He can't afford it. He's building a business, and paying for half of his mother's memory unit care. She has early-onset dementia and he doesn't want his father to lose the family home now that he can't care for his wife any longer.'

Mandy kept her shock to herself. None of this sounded like the

Reese she knew. She must really love Amrik. And he must really love her to have falsely confessed to murder. Unless, of course, he was guilty. 'I suppose he was here a lot.'

She nodded.

'Why didn't you tell me about the relationship? I thought we'd become close.'

'Remember when I tried to set you up on a date? You were scathing. I didn't want your negativity toward men to affect me.'

Mandy blinked. 'I can accept that. Was Peony really going to move in here after graduation?'

Reese shrugged.

'Let me get the timeline straight,' Mandy said. 'On Tuesday night, Amrik proposed.'

'Right.'

'On Wednesday, you went to see him at work, and Coral gave you a bad massage. Then you had the baby shower and Coral was killed just as it was ending.'

'Yes, but I told Coral I was serious about wanting a tenant just before the massage and she was going to tell Peony to confirm the details with me. They had been over to see the space already.'

'I see.' Mandy reflected. 'She must have texted Peony from work.'

'Must have,' Reese agreed.

'Then, on Thursday, Houston showed up at my house and you didn't want to rent to him.'

'No, I'd rather have a female tenant.'

'To be clear, had you heard from Peony?'

'Yes, that evening,' Reese confirmed.

'What evening?'

'Wednesday.'

Linda cocked her head. 'Before or after her sister died?'

Reese lifted a hand. 'Probably after, but I don't know. I didn't know what had happened. I think I saw the text when I arrived home, but I don't know when she sent it. It wasn't our first conversation on the subject. I was so busy with the party that I didn't check.'

'We could check now,' Linda suggested. 'It might give the police a timeline, like when Coral was still communicating with people.

If they know when Peony texted you, that's right after when Coral probably texted her.'

'My phone was dead when the police returned it,' Reese explained. 'It's on the charger. We can check later. I don't think it will help.'

'Probably not. They probably have Coral's phone records, and I'm sure they can track most of her last movements by security camera,' Mandy said. 'You're absolutely sure Amrik is innocent? No affair with Coral or anything?'

'He's a religious man,' Reese said. 'Coral was married and Christian. Not his type.'

'Where was he when she died?'

Reese poked at her brownie. 'Doing paperwork alone.'

'Has he been charged with Coral's murder?' Mandy asked.

'I called my lawyer after I was released and asked him to represent Amrik. I haven't heard.'

'What a mess.' Linda crammed a brownie into her mouth and chewed.

Mandy still felt nauseous. Thinking of not eating reminded her. 'Did you pick up the dishes on the back porch?' she asked. 'I've been feeding your cat.'

'I wondered who was taking care of Amrita,' Reese said. 'I'll clean it up tomorrow.'

'I'll do it.' Mandy rose. 'You don't want to attract strays but I didn't have keys.'

'My parents have them. I'm so glad they have not yet returned.'

'But they couldn't bail you out either,' Linda said around the brownie.

'I don't know if they would have done so,' Reese said. 'They are quite angry about my choice of husband.'

'Are you still going to marry him?' Mandy asked.

Reese licked her dry-looking lips. 'I did move much too fast,' she admitted. 'But confessing to murder for me is very romantic.'

'Unless he really did it,' Linda said flatly.

After all the drama of the night before, Mandy really needed her meditation class on Tuesday evening. She'd dutifully risen five minutes early that morning and stood in tadasana position, holding her hands in the prana mudra, which had alleviated a small amount of back pain, but all in all she felt as if she'd been five minutes behind all day, instead of five minutes ahead.

Darci had yet to follow up with her about her mysterious Bodhi Lee warning, which also had her on edge. She was still going to class, though.

'What are you going to do until class?' Houston asked. He had to work until six, but she had two and half hours between her shift and meditation, and no need to go to the jail after all.

Without customers, they were both hovering in the doorway into the back room. 'First I need to figure out what symbol I'm bringing. What did you choose?'

'I tried to be smart about it.' He pulled his wallet out of his back pocket and unfolded a piece of paper.

'Sanskrit, right?' When he nodded, she asked, 'What does it mean?'

'It's *abhaya*, meaning fearlessness.' He folded it up again and put it away. 'I looked up the mudra and it's easy, not like the one that he gave you.'

'Yeah, prana hurts. But I figure it's a good hand stretch.'

He lifted his right hand to shoulder height and held his hand palm up. 'That's all I have to do.'

'Cheater,' Mandy said with a laugh.

'What about you? You still need to bring a symbol.'

'I know.' As she said the words, an image flashed into her mind. A bullseye. 'Hang on.' She ran into the back and clocked out, then grabbed Coral's copy of Bodhi's book. By the time she found the right page, Houston was directing a couple of customers to the coffee urns. A calm voice came over the public announcement system, announcing a code.

When everything was settled again, she showed Houston the page in the book.

'Chakras are the windows to your soul. Each chakra is like a bullseye, telling a practitioner, "This is where your client's body is out of balance!"' he read.

She nodded grimly. 'I'm bringing a bullseye.' She grabbed a napkin and a black sharpie from under the counter and drew Coral's tattoo from memory. 'There you go. We'll see what he does with this.'

'Yeah,' Houston said.

'I'll see you upstairs,' Mandy said. 'I'm going to sit in the cafeteria and tackle my bunny and tea stickers for my May planner kit.'

Houston snorted. 'Now, that's a side hustle.'

Mandy shrugged. 'I should have finished two weeks ago, but life has been insane. I have my iPad Pro with me and I won't be distracted at the back tables.'

'Not on your beloved sofas?'

Mandy shook her head. 'Too much traffic down here today. I think the massage business customers sit on them while they're waiting. With Amrik being held for questioning, who knows if anyone is operating his business?'

'If I were them, I'd only take cash,' Houston said. 'Otherwise they might not ever get paid.'

'Amrik will have to be released tomorrow unless they charge him,' Mandy pointed out. 'His business should survive another day.'

'You don't think he's guilty?'

'Why would Coral's boss kill her? Now that I know Amrik had a girlfriend, I really doubt he was having an affair with Coral.' She thought about that. 'Who was lying about the domestic violence? Coral or Amrik or Darci?'

'You don't think a guy could have two girlfriends?'

Mandy thought about her ex's infidelity. 'I'm not that naive, but he was freshly in love with Reese. It doesn't seem likely, not in that phase of a relationship.'

'It all depends on what kind of guy he is,' Houston said.

She'd heard horror stories about narcissists and love bombers. Anything was possible. Including that Amrik really was a murderer. If so, was it for some reason to do with an affair with Coral or something else? 'You're right, but I need to get to sticker designing. See you later.' She went into the back and grabbed her bag out of her cubby. Knowing she'd be hungry soon, she made herself a smoothie at the blender station, then dumped the containers in the sink on the way out for Houston to clean.

'Hey,' he protested.

'Wouldn't want you to be bored.' She trotted to the elevator and found her favorite spot by the windows in the fairly empty cafeteria.

After a sip of her chocolate banana smoothie, she pulled out her planner. She reminded herself of their color scheme for May and took photos of her pages. They had managed to ink and film the spreads for their 'Plan with Me' video and she needed to finish the edits, though it wouldn't be completely done until she had the stickers ready and printed, so she could close the video with a fanned-out photo of their products.

After that, she loaded each photo into Procreate and captured the colors with the software so that she could use it to make the stickers. She used her art as the first layer, then began to turn it into her stickers, slurping at her smoothie to keep herself going.

This way, her personal planner was largely full of original art, which she preferred, and her customers could either watch her videos and paint along, or use her stickers to recreate her monthly spreads.

When her phone alarm went off at five fifty, she sat back, blinking. How had she managed to immerse herself for two hours? Her back ached despite the padded seat of the cafeteria booth, and her smoothie was long gone.

Still, she looked over her work with satisfaction. She'd completed a page containing four artistic designs for her customers' planning pages, each one with a blue or gray baby bunny in a colorful teacup and space for writing or stickers, then easily built up her standard second sheet of word stickers in the color scheme for May. Finally, she'd partially finished a sticker page featuring bunnies and teacups. She'd sell that page alone or in the monthly sticker set, imagining that women would also buy that page specifically for the special little girls in their lives.

Dashing into the conference room with only a minute to spare, she discovered the room only three-quarters full. Bodhi was up front, fiddling with a projector. Jason waved at her from the otherwise empty front row and she went to sit next to him.

'How did it go this morning?' Jason asked.

'My hands don't like prana mudra but I bet it's actually a great flexibility stretch.' She bent her neck from side to side and heard crunching sounds in both directions.

Jason winced.

She checked her phone one last time to see if Darci had responded to her texts trying to learn more about Bodhi, but her screen remained irritatingly empty. Then she heard running feet and saw Houston panting in the doorway. He saw her and dropped into the next seat.

'I wish this class didn't start until six thirty,' he wheezed.

'I'm amazed you got here this fast.'

'I sprinted up the steps and almost tripped.' He tapped his straight nose with the flat of his hand.

A few more people appeared just after Houston. When Mandy glanced around the room, it looked as full as the night before. Their teacher seemed to sense that and turned around, his dramatic dark eyes scanning the crowd. One of the cardiac nurses giggled.

'I hope you did your homework,' he said in a singsong voice.

A chorus of 'yeses' and a few 'oopses' filled the room. Mandy pulled out her napkin and set it, bullseye down, on her lap. She wanted to make sure he saw it clearly, so she could catch his reaction.

'Very well. On your feet.'

He had them do a few stretches, then sat them down again for another half-hour meditation. Mandy attempted to relax, which she needed, while simultaneously filing away the sequence of the meditation so that she could lead herself through it. Some sort of distant chime-laden music played, adding to the soporific effect.

'When you are ready, open your eyes,' he said at the end. 'Your vision may be blurry for a minute or two. That is normal.'

When Mandy opened her eyes, Houston was yawning next to her. Jason slumped in his chair, but he smiled when she glanced at him.

'Better than a chair massage,' he whispered.

'Massage is also good,' Bodhi said, overhearing Jason. 'But it has a different purpose.' He rubbed his hands together. 'Please pass your symbols up to the front so we can discuss them.'

Jason handed a piece of paper to her. Without looking at it, Mandy sent that and her own sheet over to Houston. He jumped to his feet and collected all the papers, then took them to Bodhi. He turned to the projector, then slapped down the first page.

Mandy held back a smile at the sight of the rainbow glitter peace sign.

'This is fine for meditation,' Bodhi said. 'I will teach you a mudra for it.' He had the class contort their fingers into position, then he set the sheet on the side of the table. 'You can collect it at the end of class.'

He spun through five Sanskrit words, offering mudras and even a couple of phrases, making sure they had the pronunciation correct. Then he paused to suggest an evening meditation routine they could all do, and passed out papers detailing the steps.

Mandy was excited to receive hers; it was exactly what she'd been hoping for. All she needed was to find a good selection of meditation music and she'd be set.

Bodhi patiently went through the other symbols offered. His forehead creased when he put a middle school softball team logo on the projector, but other than that he seemed pleased. Then he flipped past Houston's, noting that he'd already discussed that one, and, finally, the bullseye popped up on the screen.

'Ah, someone has been reading my books,' he said approvingly.

'What book is it from?' one of the nurses called.

'Please review any of my chakra-focused titles,' he said carelessly. 'Check your local bookstore.'

'Chakras are sometimes called the seven windows to the soul,' he said after a pause to gather his thoughts. 'We can use various techniques to reclaim our personal power through these portals. In our next session we will work specifically on the lower three chakras. In our last session, we will discuss techniques for the upper chakras. Who brought this symbol?'

Mandy raised her hand.

His gaze bored into hers. 'If this symbol is personally meaningful to you, Ms Meadows, I would suggest visualizing it over each of the seven centers of energy. See past this symbol, into the eternal energetic spaces of your body.'

She couldn't read him well enough. He didn't seem amused or shocked. But she had to take the chance. 'What does it mean when one of your pupils has actually had this symbol tattooed on to their body?'

'Perhaps they have a specific chakra that troubles them in this life,' he said.

She shook her head. 'No, like all over their torso. Not just on the chakra points.'

'Why don't you stay after class, Ms Meadows?' He paused. 'Again.'

She nodded, a sudden chill sweeping her body. No sense of helpfulness radiated from him, regardless of the useful relaxation techniques he was offering. What if he was a killer?

He turned back to the projector for a discussion of Jason's symbol, which was a photo of a spiderweb. 'I like this.'

Next to her, Jason grinned.

'Our bodies are a complex web that must stay in balance,' Bodhi explained. 'No one strand should be stronger or weaker than the others. Integrity of the system must be maintained. This is a very complex symbol and you may wish to start with a focus on one chakra; perhaps meditating on this symbol tonight will show you which strand feels weaker.'

He launched into a discussion of how they would memorize his sheet of instructions in order to meditate for half an hour a day until their next session, a longer class on Saturday.

Mandy felt like yawning by the time class was dismissed. She had less than twelve hours until the start of her next shift. At least this had been a good week for Vellum to be away, leaving her more time for self-care.

'I have to run to the bathroom,' Houston said in her ear. 'But I'll meet you in the cafeteria.'

'Why?' she started to say.

Jason leaned over Mandy. 'I can order for us. Tonight's grill special is portobello mushroom blue-cheese burgers.'

Mandy's stomach rumbled against her better judgment. 'Yum,' she said. She wanted to go home and crawl into bed, but how could she turn down one of her favorite cafeteria specials?

'Gross.' Houston made a face. 'I'll just have a double order of onion rings.'

Mandy leaned down to pick up her bag, and when she glanced up, Bodhi crooked his finger at her. She was going to have to see him after class.

SIXTEEN

M andy plucked a ten-dollar bill from her bag. 'Could you order for me? I'll be there in a second.'

'No problem,' Jason said. 'See you in a minute.'

Houston gave her a hard glance as if he wanted her to do something, but she wasn't sure how to pursue the idea that Bodhi might be his father. Besides, she had other priorities to worry about.

The class cleared out behind her as she stepped on to the dais to talk to Bodhi. Even the cardiac group hadn't stayed to fawn over their guru. She heard someone say 'thunderstorm.' Blanketed under numerous floors of the hospital and in a windowless corridor, she had no idea of the weather outside.

'That's going to be a fun drive home,' she said to their instructor. 'Are you staying near here?'

'Near Pike Place Market.' He regarded her. 'A client lets me use her condominium.'

'It's nice to have wealthy clients.' Mandy's stomach gave a rumble.

He ignored her flippant comment. 'You seem very intent on the symbol you chose. Are you thinking about tattooing your chakras?'

She blinked. 'No, of course not. I saw the phrase in your book. What—'

'You are a seeker,' Bodhi interrupted. 'You remind me of someone.'

'Coral Le Charme?' Mandy offered boldly. 'I saw her bullseye tattoos.'

He raised his brows.

'Her sister-in-law gave me Coral's copy of your book.'

'She was a dedicated student of mine, but I had not seen her in some time.' He walked around the table and leaned on it, inches from her face.

'Before she died, you mean? You didn't see her here in Seattle?'

'No. I saw her in Anchorage and Kodiak. Some students cross our paths for a time, then move on to their own wheel.'

'Right. Well, I heard you were in town when she died. Why didn't you come to her wake?'

'I don't know her family.'

She took a moment to process his words. He didn't know Peony or the others? She supposed it made sense. Peony might have been too young for the classes. She opened her mouth to clarify, but her voice disappeared when he took her hands in his.

She glanced down in shock and tried to pull away. 'Look—'

'You remind me of myself,' he said smoothly, still gripping her hands. 'Always questioning, always looking for answers. The view is beautiful from my temporary home. Stay with me tonight. We will eat, talk, and anything might happen.'

Her palms sparked, embers of stress fire, as his gentle expression became a leer. She remembered Darci's warning. Taking a step back, she tugged at her hands, but he moved with her, as if they were in a dance.

'I have much to teach you,' he said huskily.

'No,' she said loudly. 'Let me go. I'm not interested.'

Bodhi continued invading her personal space. She could smell the clove scent on his breath.

'Hey!' Houston trotted up to them.

Mandy glanced in his direction and saw irritation tightening her co-worker's face.

'No means no,' Houston spat. 'Leave her alone.'

'Let the adults talk.' Bodhi barely glanced in Houston's direction before refocusing on Mandy. 'Now, where were we? You were agreeing to my suggestion?'

She stared directly into his eyes, refusing to be intimidated by his show of strength. 'You were letting me go so I can have dinner with my co-workers.'

His face remained impassive. He squeezed her hands, a masculine display of intimidation that hurt a little, then let go.

She stepped back, feeling her hands shake. Houston put his arm around her waist and rotated her off the dais and out of the room. They walked quickly.

'Oh my God,' Mandy said, disentangling from Houston's arm as calmly as she could. 'I wasn't sure he was going to let me go.'

'You used your best don't-mess-with-me voice,' Houston said, walking down the hall. 'What a jerk.'

'I thought when women weren't interested in dating, they had a natural wall up, you know? If you don't put yourself out there, you should be invisible.' She gave a shaky laugh and followed him. 'But it doesn't seem to be working in my case.'

'Men like a challenge,' Houston said. He stopped at the mouth of the cafeteria and turned to her. 'You're a catch. You have a great house, a great life, a great daughter. I just wanted to be a part of it and I'm way too young for you.'

She was taken aback by the notion that he had interest in her rather than in Vellum. 'That's quite a speech.' And not the right time for it.

'I thought it would be easier to move down here.' His mouth worked. 'You know . . . I'd make new friends. But here I am, working with women, stuck behind a counter all day. It isn't, well—'

'The right scene for you,' Mandy said. 'It's OK to admit that. I'm going to look for a new job myself in a few months. Why don't you sit in the back on Saturday? Make friends with the cardiac group?'

He shook his head. 'I'm not going again.'

Mandy leaned toward his ear. 'What about the reason you signed up in the first place?'

He shrugged. 'What are the chances that he's my father, anyway? Besides, he seems like a jerk. Maybe I don't want to know.'

Had he signed up for the classes simply to spend time with her? Mandy didn't know how she felt about that. 'I wish he had just invited me to dinner in a public place. I could have dug into his autobiography, found out where he was and when.'

'If he has anything to hide, he wouldn't tell you,' Houston said.

Jason poked his head into the hallway. 'Guys, our food is up.'

Mandy smiled. 'Thanks. We're coming.' Her phone beeped but she ignored it until she sat down.

At her little murmur of happiness, Jason asked, 'What's up?'

Mandy pointed to her phone screen. 'Reese O'Leary-Sett talked to her boss at the podiatry office today. They want her back to work tomorrow. I think it will be good for her to go back to her routine, exhausted though I'm sure she is.'

'What about her boyfriend?' Jason asked.

She guessed, given his job, that Jason knew everything she did. 'I haven't heard and I don't want to ruin her good news by asking.'

She sent some happy emojis, then a message to get to sleep early tonight.

'Fair enough. But the hospital will have to shut down the chair massage business after this week if he doesn't return to work. There's no manager appointed and the therapist schedule was only posted through Friday.'

'None of them know what to do?'

'Right. And where are their paychecks coming from?'

A lightbulb went off. 'Amrik has a sister.'

Jason clasped his hands in prayer position under his chin. 'Can you get her number? My backup contact information for him has turned out to be one of the therapists, so it's worthless.'

'I'll text Darci DeRoy and see if she has contact info for Nandini.' Mandy's fingers flew over the keys again.

By the time she had finished her burger and her fingers were coated in gooey blue-cheese sauce, her phone buzzed again. She wiped off her fingers, seeing the message was from Darci. *Finally.* But Darci didn't have the information, and when Mandy followed up with yet another question about Bodhi, Darci simply texted a vomit emoji. 'No luck. I'll have to go through Reese.'

'That's too bad.'

Mandy shrugged. 'I doubt she wants her boyfriend's business to collapse.'

'Why not?' Houston asked. 'His actions caused her to be stuck in jail for a week.'

'We don't know that,' Mandy cautioned. 'We don't know anything.' She texted Reese.

Mandy collapsed on to her bed as soon as she arrived home, but she couldn't get the incident with Bodhi out of her head, so she texted with Reese until her eyes grew weary. Reese had given her Nandini's contact information to pass on, then insisted on Amrik's innocence and sent increasingly unhinged theories of Coral's murder, such as Bodhi attacking her during an attempted rape, to one of her fellow massage therapists killing her in a fit of jealousy, to some unnamed serial killer on the loose, until Mandy texted, *I don't know what to think, but I have to get to sleep. XOXO.*

She turned off her bedside lamp and rolled over, falling asleep instantly. Uneasy dreams of hands in various mudra positions grabbing at her filled her mind, so her sleep was not restful, despite the seven hours she technically slept.

She was holding back a yawn at the coffee bar late the next morning when Houston stiffened. Mandy followed his gaze and saw a beautiful young woman in a lilac sweater dress approach. Nandini Kurmi must keep an entire wardrobe in her signature color.

'That's Amrik's sister,' she whispered.

Houston smiled brightly at Nandini.

'Hi, Nandini. How are you?' Mandy said.

She gave Mandy a sad smile, ignoring Houston. 'It is not a good time.'

'I'm so sorry. Can I get you something to drink?'

Nandini glanced at the hand-lettered list of syrup flavors. 'An oat milk latte, please, with rose syrup?'

'Of course. What size?'

Mandy rang up the order. Houston drifted past her to make the drink.

'Were you able to do anything about the massage business?'

'I'm going to make the schedule for next week right now. We are waiting to see if Amrik is going to be charged or will be released, but it is best not to wait.'

'Administration is impatient,' Mandy agreed.

'Yes, and Amrik has competitors. They could easily replace his business.'

'What do you do? I don't think I heard when I met you.'

'I'm in law school.' She handed Mandy a five-dollar bill.

'Oh, good, so you can help him.'

'I have yet to finish the second year,' Nandini said. 'I'm on my way back to school after this. I hope we'll see Amrik home by tomorrow.'

'I hope so, too. I'm glad he did the right thing to get Reese released. I never expected him to confess.'

'He is too gallant,' Nandini said carefully.

Mandy handed over the drink and watched until Nandini was out of sight.

'Law student, huh,' Houston said.

'She's very quiet. I didn't really learn anything about her when we first met.'

'What are you thinking?'

'Right now, I can't get Bodhi out of my mind. Yesterday was intense. I don't know if it was a big deal or not.'

'I had to rescue you,' he pointed out.

'Did you?' She nudged him. 'It was effective, yes, but would he have let me go if you hadn't walked in? That's what I don't know.'

'I'm glad you didn't have to find out.' Houston smiled at some of their regular customers approaching.

When Fannah gave Mandy her break, she grabbed her phone and went into the prep room, shutting the door. Leaning against the wall, she dialed Zac Turner's number, meaning to leave a message.

Instead, he picked up. 'Turner.'

'It's Mandy Meadows.'

'Well, hello, gorgeous, I should have recognized your number. What's happening?'

She flushed at his greeting. 'Hi back. I just saw Amrik Kurmi's sister a few minutes ago. She's hoping he'll be released soon.'

'I expect he will be. Word around the station is it was a false confession.'

'Does he have an alibi?'

'It's more about him not knowing the exact details of the crime he claims to have committed.'

'Oh. I'm wondering if Bodhi Lee had a reason to kill Coral?'

'Why do you ask?'

'He came on to me pretty forcefully last night. He made me uncomfortable. And we know he used to know Coral and was in town the night she was killed. He says he didn't see her, but I wondered.'

'Right. I'd say maybe there's a reason.'

'Really?' Mandy exclaimed. 'What do you know?'

'I've heard some of the family stories.'

'How did you manage that?'

'Here's the thing. I've been seeing Darci.' He paused. 'Before this murder ever happened. That's why I was hired.'

She grimaced. While she wasn't interested in him, she was irritated that he'd asked her on a fake date. And talked in a flirtatious manner. 'I had no idea you were Darci's boyfriend.' Was the baby his? She was afraid to ask in case it wasn't.

'We've been dating for a couple of months. It's cool. Anyway, Darci told me about the Bodhi Lee situation and you've been really helpful there. He and Coral obviously had an intense relationship in the past.'

'Yeah, those tattoos.' Mandy turned to face the wall and started doing foot stretches.

'Right. Plenty to do. Any word from your pet cop?'

'No,' Mandy said. 'We don't talk like that.' And even if Justin had shared anything with her, she wouldn't tell Zac. She didn't trust him now. Too deceptive.

She quickly got him off the phone, then stood in tadasana, her fingers automatically going into her mudra, to finish stretching before she went out to the counter. While she found his knowledge useful, the one thing she was certain about was not to allow herself to be alone with Bodhi again.

Late that night, she was awakened by a buzzing from her phone. She rubbed her eyes and picked it up, then sat straight up in bed after she read a text message.

'Thank goodness,' she muttered. Amrik hadn't been charged. Then another message popped up. Reese had picked him up and was taking him home with her.

Mandy flopped back on her bed. What if Amrik really had killed Coral and the police were simply waiting for more evidence to come in before charging him? Was Reese safe?

She texted back, inviting both Reese and Amrik to dinner the next day so that Reese didn't have to worry about a meal after work.

When Reese accepted, she changed her alarm. She would get up earlier and dig out her bread machine so it could bake a fresh loaf while she was at work.

Thursday was a flurry of a full work day, a trip to the grocery store, then cooking dinner for her guests. She made a quick lentil soup and then mixed cucumber and spices into plain yogurt. With no idea what Amrik liked, she thought to stick to Indian flavors.

Dinner was awkward and quiet, especially when Justin stuck his head into the dining room and saw who her guests were. He ducked right out again, without a nod at anyone. Amrik was exquisitely uncomfortable after that, though he thanked Mandy over and over again for her kindness in helping him save his business.

Reese looked as if she'd dropped ten pounds. Her clavicle jutted from the scoop neck of her black dress. She said little, beyond telling Mandy her parents were coming home soon and that the wedding would be small.

Before they left, Mandy pushed through her discomfort. 'Amrik, did you tell me the truth about Coral's husband abusing her?'

He swallowed. 'I didn't want you to know that I hired her because of Reese. She'd asked me to keep our relationship a secret.'

'So as far as you know, Tom never hurt her?'

He shrugged. 'She wasn't happy, but I never saw a mark on her.'

Reese smiled at him and rubbed his arm.

Mandy shut the door with relief when they left. Amrik seemed far too dejected to be a killer. She'd kept reassuring him throughout the evening. Reese clearly didn't believe he was the killer, given that she'd mentioned their upcoming nuptials. Neither did Zac Turner.

With her restless sleep the previous night, Mandy fell into bed as soon as she'd cleaned the kitchen, her hair still smelling faintly of soup. Her confused brain whirred with nonsensical dreams, but she slept on.

The next night, Mandy kept busy in the kitchen after processing a bunch of sticker orders. Vellum would be home soon and she would appreciate banana bread with chocolate chips and a fresh pot of potato soup. Olivia was dropping her off after camp.

Justin came into the kitchen from the hall. 'Is the coast clear?'

'No dinner party, no kid yet.'

He shoved his hands into the pockets of his jeans. His shirt hung forward, making it clear how lean and muscled his torso was. 'I didn't think Reese would want me hanging around.'

Mandy turned away and stirred the soup, then added a touch more pepper. 'I don't know how she feels, other than she's too tired to raise a fuss about anything.'

'How do you feel?' he queried.

'I won't be happy until we have the real killer arrested.'

'Understandable.' Justin rubbed the top of one bare foot against the back of his jeans.

Mandy wished he'd be less sexy around her. 'You know I was right about Reese.'

'Are we going to play the I-told-you-so game?' Justin countered. 'SPD follows the facts, not emotion.'

'I know that.' Mandy dipped her spoon into her soup and pulled out a teaspoonful, then held it to Justin's lips. 'What's your best fact now?'

He blew on it gently, holding her gaze, then cleared the spoon. 'Needs salt. The person who killed Coral Le Charme had access to Reese's house.'

'Right.' Mandy's phone rang. She handed him the pink Himalayan salt shaker as she glanced at the screen. 'It's the forge.'

'This ought to be good.' Justin shook some salt into the soup.

She connected the call. 'This is Mandy.'

Justin leaned against the refrigerator and crossed his arms, a cynical expression on his face.

'Hi, Mandy, I don't know if you're aware that tomorrow's class at the forge will teach you how to put a handle on that blade you made.'

'Darci told me,' she said, recognizing Rod Portilla's voice.

'I didn't see you on the roster. How about I add your name? I'll take you to dinner after. I feel like we haven't had a chance to get to know each other yet.'

Mandy closed her eyes for a second. 'No, sorry, I'm too busy with my business this weekend.'

'Your blade isn't much good without that handle,' he wheedled.

'I'll live,' Mandy said. 'Look, Rod, you guys aren't going to turn me into a bladesmith. I already have a demanding side hustle.'

'It's your loss, Mandy,' he said with a new edge of irritation in his voice.

'I know, Rod. Have a great evening.' She disconnected before he could come up with another approach.

When she glanced up, Justin gave her a long, hard stare.

'Trust me, I never encouraged that guy. I'm sure he's a suspect.'

He set down the salt shaker. 'Then why is he calling?'

'I guess they are desperate to drum up business,' Mandy insisted. 'Speaking of pushy men, Bodhi Lee hit on me on Tuesday night.

I wasn't sure he was going to let go of me, but Houston came to my rescue.'

Justin put his hands on his hips. 'Do you want me to teach you some self-defense moves?'

'I know how to break a grip, or I could have stepped on his foot or something like that, but I was paralyzed by the idea that he might be a murderer.' Her collar tickled her ear and she realized she was canting her head at a strange angle. Straightening, she asked, 'Is he dangerous?'

'I haven't interviewed him, but if he makes you uncomfortable, you should listen to your instincts. Don't go to the classes anymore.'

'He's a good teacher; that's the frustrating thing.'

'I'm sure there are lots of good teachers of whatever he's peddling.'

Mandy's ears picked up sounds behind the house. 'That will be Vellum.' Her timer went off. 'Perfect.' She grabbed an oven mitt and pulled her bread out of the oven.

'I was wondering what smelled so good,' Justin said.

'Chocolate and the world's most perfect quick bread flavor,' Mandy said.

Voices floated from the yard. Mandy forced herself to walk to the back door, rather than run. She had to get used to her daughter being older, having a life that took her away for long periods, but after almost losing her to her former mother-in-law in February, she'd gone back to clinging.

She flung open the back door. 'Need help?'

'The zipper broke on my duffel bag,' Vellum called, muffled by the fabric in front of her face.

Mandy laughed and went down the back stairs, then helped Vellum and Kate gather up armfuls of belongings that had spilled on to the damp grass. 'Was this a week of camp or half a year on tour?'

'My backpack is full of art. Everything else got shoved in here.' Vellum pointed to the broken zipper. 'I'm so glad I'm home.'

Mandy attempted to hug her around the armful of clothing.

'Can I help?' Justin called from the porch.

'Your feet are bare,' Mandy called. She ran up the steps and thrust an armful of clothes at him. 'Here, take these straight to the washer. I can smell the campfire on them.'

Her phone buzzed as she reached the backyard again. Ignoring it, she scooped up the last of the spilled items and told Vellum's friend to say hi to her mother. By the time they had all the clothes dropped on the floor by the washer, Mandy's phone buzzed again.

'Does Linda have brownies ready for me?' Vellum joked.

'No, she's with George tonight.' Mandy pulled out her phone, then blinked after reading the message.

Dr Burrell had texted to see if she'd like to go to the Arboretum the next day.

She threw her arms up in the air.

'What, Mom?'

'I've been asked out twice tonight.'

Justin snorted.

She fixed him with a glare. 'It *is* Friday night and I *am* single.'

'And just because you aren't interested doesn't mean they can't ask,' Justin said, singsong. 'Maybe you should stop giving out your phone number.'

'I never gave it to Rod.' She quickly texted back to Dr Burrell, explaining she had plans with Vellum and suggesting another weekend instead.

Vellum glanced between the two of them, amused. 'Maybe I shouldn't have left the two of you alone all week.'

Justin forced a smile. 'I need to make a call. Nice to see you home safe and sound.' He walked past them into his sitting room and shut the door.

Mandy shrugged. 'I don't know what to say.'

'Did you hook up?'

'No.' She lowered her voice to a whisper. 'But I think that one kiss might actually have meant something to him. And he's still irritated by my reaction. Don't tell him I told you about it, OK?'

'Don't give in. If you have a relationship with him and it doesn't work out, he'll move,' Vellum warned. 'Then we're back to where we were two months ago.'

'That's why I'm not going to play that game,' Mandy said. 'Even if I wanted to.' Which she didn't. She didn't think she did. Did she?

SEVENTEEN

'**A**re you ready to start the livestream?' Mandy asked Vellum on Saturday morning, after she brewed her second cup of coffee.

'It feels strange to do this today.' Vellum set her juice glass in the sink.

'We've got brunch with your grandmother tomorrow. Besides, it's good to switch it up. That survey I did showed that only sixty percent of our Mandy's Plan audience could be online on Sunday mornings.'

Vellum yawned. 'Fingernails ready? Mine are still wet.'

Mandy inspected her daughter's dark purple nails. 'Cute but the wrong season.' She displayed her baby-blue nails.

'Should I change them?' Vellum asked.

'Nah, not for a livestream. Let's go.'

Mandy and Vellum set up their table in the art studio. Mandy cradled her phone to film over their planners while Vellum grabbed stickers.

'Let's use the garden stakes,' Vellum suggested.

'I'll follow your lead. You want to focus on a school layout and then I'll talk about how to make it work for me?'

'Perfect,' Vellum said.

'OK. Filming in three, two, one.' Mandy turned on the live part of a popular social media app on her tablet and hit the button to start their feed.

'Hi, everyone!' Vellum said as they drummed their fingers on the table by their planners. 'I've been on spring break and it's time to buckle down again. Mom's going to let me take the lead on our weekly set-up with these cute stickers. I'm going to be stuck inside studying all week, but at least these garden drawings will bring spring into my life.'

'You bet,' Mandy said. 'Besides, we live in Seattle. It's just going to rain all week, anyway.'

'And it's going to take a few days for the moss to stop growing between my toes after my week at art camp.'

'Vellum did some adorable pieces there,' Mandy enthused. 'I can't wait to see how we incorporate some of her animal paintings into our planners in the future.'

'But first . . . bunnies are coming,' Vellum said. 'Did you get the sticker set finished, Mom?'

'Oh, yes. Lots of free time while you were gone. I'll show them to you after the livestream and maybe we'll get them uploaded sooner rather than later!'

They kept the banter going for forty-five minutes, answering questions typed in by viewers, and completing two-page weekly spreads for the next week, full of botanical drawings of local garden flowers. That part went very quickly, so Mandy chatted about her meditation class and sketched her assigned yoga pose and mudra on another sheet. Some of their watchers were very enthusiastic and posted supportive messages.

'I have to go to class in half an hour,' Mandy told Vellum after they ended the livestream.

'Can I go?' Vellum asked. 'I do have a kink in my neck after sleeping on that worn-out camp bunk all week.'

'I suppose, but this is mediation, not yoga.' Mandy paused at Vellum's look of confusion. 'I know I was talking about the pose, but it's all integrated.'

'I should call Dad first.'

'Do that and then we can go,' Mandy suggested.

Vellum called Cory while Mandy cleaned up.

Mandy ignored the call deliberately, but her attention focused when Vellum exclaimed, 'Still in the hospital?'

Mandy patted her daughter's shoulder as she said, 'Should I visit Grandpa?'

Vellum listened, then leaned against Mandy, her face taut with frustration. 'Mom could drop me off. She's going over to USea anyway and that's only a couple of blocks away.'

Mandy tried to hear Cory's response, but Vellum held her phone too tightly to her ear to let sound escape. 'OK, Dad, but I'm happy to sit with Grandpa.'

She ended the call, her mouth tight. 'Why does he always push me away, Mom?'

Mandy wrapped her daughter in her arms and remembered how Cory had hit on her. 'He's focused on the wrong things. His priorities are all wrong.'

'He doesn't control access to Grandpa.'

'No, but it's possible that your grandfather doesn't want you to see him like this.' She released the hug.

'The men in this family all suck.' Vellum shoved her phone into her pocket.

'Maybe you *should* go to the class with me. I know there's at least one empty chair today. Houston is dropping out. I think we both need the stress relief.'

'I agree,' Vellum said.

'I don't like the teacher,' Mandy warned, 'so stay away from him, but the meditation portion of the class is great.'

Mandy's phone buzzed as soon as she and Vellum took their seats in the back row of the class, clad in stretchy yoga pants and cotton sweaters. Eager students had filled half of the room already. Instruction would start at noon, so to stave off hunger they'd both devoured protein bars on the way. She glanced down to see a text from Houston.

Did you make it to class? it read.

Yes. Hasn't started yet, she texted back. *Did you decide to come?*

He sent back a thumb's down emoji.

'Hello,' Jason said, appearing at Mandy's side.

Mandy smiled at him. 'Hey, Jason, this is my daughter, Vellum.'

He nodded at her and reached over Mandy to fist bump Vellum. 'Hi.'

Mandy nudged Vellum. They both got up and moved over a seat so Jason could sit next to her. Bodhi Lee arrived at the door, trailed by the cardiac gang.

He went to his table. Mandy had explained his history with Coral to Vellum during the drive. She gazed at him, clearly curious.

Bodhi had kept his back to the group, apparently to shut out his groupies. With a theatrical flourish, he turned around and hit a button on the console to lower the room lights. 'With a soft gaze facing forward, take a deep breath through your nose and release it through your mouth.'

Mandy followed the opening part of the meditation. After Bodhi told them to close their eyes, his chime-accented music began to tinkle in the front of the room. The meditation went on much too long, with long pauses of blank space filled only by the chimes. When they were finally told to open their eyes again, Mandy saw an hour had passed.

'I know my limit,' Mandy whispered to a glazed-over Vellum. 'Half an hour of that is perfect. Not an hour.'

Bodhi told them to stand and took them through a series of stretches to realign their bodies. Then they all had to confess if they'd been doing the mudras and yoga poses they'd been assigned.

Mandy had done her homework, and Bodhi didn't ask where Houston was or comment on Vellum's taking his spot. He seemed bored today.

Without giving them a break, he launched into an overview of the chakras, expanding on what he'd taught them before. After a ten-minute break, he went into even more detail, but Mandy recognized all of the information from his book. She was disappointed by the lack of new material, though Jason took notes from time to time on his phone.

She hoped Bodhi would call for questions at the end, because she wanted to ask him for more meditation tips, since, after all, that was the point of the seminars, not how chakras fit into medicine, but he abruptly ended the class after three hours.

One of the cardiac gang raised their hand and spoke. 'What is our homework this time?'

Bodhi stared down at his papers, spread out on his desk. 'Meditate for an hour a day, focusing on opening your weakest chakra.'

'How do we know which one is the weakest?' the woman asked.

Justin raised his hand. 'Can you meet with us individually for a brief consultation? Maybe we can wait in here, and you can go into the hall and speak to each of us privately in turn?'

'As you wish.' Bodhi glided out of the room, followed by the women at the end of the first row. The rest of the cardiac gang went to the glass wall of the room and stared at Bodhi and his first student.

Vellum stood up and bent her neck from side to side. 'If this was supposed to be a meditation class, that guy is a charlatan. He didn't teach anything you couldn't learn online.'

'A lot of people still need the live instruction,' Mandy said defensively. 'We all have different learning styles.'

'I guess,' Vellum groused. 'He's actually written books?'

Jason pointed to the desk. 'He has a few of them up there.'

'I think he was just reading from them, or has them memorized,' Vellum said. 'That was so boring.'

Mandy realized a fair number of the original attendees had not shown up today when Vellum made her way to the front of the room so easily. A quarter of the seats were empty.

Jason followed her gaze. 'Lots of people have to get their kids to activities on Saturdays.'

'True,' Mandy said. 'But he didn't do his best work today. I expected more from him.'

'It seemed shallower,' Jason agreed. 'Or maybe not. Maybe just too esoteric. The meditation practice was much more interesting than the chakra material. He didn't talk about them to this extent in the executive training.'

Mandy followed Vellum to the desk. She had one of Bodhi's books open, not the one that Mandy had. This book was indeed a scholarly-looking text on chakras. She didn't doubt his knowledge, just his character. At the far end of the room, the door opened and closed to let two of the students switch in and out of the consultation.

Mandy wandered behind the desk, wondering what was written on all those sheets of paper. With her elbow, she knocked one of the books on its side and scattered a stack. When she bent to pick it up, she saw the official-looking font at the top.

'What?' She frowned.

Vellum glanced up and Jason walked around the desk. 'What is it?'

'It's a birth certificate.' Mandy held it up, her heart starting to pound when the name crossed her vision. Something was very wrong here.

'For Peony Le Charme,' Jason read. 'Who is that?'

'Coral's younger sister.' Mandy checked the dates. 'You know, the murder victim? Yep, this is Peony's. I already knew how old she was.'

Vellum leaned over. 'I thought you said this person was Coral's sister.' She pointed to the mother's name.

Mandy stared. 'Wait. What?'

Jason pointed, too. 'Mother's name is Coral Le Charme. Father's name is blank.'

Mandy's eyes went wide. 'Maybe Coral had the same name as her mother?'

'Why would the teacher have this?' Vellum asked.

Exactly her thought. 'Coral was his student back in Alaska. No one has ever denied that.'

'Does he hold on to all his disciples' personal papers or something?' Vellum asked. 'Like a cult?'

'It's very odd,' Jason said. 'It shouldn't have been brought here, whatever the reason for him having it.'

'I've got such a bad feeling about him,' Mandy said. She scooped up the rest of the papers she'd spilled and pulled out her phone to take a quick picture of the birth certificate. 'What if he's stealing identities or something like that?'

'She's a minor,' Vellum pointed out. 'I think we should get out of here, Mom, and talk to Justin.'

The door opened and shut again, more students moving in and out. Mandy quickly flipped through the rest of the papers, aided by Jason, but everything else appeared to be photocopies of pages of Bodhi's books. She sent her photo of the birth certificate to Justin and asked why Bodhi would have this, then tucked her phone away as the last of the students went into the hall.

'Do you want your consultation?' Jason asked.

'Of course not,' Mandy said. She already felt unsafe, and Bodhi Lee had just become her chief suspect in Coral's murder. Bringing Vellum here had been a terrible idea.

'There's only one door out of here,' he remarked.

'After last time, he won't be surprised if I don't want to speak to him privately, or allow Vellum to,' Mandy pointed out. 'If he even recognizes he was being inappropriate, that is.'

'We'll go out together. You two can be on your way while I have my consultation,' Jason said. 'Do you really need to speak to the police?'

'As far as I'm concerned, Bodhi is a murder suspect. They've released Reese and Amrik. I'd like to know who Seattle PD's primary suspect is.'

Vellum sighed. 'Let them do their job, Mom. Reese is free and that's all you care about, right?'

'I know you're tired, honey, but this man has a teenage girl's birth certificate in his possession. As a mother, I can't ignore that, particularly when her sister was just murdered. I'm going to drop you off home and go see her brother-in-law.'

'At the forge?'

Mandy checked her phone. 'By the time I get there, the class will be over. He needs to know what I saw before Bodhi Lee returns to Alaska.'

Mandy dropped Vellum off at home and drove north.

Only a couple of cars were parked outside the forge, which probably meant the class was over. Her class the previous weekend had ended by now. She walked into the building. No one stood in the anteroom, but the door to the forge area was open and Tom and Peony were setting tools on to the pegboards along one wall.

'Hello,' she called.

The more pleasant of her classmates from the previous weekend walked past her. He smiled faintly but kept moving. Tom and Peony both spun around.

'What brings you by?' Tom asked, turning back and grabbing a tool she didn't recognize. 'I thought you had other commitments today.'

'I had a meditation class all afternoon,' she said as he set it in place. 'Prepaid. And worked my second job.'

'Got it.' He hefted a massive hammer into place between two pegs. 'What's up?'

She cleared her throat. 'The class was with Bodhi Lee.'

'With Bodhi Lee?' Peony picked up a sanding belt. 'That's odd.'

'My employer brought him in for training and I paid for a four-session series after liking the free seminar. Why do you call it odd? Darci told me that Coral had been his student.'

Tom glanced at Peony, then winced. 'Bodhi Lee is Peony's biological father.'

'Oh,' Mandy said, remembering the paper had a blank space where the father's name should have been. What did all this mean? 'Your mom had an affair?'

'Not my grandmother,' Peony corrected. 'Coral's my mom.'

Mandy's brain blanked. Bodhi said Coral had lied about her

age, but she'd never considered that she was old enough to be Peony's mother. 'You aren't really Coral's sister?'

Peony shook her head. Her hair covered her face as she hung up the belt and grabbed another.

Mandy continued gamely. 'The reason I'm here is I accidentally tipped over some papers Bodhi had in class and saw a birth certificate for you. That was concerning enough that I thought I ought to tell you and your guardian.'

She frowned. 'My birth certificate?'

Mandy nodded. 'Exactly. There was no father listed. Why would he be wandering around Seattle with your birth certificate?'

'You came to gossip?' Peony asked, her hair shifting again as she placed the belt.

'No.' Mandy wondered if Peony risked having her hair caught in machines or burned. 'I was concerned for your safety. You should tell the police. Maybe Bodhi was the person who tried to kidnap you.'

Tom sighed. 'Coral was only fourteen when she had Peony, so her parents raised Peony as their own until she became certain that Peony would be healthier with her.'

'I see.' Mandy shuffled her feet. 'I guess I'm interfering in your business, but I was so alarmed that I wanted to tell you right away. I took a picture.' She held her phone out to Tom.

'I appreciate it,' Tom said, glancing at the screen. 'Coral was afraid of Bodhi, but she never publicly stated what had happened, so Bodhi wasn't arrested for rape or anything. He just walked away from all of it.'

It didn't seem like the dead woman had entirely let go of her lover, though. 'Why did Coral have that book he wrote, the one he autographed? She must have been in touch with Bodhi again when she was older. What's the history there?'

'I didn't know about that,' Tom said. 'Must have been in the back of a closet.'

'Darci gave it to me when I told her about the class. She saw it somewhere.'

'It wasn't any of Darci's business,' Peony said. 'But yeah, why would Coral have had it?'

'I'm worried that his appearance in Seattle right before Coral died is suspicious,' Mandy suggested.

Peony walked stiffly to a metal folding chair set up by the door and sat down. She put her head in her hands.

'I'm so sorry,' Mandy said, feeling helpless. 'I wanted to warn you. I should have just called. I don't know what I was thinking.'

Tom looked equally upset. 'I don't get it. Tell me about this book.'

'Umm, I think it was published about seven years ago. The autograph wasn't dated, but if the book didn't come out until Peony was ten or so—'

'She was back in touch with Bodhi at some point,' Tom agreed. 'I wish I could be totally surprised, but I'm not. She really believed in that meditation stuff. It was still before we met.'

'That was about five years ago?'

'Not even that,' Tom said. 'But, yeah, after that book was published. I doubt she'd have told him about Peony, though. She was so protective.'

'She loved me,' Peony said. 'She thought she could fix everything she did wrong.'

'What do you mean?' Mandy asked.

Peony coughed. Tom started to go to her, but she caught up on her breathing after several breaths. 'I thought I could learn something about my health problems. You know, all those ads that companies run about testing your DNA to learn about what's hiding on your chromosomes.'

'Yeah, I've seen a ton of those,' Mandy agreed.

Tom opened another chair and sat on it, putting his hand on Peony's knee. He seemed to have forgotten Mandy, and there weren't any other chairs.

'Anyway, with a lot of those sites, they match you up to your family if you want and I didn't care about that. But I guess I clicked the wrong button when my test came back last month.'

'What does that mean?' Tom asked.

Peony slid her body around on the chair. 'A bio-dad popped up on the site for me.'

'Bodhi,' Tom guessed.

'I changed my privacy settings but it was probably too late. He'd probably already seen it, or someone had,' Peony said.

'Did he try to contact you directly?' Mandy asked.

'No. I'm not sure it was even Bodhi.' She licked her lips. 'Coral never talked about my dad and I knew she was only fourteen when she got pregnant, so obviously something was wrong with him. I deleted my account completely to avoid the guy.'

'Do you think your mom gave Bodhi your birth certificate?' Mandy asked.

'Maybe she wanted to prove she'd never asked for money,' Tom said. 'Since the father box was blank.'

'It makes sense that Coral gave it to him,' Mandy said. 'It can't be easy to get the birth certificate of a minor unless you're the guardian. Maybe he came down here from Alaska to confront her after he saw your DNA test?' She shivered. 'What if he's going to try to kill you, too?'

'Was there any blood on it?' Peony asked abruptly.

'What?' Mandy gasped.

'Maybe he stole my birth certificate from Coral after he killed her.' Peony put her fingers into her hair and twisted the strands.

'You do think he killed her?' Mandy asked. She didn't remember seeing any belongings near Coral's body. Had the certificate been in her tote bag or purse? Had the killer taken everything?

'Maybe,' Peony said carelessly.

'Did you always know Coral was your mother?' Mandy asked, confused as to why Peony kept calling Coral by her name.

'No. I started wondering when she wanted me to move here,' Peony said. 'But she wasn't motherly, really – just sisterly. I figured it out after I took the test.'

Tom stood up and paced across the concrete floor, then back again. 'I have a bad feeling that Bodhi is trying to get to Peony.'

'Someone did try to kidnap her,' Mandy agreed.

'Exactly.'

Mandy spoke her thoughts aloud. 'Why? She's almost an adult. Is there money involved?'

'About one in ten cerebral palsy cases are caused by birth injury, something you can sue for,' Peony said. 'Mine wasn't, but maybe he thinks I'm rich.'

'Oh,' Mandy said. 'Maybe he thought this property was yours?'

'Maybe,' Peony agreed. 'I mean, it is. My grandma, who was really my great-grandma, left it to me. My parents, I mean, grandparents, are hippie types but my great-grandma had money. She didn't leave them anything in her will.'

Wow. Did Rod know? They'd talked about forcing Peony to move out, after all – off her own property. 'Since Zac is Darci's boyfriend, why didn't he take all of this information to the police?' Mandy asked.

'There has been no proof of Bodhi's involvement in my wife's death until now, but Zac has been tailing him,' Tom said. 'As soon as he has any real evidence, he'll tell the police.'

'I told the SPD about the birth certificate. Maybe you should tell them about the property, too.' Were Tom's businesses at risk if Peony died or was handed off to a new guardian?

'I'm not allowed to be alone right now,' Peony volunteered. 'They make sure someone is always with me.'

'There's only one meditation class left,' Mandy said, changing the subject. 'As far as I know, Bodhi has no reason to stay in Seattle much longer.'

'When is the last class?' Tom asked.

'Monday night. It was four seminars over seven days.'

'We'll be on our guard,' Tom said. 'If he wants something, he'll have to make his move soon.'

Mandy remembered something that had bothered her all along. 'Did Coral have those tattoos when she met you?'

'The bullseyes?' Tom asked.

Mandy nodded.

'Yeah. She said she'd had them for years.'

'I've attended my last meditation class,' Mandy said. 'I think you'd better come clean to the police about Peony's family history and how Bodhi probably found out about her.'

'Did I break any laws?' Peony asked tremulously.

Mandy wanted to hug the girl. 'I don't see how, honey. I'm so sorry for what you've been through.'

Peony sniffed, tears appearing in her eyes. 'It's been horrible.'

Tom crouched down and patted her leg. 'You'll be fine. We'll keep you safe.'

He'd better, or he could lose his business on the land he'd developed.

Mandy's stomach growled as she parked her car by her back gate. She went up the stairs to her house, debating what she should have to eat. Maybe Vellum had whipped something up.

She was shocked to smell the heavenly scent of fresh chocolate chip cookies when she opened the back door. 'Have I died and gone to paradise?' she asked.

Justin turned away from the counter. He held a spatula in one hand and had a kitchen towel tucked into the front of his jeans. Vellum stood at the stove, a spoonful of dough poised above another cookie sheet.

'I'm going to have to leave you two alone more often . . .' She trailed off, realizing how inappropriate that sounded.

Vellum rolled her eyes. 'You have nothing in the house, Mom – not even frozen muffins. We ate all the banana bread.'

'If you aren't home, it all just goes in my belly.' Mandy patted her somewhat flat central region.

Justin held up the spatula to her. She picked up the still warm cookie, leaving oozing chocolate behind on the silicone. Small enough for one large mouthful, it melted in her mouth.

Yummy. 'When you're done, leave the oven on and I'll whip up a batch of cherry almond muffins. I still have frozen fruit in the freezer.'

'No, you don't; you used it for baked oatmeal.'

Mandy opened the freezer and peered into it. 'Wow, we really are running on empty.' She poked around and came up with frozen pineapple. 'I can do something with this.'

Justin lifted the empty tray. 'Do you still need this tray?'

'No,' Vellum said. 'Just used up the last of the dough.' She pushed the filled tray into the oven and set the timer.

'Justin, before you go, did you see my text about Peony's birth certificate?'

'I did,' he said. 'I suppose you asked the family about it?'

'Yes,' Mandy said defensively. 'Tom said Coral got pregnant at fourteen with Peony.'

'Gross,' Vellum said.

'Exactly,' Mandy agreed. 'Bodhi is the father. He must have been more than twice her age. Tom also said her tattoos were from before he and Coral met.'

'Has Bodhi paid child support?' Justin asked.

'No. It doesn't sound like Coral wanted anyone to know Peony was her daughter, but we know Coral ended up around Bodhi again later. Still, Peony thinks he only found out he was her birth father when she did a DNA test to get genetic health information and wound up with a father match instead.'

'She thinks she tested on a site he was on?'

Mandy inhaled fresh cookie nirvana. 'They think he tried to kidnap her. Maybe because he thought she was wealthy. She inherited the land their buildings are on.'

'I thought it was Tom's?'

'I guess not; just the buildings are his.'

Justin washed his hands and dried them on his towel, then pulled it from his waistband. 'If Zac had seen Bodhi trying to kidnap Peony, that would have been useful, but he didn't.'

'He can't be everywhere.'

He grimaced. 'Why didn't he catch that if he was tailing Bodhi?'

'I don't know. Is Amrik still your chief suspect despite all this?'

Justin shrugged. 'It's out of my hands, but he did confess, and the needles were found in Reese's house.'

'Why wasn't he charged then?'

'I'm guessing the district attorney was more cautious after the Reese disaster.'

'What happens next?'

'We're waiting for a search warrant on Amrik's—' He stopped talking. 'Mandy, you aren't a cop.'

She smiled sweetly. 'Just a concerned citizen. If I were you, Saturday night or not, I'd get a search warrant for Bodhi Lee's borrowed condo, rental car, and whatever, before it's too late.'

EIGHTEEN

On Sunday, Vellum woke up with a sore throat. Mandy plied her with hot tea and lemon, then went to brunch with her mother alone, leaving Vellum with the copy of *The Book Thief* she was supposed to finish reading by Monday.

'I wish kids didn't have to read such depressing books,' her mother fretted when Mandy updated her on Vellum's Sunday.

The front-desk staff at the popular weekend breakfast place directed them to a booth, giving Mandy time to phrase an answer.

'Those who do not learn history are doomed to repeat it,' she quoted. 'Take Coral Le Charme. I get the impression she couldn't completely stay away from Bodhi Lee and now I think her compulsion or obsession or whatever led to her death.'

Her mother took off her coat and tucked it next to her, then opened her menu. 'That's why you shouldn't let Vellum date yet. She's too young. Not enough prefrontal cortex development.'

'I can't fold her in bubble wrap until she's twenty-five,' Mandy pointed out. She already knew what she wanted, and held up her cup as a waitress walked by with a full coffee pot. 'But so far, no dating. It has to be coming any second now.'

'Maybe they don't date anymore at her age,' her mother said, turning up her cup to be filled. 'Does she have one of those swiping apps on her phone?'

'Eww. No, Mom. She went to a bowling party on Valentine's Day. A big group of kids – boys and girls. I think they are still just doing group stuff. And she spends Friday nights with her best friend.' Another waitress appeared and they made their order.

'I hope that girl is a nerd,' her mother said stoutly as she poured creamer into her coffee. 'Because as soon as the best friend starts dating, there goes Vellum's attention to schoolwork.'

'She didn't avoid brunch to do schoolwork,' Mandy soothed, following suit. 'She's fighting a cold. No surprise since it rained all week at camp.'

When the waitress checked on them after they were served, Mandy added an order of a vegetable omelet and fried potatoes for Vellum.

The container still felt warm in her hands as she went up the back steps of her house after brunch.

When she opened the door, she heard voices in the dining room. Vellum and Justin seemed to have become close. Mandy didn't mind. Vellum needed a father figure, given Cory's indifference and immaturity.

She grabbed a fork from the silverware drawer and brought the takeout into the dining room, but she didn't find Justin in the room with her daughter. To her astonishment, Houston sat there, casual as could be, in the chair next to Vellum, who still wore her bathrobe.

Her breath seized in her chest. As gently as she could, she set down the food. Eggy, starchy scents filled the air.

'Did you bring enough for two?' Houston said with his winning grin. Then his expression slipped when his gaze went to the fork.

Mandy glanced down and saw she was holding it, tine-first, in his direction. 'I'm very sure I told you to leave my daughter alone.'

'But we're all friends now. I saved you from Bodhi Lee.'

'That doesn't change the fact that she's a minor and you are not.' Her voice was crisp and precise.

'I didn't know she was home alone,' he insisted.

Vellum sat frozen, staring at her mother. All of a sudden, her body convulsed and she let out a mighty sneeze.

This seemed to set Houston into motion. 'Sorry you're sick, Vellum. Feel better.'

He made eye contact with Mandy, as if to prove he could, then walked around the other side of the dining-room table. Her ears tracked his footsteps across the living room and into the tiny entryway, then out of the door.

Mandy's mouth tightened. She slowly set the fork down on the container and stalked through her house. At the front door, she slid home the bolt lock and went back to the dining room.

Vellum hadn't touched the food.

'Eat before it gets cold,' Mandy said brusquely, opening the paper bag and taking out the clamshell. She lifted the lid and set the food in front of Vellum.

Her daughter's lips trembled. 'I'm sorry, Mom. He just showed up and zoomed right past me, like a puppy or something.'

'Aggressively?'

'No, just completely at home. I didn't know how to say no.'

Mandy considered her daughter, then handed her the fork. 'That's a good way to get yourself in a bad situation. You need to set clear boundaries.'

'I know but—'

'Men are raised to have self-confidence, to look out for number one. Women are raised to doubt themselves and take care of people. Can you imagine how much shame I would feel if I treated us the way your father has?'

'You'd never do that,' Vellum said quietly.

'Exactly, but he thinks he's done nothing wrong. I'll bet Houston doesn't either. He's now ignored a clear directive from an adult.'

'He really didn't know you wouldn't be here, right?' Vellum asked, still in a small voice.

'It doesn't matter. He knows we work on Mandy's Plan on the weekends. He's been told not to come here.'

Vellum sniffed. 'Nothing happened.'

Mandy sat down next to her. 'Not this time, sweetheart. In the future, use the peephole on the door and text Justin for backup. Talk through the door. People can hear you. Or at least keep the chain on. It's not perfect, but it would probably deter a Houston type. He doesn't have any muscles.'

Vellum's mouth quirked. 'Yeah. Pretty face and scrawny body.'

Mandy leaned back. She'd never heard her daughter critique a man's form before. Sixteen was only a few months away. 'It's not like you go to a girls' school. There are boys your own age in your life, right?'

Vellum frowned and stabbed a fork into her eggs. 'Can I have some ketchup?'

'I'll get it. But you can tell me if you want to start dating. That time I said no was when you were thirteen. That was too young.'

'It was. I heard that kid already got someone pregnant at another school.'

Mandy's eyes widened. 'It happens. That's why you have to be careful.' She went and grabbed the ketchup and brought it to Vellum.

'Yeah. Who wants a baby so young? Anyway, Mom, I haven't met anyone I liked enough to give up my free time yet. I don't have much.'

Mandy kissed the top of her daughter's head. 'No, you don't. Between school, extracurriculars, Mandy's Plan, and your friends, you have a full plate.'

'But you'd let me date?' Vellum asked.

'Someone age-appropriate and a good guy. I'd want to know something about the family.'

Vellum nodded. 'Yep, me too. Sorry, Mom.' She sneezed again.

On Monday morning, Fannah sent Houston on his break during a lull in customers.

'Can I talk to you for a minute?' Mandy asked.

Fannah gestured her into the back room, leaving her standing while she took the one chair. 'What is it?'

'Houston.'

'Oh?' Fannah touched the keyboard and her monitor lit up.

'I don't trust him,' Mandy said. 'He's shown up at my house a couple of times even though he knows he's not welcome. I've told him point-blank to stay away from my daughter, who is five years younger than him, and yet he turned up at my house again yesterday.'

'Why does he have your address?' She typed in her password.

'He figured it out from things I'd told him. Creepy, right? He just showed up at my house one night, a couple of days after the massage therapist was killed.'

Fannah looked amused. 'Do you think Houston killed her? Are you afraid for your life?'

Mandy gritted her teeth. 'I just think he's not a rule follower. You must remember how difficult it is to deal with teenagers. We were both teenagers. He's twenty and that isn't much better. He's fixated on my daughter.'

Fannah glanced at the computer screen as if to make clear the conversation didn't interest her. She clicked through a couple of screens with a manicured nail. 'He's still on probation, but he's done nothing wrong here at work except for eating the cookies, which I dealt with immediately.'

'So he only has one strike against him here, and I'm sure he'd point out to you that he got me away from Bodhi Lee when he was harassing me after class. But that didn't make him welcome in my home.'

'Do you think he stole your address from files here? Found it on the computer or something?'

Alarmed, Mandy asked, 'You don't leave anything personal up on screen, I hope?'

'No, and even if I did, it goes to the protected screen in five minutes.'

'I think he really did figure out my address. He told me how he had.' She re-tied her apron until it felt tight.

Fannah cleared her throat. 'I would suggest you make your personal boundaries clear. Don't socialize with him outside of work, so he understands you only have a business relationship. From my perspective, the customers love him and business is up. The younger women especially love to come and chat with him, and that makes sales.'

Mandy heard rustling and peeked out of the door. Houston was back from his break. 'I have made my boundaries clear,' she said, trying to keep temper out of her voice. 'And we're both done with the meditation class.'

'Don't discuss your personal life at work,' Fannah advised. 'No more talk about your daughter.'

Mandy saw customers approaching. As she went to the cash register, she thought that Fannah was basically telling her to be a robot. For the first time in ages, she missed her former co-worker, Kit, who, for all her faults, at least hadn't harassed Vellum.

Since Fannah had made it clear she wouldn't help, Mandy decided she'd better handle Houston herself. Fannah left an hour before she did and there was usually a quiet fifteen or twenty minutes between the time she left and the end of the nursing shift. She'd confront him then.

Reese had returned to work, so she texted her friend during her break and asked if she could stop by the coffee bar around then, so she'd have backup if she needed it.

Then she spent the early part of the afternoon working extra hard, so she wouldn't feel guilty for taking a few minutes to deal with her personal issue.

Fannah watched her slinging cookie dough in the prep room with approval. Mandy ignored her and finished the cookie work ten minutes earlier than usual, just as Fannah left for the day.

'The blender station could use some love,' Fannah said on the way out.

Mandy groaned inwardly. This is why shift workers didn't burn themselves out working fast, because there was always more work to fill in the cracks.

She puttered for a couple of minutes, cleaning the most obvious spills away, then brought a load of blender parts to be washed in the sink behind the counter.

'Why don't you do that in the back?' Houston asked. He had an earpiece in and must have had his cellphone tucked away, because his head was bopping rhythmically.

'You aren't supposed to have your phone up here,' she said sharply.

'Calm down, Mandy. Geez.' He pulled the earbud out and tucked it into his apron. 'What do you care? There isn't anyone here.'

The up and down escalators hulked in front of the coffee bar. Just as Houston spoke, Reese stepped off the escalator and approached.

'It's against the rules,' she said.

'You're hardly perfect,' he scoffed.

'I don't claim to be.'

Houston held up his hand, as if to hush her in front of Reese. Her face flushed with fury at his behavior.

The nurse glanced at his hand dismissively. 'What's going on?'

'I'm frustrated,' Mandy said. 'Look, Houston, I'm starting to see a real similarity between you and Bodhi Lee – not just in your looks but in your behavior.'

'Excuse me?' he spluttered. 'I'm the one who rescued you from him.'

She ignored that truth. 'You are not welcome at my house. You know this.'

'Don't get personal in front of a customer,' he spluttered.

'She's here as my friend.'

'Vellum invited me in,' he insisted.

Reese's eyebrows went up.

'No, she didn't,' Mandy said. 'She opened the door, which was an error, but then you stepped around her, and she's too young to know how to deal with that. Emulating Bodhi's behavior toward me, mimicking it with young girls, is unacceptable.'

'Oh, come on,' he snapped, his face darkening.

'You did the same kind of thing at my house,' Reese said. 'You couldn't comprehend that I would have a room in my house you weren't welcome in. It's a definite pattern.'

Mandy nodded. 'Exactly. Let me be clear, yet again. You are not allowed in my house or around my daughter. Vellum knows this rule as well as you.'

Houston snorted. 'Vellum likes me, and if you think you can control teenagers, think about Coral Le Charme having Bodhi Lee's baby at fourteen. If he's my father – well, my mother was sixteen. Think about that.' Lifting one side of his mouth in a lazy smirk, he pushed past Mandy and went into the back room.

Mandy heard the prep-room door slam. Houston seemed to be intent on following in Bodhi's footsteps, whether or not Bodhi was his biological father.

Reese had far too much control of her face to let her mouth hang open, but her face seemed to lengthen with the shock of his words. 'Such arrogance. If only Fannah had heard that.'

Mandy shuddered. 'I don't feel safe, but Fannah won't do anything because she thinks he's good for business.'

Reese scrunched up her forehead. 'Write this conversation down. I'll do the same. Everyone does something they could get in trouble for.'

Mandy nodded. 'Yeah, he's listening to music on his phone, but I've carried mine at times, too. I'm not sure I should point the finger at him.'

'Maybe he'll quit and leave once he's figured out who his father is.'

At those words, Mandy felt struck by lightning. 'We know Bodhi did a DNA test. Peony found it when she did her own.'

'Has Houston done a DNA test?'

Mandy nodded. 'But I don't know which company he used. I'll text Darci and see if she knows what site Peony did her test on. Maybe he can get the answer he wants. Then maybe he'll move on. He isn't happy working here.'

'I wonder if we'll ever know who killed Coral,' Reese said.

'It has to be Bodhi. I hope he'll be arrested soon.' She touched Reese's arm across the counter. 'You need to be certain your boyfriend didn't do it.'

Reese tugged on her earlobe, then played with her earring. 'He let me sit in jail for days. I know you're the one who persuaded him to talk to the police.'

'But then he took the blame, even though there's no proof he's responsible either.'

Reese nodded. 'I don't know if I'm depressed or just feeling that the bloom has gone off the relationship. I'm not sure Amrik is quite the man I thought.'

'You're very young still,' Mandy said softly.

'I don't want to find out my parents are right about him.'

'No one could have foreseen this set of circumstances. It could have broken up anyone.'

'I know,' Reese said. She forced a smile as a group of nurses appeared from the elevator bay. 'I'd better get back to the office.'

Mandy sighed. 'The rush is starting, and just when I've made an enemy.'

'Don't go into the back room alone with Houston,' Reese warned.

'I'll stay behind the front counter,' Mandy said. 'In full view of the security cameras. Thank you so much for helping me, especially when you're dealing with your own issues.'

'You're welcome. I'll come get you at the end of your shift. I'll be done at the same time.' Reese sketched a wave and walked toward the escalator.

'The usuals?' Mandy asked the crowd of five.

The nurses all nodded, and one of them asked, 'Where's the cutie?'

As if on cue, Houston appeared in the doorway and spread his arms wide. 'Here I am, ladies.'

Mandy considered him, so different from Peony, so charismatic and theatrical. Although his appearance mimicked Bodhi Lee, his energy had no self-containment like the other two. But that meant nothing. A person could easily inherit looks from one parent and personality from another.

After four, Mandy trudged up her slick back steps, trailed by Reese. From her landing, Mandy saw Linda crossing the street, a container in her hands. 'Brownies incoming,' she told Reese, and unlocked the door so she could enter.

Mandy waited until Linda climbed the steps and went inside herself. A blast of warm air greeted her. It wouldn't be too much longer before she could turn off the thermostat for the season.

'I think the grass grew an inch overnight,' Linda exclaimed as they all pulled off their coats. 'Have you checked your front yard?'

'Not yet.' Mandy gave her friend a one-armed hug. 'I missed you.'

'I don't know why I waste my time with George,' Linda said. 'But you have a lot to do.'

'I suppose, but I don't think my mind is going to focus on work again until we get this murder sorted out.'

In the kitchen, Vellum gave Reese a hug. They had bonded over journaling the past couple of months. Vellum already had the electric kettle warming. Reese chose tea from the tins stacked on the stove's ledge.

Linda cut her brownie into four large pieces while Mandy pulled down plates, deciding not to argue about the size. She could use some chocolate after the unpleasant encounter with Houston.

They had an enjoyable chat about garden planning now that the rains were diminishing. Linda suggested they plan a trip to the nurseries in south Washington. She wanted to clear out some of her dead trees and plant new lilacs.

They were checking on bulb prices when Vellum's phone buzzed. Mandy saw her daughter's eyelids half close, then she tucked her phone away.

'What is it?' Mandy asked.

'Nothing.' Vellum forced a smile at her mother.

But Mandy knew her daughter too well. 'It wasn't nothing. Show me. Is your grandfather OK?'

Vellum sighed. 'Don't blame me. You can scroll up.' She pulled out her phone from her jeans and handed it over.

Mandy typed in Vellum's password, her birthday, and chose the app that had a waiting message. Mandy's jaw clenched when she saw who the text was from. Finger shaking, she scrolled up.

Her daughter had twelve messages from Houston over a period of time. Vellum had never responded, but Mandy knew he could be sending through the other apps, too.

Justin walked into the room. 'Brownies are back?'

Linda put her hand over her mouth. 'I'm so sorry. We ate them all.'

Reese held up her dish. 'Half of mine is up for grabs.'

Justin laughed. 'Actually, I ordered a pizza. Should be here in a minute. Thanks, though.'

'What does it take to get a restraining order for harassment?' Mandy asked, holding up Vellum's phone.

He frowned. 'What's going on?'

'No matter how many times I confront Houston, he keeps contacting Vellum, even showing up here. Reese and I had a pointed conversation with him today, yet he's just texted Vellum again.'

Justin sat down next to Reese. 'Vellum, do you want to talk about this privately?'

She shook her head. 'No. I don't encourage him. Mom can show you. I'm not responding to his texts and he pushed past me into the house. I swear I didn't invite him in.'

'It's time to take precautions. You could have been raped,' Justin said gently. 'You aren't going to open the door to him again, right?'

The color leached out of Vellum's face. Tears sprang to her eyes. 'I've learned my lesson. I think he's trying to play some kind of head game with Mom, more than anything.'

'Why do you think that?'

Vellum shrugged. 'I've seen him looking at her. Like he's laughing at his own private joke.'

Justin exhaled heavily and rubbed his fingers over the stubble on his cheeks. 'You could consider a restraining order, but we don't know what is making this kid tick. Does he have intent to harass or stalk one or both of you?'

Mandy sighed. 'My issue is obviously his pursuit of Vellum. He's never been particularly threatening to me at work. Fannah, our boss, has no problem with him, so I have no recourse there.'

'Perhaps if you left the coffee bar, Houston would forget about you guys,' Justin said.

Mandy set her fork down. 'We need the health insurance.'

Reese put her hand on the table. 'Why don't you train as a medical assistant? I could help you find a different job. There's always a spot for good people.'

'I don't want to take the time to do the training,' Mandy explained. 'My business pays too well to give it up for months.'

'It would be a higher-paying position in the end,' Reese said. 'With a career path, too. You could continue on to nursing.'

'I think you're moving away from the main point,' Justin said.

'Not really,' Linda interjected. 'Mandy always said she'd job hunt in May, when her first year was up. That's only a few weeks away.'

The doorbell rang just as Mandy was about to call pause on the conversation about her life choices.

Justin stood. 'My pizza.'

Linda followed suit. 'I need to make some calls to the East Coast before it gets too late.'

Mandy stood and gave Linda a hug. Reese hugged her, too. Mandy watched with maternal pride. Seeing her friends form bonds made her happy.

By the time Linda had headed out the back door, Justin had returned to the dining room with his pizza.

'Is that for just anyone?' Vellum asked.

Justin snorted. 'You can have one piece. I'm hungry.'

'And you didn't get any brownies,' Mandy added.

'Exactly. Seriously, though, if you feel Houston is presenting a danger, then the time to act is now, and that's not career retraining. Go over your boss's head if you need to. Explain this kid is harassing you and your minor daughter at home. Tell them you never gave him your address.' He sat down and flipped open the pizza lid, then pointed to Vellum.

She took a piece. Mandy eyed the long strands of cheese between Vellum's piece and the pizza box, but told herself she was too old for back-to-back brownie and pizza. 'If he was fifteen, then we could give him the benefit of the doubt, but twenty?'

'Especially when he knows right from wrong,' Reese added. 'He knew Bodhi wasn't behaving appropriately when he grabbed you.'

'Yeah, *he* wants to be chief harasser,' Mandy agreed.

Justin shook his head and pulled out his phone. 'Hell, I should have put in a security system. I know better.' He started typing into his phone.

'Good idea,' Reese said.

'I can pay for it.' Mandy hoped it would cost less than four figures for a few cameras. 'I'm not broke thanks to having a tenant.'

Justin shook his head. 'I can get some cameras up tonight. My buddy Burns just installed some for his new girlfriend.' His phone buzzed. He glanced at the text then said, 'Great, he'll pick up what we need and bring it over tonight.'

'Which one is Burns?' Reese asked, with an innocent flutter of eyelashes.

'The one who had tattoos,' Mandy reminded her.

'Ah,' Reese said, slumping slightly.

Justin's eyelids lowered. 'Did you break up with Amrik?'

Reese shook her head. 'But I remember one of your friends was really cute.'

'Frost,' Mandy said, watching with avaricious eyes as Justin took his first bite of pizza. It looked so good going into his mouth. 'Burns looks like a pro wrestler. Super tall, muscles for miles.'

Justin chuckled. 'Basically, Amrik's opposite.'

Mandy waited for Reese to rush to her boyfriend's defense. After all, Amrik was very handsome, but Reese said nothing. She shrugged, not sure how she would react in Reese's current situation either.

'OK,' Mandy said after a moment. 'I'll let Darci know how pushy Houston is. He's been to the forge and we don't want him fixating on anyone there next.'

'You wish, Mom,' Vellum said, then took a huge bite. Pieces of red pepper dropped to her napkin as the slice bent.

'I'm not so sure,' Mandy told her. 'If Houston finds out that Peony is Bodhi's daughter, that might spark his interest. He'll want to know if she's his half-sister.'

NINETEEN

Mandy called Darci while the others enjoyed their pizza. When she answered, Mandy said, 'Hey, how's my favorite pregnant lady?'

'Stressed,' Darci said. Mandy heard her say something else in a tone too muffled to hear, as if she'd covered the speaker.

'I hate to add to your stress, but I wanted to tell you that I don't trust Houston Harris. I don't know if you've seen him around since the knife class, but don't let him near Peony. Long story.'

'What?' Darci asked.

Mandy had the sense she wasn't really listening. Pregnancy brain, maybe. Mandy remembered the fog that had descended over her brain late in the first trimester. 'He's getting kind of stalkerish, so I wanted to let you know.'

'Hey, Mandy, I don't know about any of that, but we've got our own problems here.'

Mandy heard an exclamation, someone else in the room with Darci. 'What's going on?'

'I was just texting with Zac.'

'Did he learn something new?' Mandy heard a sharp-pitched scrape, as if someone was moving furniture, then a man's voice.

Darci's voice shook. 'Zac says he saw Bodhi at a home improvement store just now, buying duct tape and rope.'

Mandy put her phone on speaker and held it out to Justin. 'Say that again?'

'Bodhi's buying duct tape and rope at the Home Depot on Aurora.'

Justin frowned and finished his first slice of pizza. 'Isn't this guy just here temporarily?'

'At a condo downtown,' Mandy said. 'He tried to take me there. There's lots of reasons to buy duct tape, but rope? And why on Aurora? That's way north of downtown.'

A shriek came through the line. Mandy heard the man's voice again and recognized Tom's voice.

'I need help,' Darci panted. 'Peony is so upset. Dealing with all this crazy energy isn't good for my baby.'

Mandy's mothering instincts went on high alert. 'Of course it's not good. But Zac isn't going to lose Bodhi between Home Depot and your house, if that's where he's heading.'

'What if he has a gun?' Darci asked. 'And we have all these weapons – knives just everywhere, and daggers and swords and axes.'

'Have you called the police?' Justin said into the phone.

'Who is this? What am I going to say?' Darci cried.

'She's losing it,' Reese murmured.

'I don't blame her,' Mandy whispered.

'What am I going to tell the police?' Darci asked. 'Nothing's going on except Peony is freaking out. I need help, Mandy, please come over.'

Mandy heard the furniture scraping sounds again, then Tom swore. She stood, unable to stay calm with all the commotion. 'Darci's right, Justin. What are you going to do? Send people over to protect them?'

'I can ask for a wellness check,' Justin said. 'Do you want me to come with you?'

'No,' Vellum said in a forceful voice. 'Mom, we need the security cameras here. Houston's harassing us, not them.'

Justin looked at Vellum. 'Have another piece of pie, kiddo. I'll call Lynnwood's Patrol Division and see what they can do.'

'Has anyone checked into Bodhi Lee's background?' Reese asked.

'Zac is primarily a bail enforcement guy,' Mandy explained. 'If he had access to an open warrant for Bodhi Lee, he'd be all over it.'

'What about Houston?' Vellum lifted her eyebrows as she pulled another slice of pizza away from the pie.

'I'll ask Zac to run a background check on Houston when I get up there,' Mandy said.

'I'd rather you didn't go,' Justin said. 'Someone from that family was murdered a few weeks ago and we don't know who did it.'

'Darci's pregnant,' Mandy said. 'She should be resting, not calming a hysterical teenager. This is in my wheelhouse.' She kissed the top of Vellum's head.

'Call when you get there,' Justin said, resigned.

Reese pushed her chair back. 'I'll go with her.'

Justin rubbed his temples. 'Are you sure that's a good idea?'

'I won't feel safe until the real killer is found,' Reese said crisply. 'I want this to be over.'

Soon after, Mandy and Reese pulled up alongside the forge.

'It looks quiet,' Reese said.

Mandy saw lights on in the house. 'Let's check on Peony and try to get her to take a shower and go to bed.'

'OK.'

Mandy nodded. 'Darci needs to put her feet up. I remembered to grab some hibiscus tea, so I'll make her a cup and settle her down if you want to focus on Peony.'

'Sounds like a plan.' Reese reached for the door, then hesitated. 'They know I didn't kill Coral, right?'

'I'm sure it's far easier for them to blame Amrik than you.' Mandy frowned. 'Though he was at the memorial with his sister.'

'At least the police released me. That's got to count for something.'

'I have the impression that whatever Amrik said, it exonerated you completely.'

Reese's mouth twitched. 'He knew I'd done some online shopping that night. I was on the platform that we both use. The police found a time-stamped conversation I had with a seller right at the time Coral died. Thanks to you, we know exactly when that happened.'

Mandy frowned. 'But you were at the party.'

'I was feeling shaky from all the sugar, so I went to my car. I had a bag of trail mix in my glove compartment. So I ate the nuts in my car and talked to the seller over the messaging function on the website.'

Mandy had to ask. 'What did you buy?'

'The most delicate caftans,' Reese said. 'They're perfect for summer but they take a month or so to come from India.'

Mandy clapped a hand to her forehead. 'You were haggling on arrival time?'

'No, fabrics. The seamstress didn't have the fabrics she was advertising, so we were trying to choose acceptable alternatives. I'll order you one. They're the best.'

A skidding shriek of tires on gravel swiveled Mandy's head away from Reese. A black pickup turned on to the DeRoy property and came to a halt next to Mandy. The motor turned off, but the truck kept making pinging noises.

'Is that Tom or Rod?'

'I can't tell.'

Reese's voice went edgy. 'Let's stay here.'

The driver's side had opened. A man stepped around the hood of the truck. Mandy recognized him and got out of the car.

'Hi, Zac,' Mandy greeted the bounty hunter. 'What happened at Home Depot?'

He didn't speak, just swaggered to the passenger door and unlocked it. Reaching in, he helped another man out.

Mandy's mouth dropped open. Behind her, Reese squeaked in alarm. Zac pulled Bodhi Lee out of the way and slammed his door shut, then took his arm.

Mandy gasped. 'You handcuffed him?'

'Call the police, Mandy,' Bodhi huffed. 'You have to help me.'

'He's a bounty hunter.' Mandy shrugged. 'Maybe there's a warrant out for your arrest. How would I know?'

'I was working on my social media,' he said, fixing her with that teacher's gaze. 'He misunderstood. I'm no kidnapper.'

She shrugged again, telling herself that he wasn't a safe man for multiple reasons.

He continued. 'I was merely planning for a video.'

'On what?' Reese said behind Mandy. She put her hand on Mandy's shoulder.

'I planned a video about how to meditate in difficult situations.'

'Using rope and duct tape?' Zac said in a sarcastic tone.

Mandy had a flash of memory from her video watching. 'Actually, I think I have seen something like that.'

'Seriously?' Zac demanded. He tugged Bodhi toward the forge. A narrow path between the wall and the cement parking-spot markers led to the DeRoy house.

Mandy tried to remember. 'I think someone was using the rope and tape to make a hammock or something to suspend them from a tree? Maybe? I'm not quite sure, but I did see something of the sort.'

Bodhi stumbled, then balanced himself against the wall. 'See? I'm not trying to kidnap anyone. I'll sue you for unlawful arrest. Call the police, Mandy!'

'My housemate already did,' she said, though she wasn't sure if Justin's request for a drive-by would be sufficient. Regardless of what she thought of Bodhi, Zac had put himself into a dangerous position with his handcuffs and manhandling. His attempt to keep Peony safe from kidnapping might result in kidnapping charges of his own.

'Call your lawyer, Zac,' Reese advised. 'You don't want to spend a week in jail like I did.'

'When I have time.' Zac towed Bodhi toward the house. 'I promised Darci I would keep her family safe.'

'Then why did you bring him here?' Mandy walked behind the cars to parallel Bodhi and Zac's walk to the house, wondering why Bodhi wasn't attempting to escape. From the way he carried himself and the muscles she'd sensed under his shirt, he probably had studied a martial art. Also, he had a grip like steel, as she well remembered.

'I want him to look Peony in the eye and admit he tried to

kidnap her.' When the men reached the front door, Zac pulled out his cell phone and glanced at a text. Before he could put it away, the front door opened.

The light in the overhang flickered on. Instead of Darci in the doorway, Peony stood there, her face contorted with rage. Moving faster than Mandy would have thought possible with her braces, which weren't visible, she launched herself at Bodhi.

Zac's phone dropped on to the gravel. Bodhi stumbled back, which broke Zac's grip on him. Zac entered the house, disappearing from sight.

'What's happening?' Mandy cried as Reese pulled out her cell phone.

Peony pummeled Bodhi's chest, screaming, 'You and my mom destroyed my life! You jerk! You douche!'

Spittle sprayed into the air, spattering on Bodhi's chin. He remained impassive and Mandy didn't know why. Was he accepting of the physical abuse or merely stunned by the handcuffs and the crazed girl? She had a flash of insight. Had Peony displayed this out-of-control anger toward Coral? Did she have the capacity for murder?

'Stop it!' Mandy cried. She reached for her phone with jerky motions, but Reese was already speaking into hers.

'Yes, I need the police,' Reese said. She sounded much calmer than Mandy felt. 'We have an assault going on and maybe a kidnapping?'

Peony's foot slipped on the gravel. Mandy raced forward and grabbed the girl's arm.

'Peony, back off!' Mandy ordered. 'The police are coming. Don't make this any worse.'

Peony wrenched her hand away and slapped Bodhi's face. His head snapped to one side. He winced as Mandy grabbed for her again. Reese glanced between the two of them, still talking on the phone, and backed away from the confrontation toward the house.

'Why did you have to do the test?' Peony screamed. 'I was better off not knowing.'

Bodhi worked his jaw. 'I didn't care about finding relatives. I just wanted to see what my cancer risk was.'

Peony sniffed and coughed. 'I didn't know Coral was my mom

before that stupid test! She said she trusted you, but you got her pregnant.'

Mandy put up her hands. 'It's OK, Peony, let's go inside before more people call the police. You have neighbors.'

Zac appeared from the house and grabbed Reese's arm, pulling her inside with him.

Peony ignored everyone but Bodhi, her hands fisting. 'I thought my grandparents were my parents. But I never belonged to them at all.'

'Of course you did,' Mandy soothed. She heard the house door slam.

Peony turned to Mandy as if noticing her for the first time. She took a breath, then screamed right in Mandy's face. 'Shut up! You don't know what you're talking about.'

Mandy took a step back, horrified by the vicious anger in the girl. Why she felt compelled to protect the loathsome Bodhi was beyond her. Except he couldn't defend himself with his hands cuffed behind his back and she wanted to protect Peony from assault charges. 'Why don't you take a deep breath, Peony, then explain?'

'There's no cause for anger,' Bodhi said in his soothing voice. 'You had parents, a good life.'

Peony ground her teeth together, her lips flaring away from them. Her voice, when she spoke again, was garbled. 'Grandpa abused me, just like you abused my mom. He told me he loved me and taught me how we could share our love.'

Mandy felt the blood drain from her face. *Oh, Peony.*

Bodhi swore. 'Coral didn't know. I promise. She thought she was doing the right thing. We'll get you some help.'

'I want all of you dead,' Peony said, her face contorted by rage, tears, spittle, and snot.

Mandy's heart skipped a beat as Peony pulled a knife out from under her shirt. Who was this girl? She had misunderstood the situation all along. Moving fast, Mandy grabbed for Bodhi's arm and turned blindly, steering him away from the house and toward the vehicles. They stumbled on gravel.

'Did you kill Coral?' she called behind her, hoping to make Peony pause.

Instead, she heard a thwack on the side of the forge. She ducked, frantic for a place to hide.

'She threw the knife,' Bodhi said in a choked voice.

Grimly, Mandy held on to him, moving between the cars for safety. When she tried her doors, they weren't locked. She shoved Bodhi in the back and jumped into the front as Peony pulled the knife from the forge siding and staggered toward them. Mandy hit the auto-lock button just in time.

Her hands shook as Peony pounded on her car, her contorted face peering inside. Her shrieks penetrated Mandy's bones. Peony's dead eyes sent chills down her spine. She was sure now they'd found their murderer. Grabbing for her purse, Mandy scrambled through it for her phone.

'I think I pulled something in my back,' Bodhi groaned.

'Calling the police,' Mandy said, attempting to type in her security code with shaking hands. 'Where is Tom? And Darci? We could really use their help about now.'

'Get him out!' Peony screamed. 'I want him dead! He ruined my life!'

On the third try, Mandy's code went through. But she hit the wrong button and her email came up instead of phone dialing.

Peony pushed the car and it rocked slightly.

'I didn't do anything wrong,' Bodhi moaned from the back. 'I didn't kill Coral.'

'That's a load of baloney,' Mandy snapped. 'You practically tried to drag me to your hotel. And you tried to kidnap Peony from school.'

'I did not,' he said with a groan. 'I don't know where she goes to school.'

'Why should I believe you after you grabbed me after class?'

'That was different, I—' His words were interrupted by the sounds of fists on the window.

'Shut up!' Peony screamed. 'I killed Coral! I want you all dead.'

'Oh, Peony, why?' Mandy asked, the words falling from her numb lips. She was past surprise, but sorrow filled her at the lives destroyed. Her finger slid around on her screen, damp with sweat. Just as she finally had the call icon successfully pressed, she heard sirens. Justin's or Reese's call must have set the police into motion.

'She let Grandpa hurt me!' Peony slammed the knife into the windshield right in front of Mandy's eyes. She yelped and dropped her phone.

'That brat is going to kill us,' Bodhi whimpered.

'She's your daughter. Why did you have her birth certificate?'

'We'll be just as dead, whoever she is. Coral sent it to me to prove she hadn't listed me as father.'

Peony's knife made contact again. The windshield seemed to give a little. Mandy winced, covering her eyes. Peony probably couldn't do too much damage to the windshield. If she came for the side windows, that was another issue.

The sirens grew louder, making any communication with Peony impossible. Had Coral known how much her daughter had hated her or was her death a surprise?

Mandy felt numb, hours later, as she pulled into Reese's driveway. Peony had been arrested. Tom had needed to drive Darci to the hospital for abdominal pains. Zac hadn't backed down on his claims that Bodhi had been planning to kidnap Peony. Bodhi had insisted *he'd* been kidnapped, so they'd both been taken for questioning. Mandy had no idea what all their lives would look like come morning.

'What are you going to do now?' she asked her passenger.

'I don't know,' Reese said quietly. 'How about you?'

'I've been outside for hours. It might be April, but I feel like a block of ice. I'm going to thaw out under my blankets.'

'I can hardly feel my hands or make sense of my thoughts,' Reese admitted.

'Amrik is innocent,' Mandy pointed out. 'That's the important thing, right?'

Reese rubbed her eyes. 'Do you think he confessed to save me?'

She considered. 'Yes, but it wasn't a very smart thing to do. Do you think he'll get arrested now for – I don't know – wasting police time or something?'

'I doubt it,' Reese said quietly. 'The police realized he was lying, but they didn't arrest me again.'

Mandy rubbed her hands together. 'Yeah, well, they had the wrong person.'

'But he waited to talk to them – that's what I can't forgive.' Reese undid her seatbelt, then let it slowly retract through her hands.

'I get that. Maybe he didn't have all the facts at first. The police must have realized more people had access to your house than they thought. It opened up possibilities they hadn't considered.'

Reese nodded. 'Peony used to visit Coral at the hospital pretty regularly. She even showed up at the podiatry office a couple of times.'

'How did she get the syringe?' Mandy asked.

'A month or so ago, she said her braces were bothering her and she was afraid she was going to fall. She'd started using more visible braces again.'

'You helped her?'

Reese lifted her hands. 'I led her into an open treatment room and took a look at the brace. I didn't see anything wrong with it. I went to see if the doctor could take a quick peek and she must have swiped the syringe then.'

'Was she in your house after that?'

'I had Coral and Peony over for lunch right when Coral started working at the hospital. That's when Peony saw the basement. She showed up—' Reese put her head in her hands. 'Wow, that was before Coral died, though.'

'What did she do?'

'She brought me a trivet, an iron trivet. As a thank-you gift. And she talked to me about renting the basement. I didn't see where she'd get the money. But then, of course, right after Coral died, she confirmed that she wanted to move in.'

'There seems to be some confusion. People seem to think she has money. But I only know about the land.'

Reese lifted her head and leaned against the headrest. 'There's more. I think it has something to do with her Permanent Fund dividend. That's what she said.'

'That money that people who live in Alaska get?' Mandy asked.

'Right. Coral said her money and Peony's had been invested in a fishing boat over the years. When the catch was good, they made quite a bit.'

'Then she might have had her rent covered.'

'Yeah, maybe. She must have figured out how to sneak in when she visited.'

'Do you have an emergency key somewhere?'

Reese pulled her purse into her lap. 'Not anymore, but I did, hidden on the porch. I guess she found it when she was looking around. I had a call from India that went on quite a while that day. I didn't think anything of it.'

'I knew Peony had a lot of upper body strength, but it never occurred to me that she had the agility to stab someone. Coral was on the ground.'

'She was upright when she was stabbed,' Reese told her. 'My lawyer went through it all with me. Besides, Peony just uses ankle braces, or she had been until recently. It would have been difficult for her but not impossible.'

'Maybe she'd been wearing the knee braces to make her disability seem more severe.' Mandy slid her hand over Reese's and squeezed. 'Darci said she had no reason to think she'd actually had deterioration in her stability.'

'She really had it thought out. Paying her friends to stage the fake kidnapping to throw everyone off the scent. They gave her an alibi, too, claiming she was at a prom meeting.' Reese squeezed her hand back. 'It's hard to believe.'

'It was such a cold-blooded thing to do. I'm sure Coral did her best. She and Tom and Darci put so much time into helping Peony.'

Reese's voice dropped to a whisper. 'Peony lured Coral into the garage, saying a friend had driven her to the hospital and they had a gift waiting for her in the car. Then she stabbed her to death.'

Mandy shivered. 'She would have killed Bodhi too, if she'd had the opportunity. Only seventeen and she thought they had ruined her life.'

'Peony ruined theirs instead.'

Mandy sighed and forced herself to change the subject. 'Enough about her. You have a lot of thinking to do, but we'd both better get some rest. I can't believe it's only Monday.'

'At least we'll both be waking up free tomorrow.'

'And alive,' Mandy added. 'Unlike poor Coral. One thing, though. I've never understood why you wouldn't admit you and Coral were friends, when you obviously were. And what about Rod? Justin said you grew up in the same neighborhood?'

Reese frowned. 'I don't remember ever seeing him around back then. As for Coral, she wasn't like you, Mandy. I didn't really want to be friends with her. She had lived a rough kind of life, didn't have much education, didn't dress with any class. This new Goth phase – good grief.'

'But you liked her.' Reese's snobbery was not one of her better qualities, but she knew her friend's parents were even worse.

Reese shrugged. 'I was never sure of how I felt, except I knew she liked me. I was flattered, but not exactly willing to introduce her to my social circle.' She folded her hands under her arms. 'I mean, I never could have seen her having tea and brownies with you and Vellum and Linda.'

'We're not fancy people,' Mandy pointed out.

'You don't talk in slang or discuss private topics or – I don't know.' Reese huffed in frustration. 'She didn't have much ambition.'

'Maybe she did want more. After all, she wanted to be your friend.'

'I guess, but I suppose her life was just too broken. Even if Bodhi Lee walks away tonight or tomorrow, he's still responsible for getting a young girl pregnant and generally messing her up.' Reese nodded, almost to herself, and got out of the car.

Mandy waited until she'd gone inside, thinking about the dangers of using charisma on vulnerable people. She didn't really think Bodhi had intended to kidnap Peony, but she wouldn't put some sort of mind game past him. Even though she actually believed his story about his video plans, he had been way north of his condo. That was for the police to figure out, and she was more on Zac Turner's side than Bodhi Lee's. She reversed out of Reese's driveway and drove down the dark streets to her own house.

After she parked, she couldn't find the energy to climb out of her car. She unlocked her phone and sent an email to herself to remember to check the windshield in the morning and make sure it didn't have any chips or other damage from Peony's onslaught. Only luck had allowed her to drive away. The police could have insisted it needed to stay as evidence, but in all the confusion of Peony's hysteria and the arrest, the attack on the car had been forgotten.

In the case of Houston, she was glad to know he had nothing to do with Coral's death. Regardless, she'd keep her contact with him to strictly coffee-bar business and hope he'd move on soon. Her toes felt icy. Time to get into the house. Feeling as if she'd aged twenty years, she climbed out of her car, went through the backyard, and walked up the steps to her house.

Justin's friend had put a lock box on the back door with a new key inside. She had a text with the code for it and the security system. After she juggled her phone flashlight so she could see, everything worked smoothly and she slid the new key on to her keychain.

She dropped her coat in the mudroom, then stared blearily into the kitchen. Her bed beckoned her but she didn't think she'd fall asleep until she warmed up. After rejecting the thought of a shower, she decided a cup of hot cocoa might do.

She turned on her coffee maker, found a hot chocolate pod, and grabbed a clean mug from the dish drainer. The house was silent, though she heard cars on the street.

She peeked at Vellum's door while the coffee maker warmed up, and only saw the faint glow of the night light. Vellum must be asleep.

Mandy's phone rang. She slid the call open without checking to silence it as quickly as possible.

'Hey, Mandy.' *Cory.*

'What?' she asked wearily. The coffee maker stilled, so she shoved in a pod and punched the button to send hot water into the chocolate powder.

'I wanted you to know I'm making changes.'

She turned on the speaker so she could hear him over the noise of the coffee maker. 'Why? Because of your father?'

'Yeah. We had a long talk in the hospital. Several.'

'I don't need to be involved in your life anymore,' she said. 'I don't even want to be, other than making sure Vellum sees you sometimes.'

She heard rattling behind her, but then his next words focused her back on the call.

'Look, I took a job. One of Dad's friends offered me a management job at a startup in Kirkland.'

'You took a job?' she asked, incredulous.

'Yeah. I'm going to do better. I'll pay child support.'

'Why?' The door opened and closed in the mudroom.

'Vellum says you're working too hard. And I feel like having a cop in your house is attracting danger. You can dump the tenant, Mandy.'

'I'm glad you're taking the job. And I can't wait to get child support checks.' Mandy turned around. Wasn't Vellum here? Had she been over at her mother's house?

Justin stood there in the doorway, not Vellum. Mandy realized he had overheard Cory speaking.

'Thanks for the update, Cory, but I have to go now.' She disconnected the call, staring at Justin. 'I thought you'd be gone all night with the drama.'

He shrugged. 'It's not my case anymore. I was reassigned because of your involvement.'

'Oh, sorry.' She heard the final gurgle on her coffee maker and grabbed her hot chocolate. 'Here.'

He took the cup and stared into it. 'So, are you ready to kick me out?'

'No. I can't trust Cory to do what he claims.'

'Is that the only reason?' He looked up at her. 'Am I any better than he is?'

'You haven't broken my heart yet,' she whispered.

He stepped into her personal space, the cocoa steaming between them. 'In that case, are you going to tell me not to kiss you this time?'